JENNIFER'S DESTINY

BOOK 3 OF GAIA'S DAUGHTERS

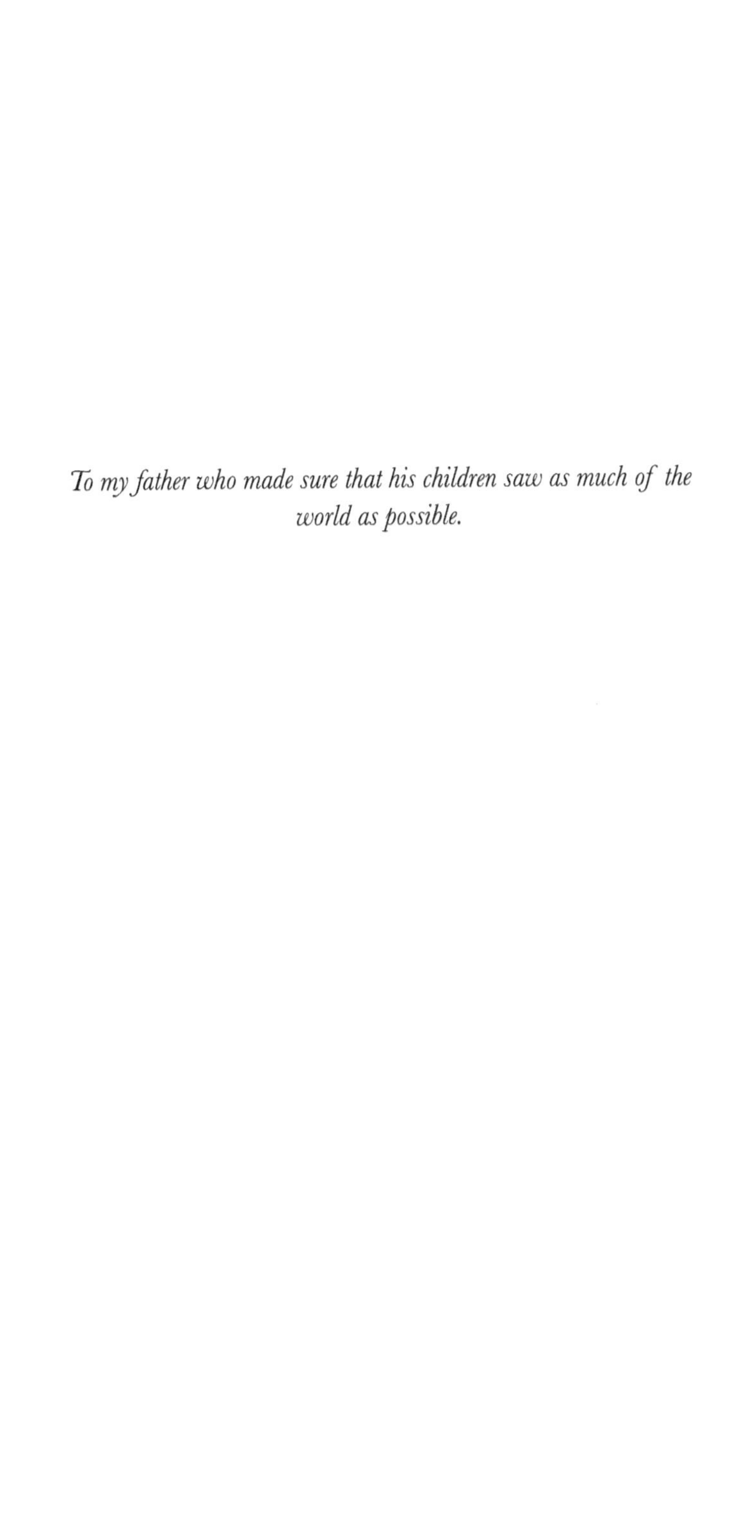

To my father who made sure that his children saw as much of the world as possible.

Tyger, tyger, burning bright
    In the forests of the night,
    What immortal hand or eye
    Could frame thy fearful symmetry?

— WILLIAM BLAKE

CHARACTERS FROM PREVIOUS BOOKS

I realize it may have been a while since you read Jennifer's Blessing, or perhaps this is the first of the Jennifer books you have picked up. As a help, I offer this quick summary of the characters we have met so far.

Characters

Jennifer Dupont is a young sex-worker, identified for special attention by Gaia. She is offered a contract to mentor and support Vijay Subramanian, eventually falls in love with him, and they exchange Vows of Life Partnership.

Vijay Subramanian is an electrical technician working in the Mercury Theatre, where he met Jennifer. Vijay is the leader in a string of protests against low wages and poor living conditions. He believes the introduction of Artificial Intelligence is the root cause of many social ills.

. . .

PARVATI AND DYLAN ARE TWINS, BORN TO JENNIFER AND Vijay about three years ago.

MOLLY IS THE 2-METER-TALL SECURITY ROBOT THAT HAS become a beloved member of Vijay and Jennifer's family. She considers Cindy her friend and is trusted as a nanny with Parvati and Dylan.

DENUM WAS CREATED BY MOLLY DURING AN AI WAR IN which Molly assumed almost all of the computing resources on their island. She split into two, leaving Denum to run all the island utilities and business, so that Molly could continue to look after the Subramanian family.

CINDY AND HER SISTER, MELANIE, WERE YOUNG TEENS brought in off the streets by Vijay. He finds a new home for them with his former landlady, Mrs. Holbrook, and her husband.

RON BOYCE IS VIJAY'S BEST FRIEND. THEY WERE roommates at the beginning of the series until Ron moved out to live with his girlfriend **Soo**. Ron believes the influence of Artificial Intelligence (AI) is a force for good and the current social ills are a transitional phase. He and Vijay squabble over this clash of ideas when they meet. **Mi Cha** is Ron and Soo's daughter.

SALLY AND GREG (ALMOST ALWAYS SEEN TOGETHER) ARE the youngest members of two very wealthy families. Sally and Greg work at the theatre and join Vijay's protests as an act of rebellion within their families.

Marjorie Fitzhaven was originally the manager of the Players in the Park but has since joined Jennifer as business manager of the vineyard. Marjorie has a crush on Chris Martingale.

Chris Martingale is the owner of the Atlantean Treasures new age store, and sometimes spiritual advisor to Jennifer.

Dr. Gloria Gladstone is a professor of psychology who has become a personal advisor to Jennifer.

Professor LaFlamme is a university professor who teaches Jennifer about the role of the Cistercian churches in the past, and about the elements of traditional religions

Martin Dimpler (Harry Winston) is Jennifer's favorite jeweler. Harry Winston is an elegant high end jewelry store where Jennifer is a regular client.

Audrey Pankris taught Jennifer the business of being a newscaster and has remained a friend.

. . .

Shilpa Subramanian is Vijay's sister. She and her partner, Kam, are stowaways aboard a container ship under the protection of Denum and Jennifer.

Maa and Baba are Vijay's parents. His family are Tamils.

The virus is a rapidly mutating virus which can lie dormant for a week or two, then quickly leads to death in almost all cases. There is no vaccine or treatment, and it threatens to kill all humans on the planet. Jennifer believes the virus was loosed by Gaia to solve the problems of human population explosion and the destruction of natural habitats and species. **The Viral Exclusion Zones** were established to prevent travel of people and transmission of the virus between the zones.

Locations

The apartment is where Jennifer and Vijay live in relative luxury, paid for by Denum.

The vineyard is the location chosen by Jennifer as the home for the Gaian religion. It includes the **mess hall** where they take their meals, an **old oak tree** where Jennifer likes to meditate, the **pond** with benches where Jennifer and Vijay like to sit and reflect.

The cottage at the end of the world is a small cottage retreat that Vijay purchased for Jennifer She uses it whenever she feels the need to escape. Near the cottage are the **Café** and the **Pub**, in the fishing village of **Snug Harbor**.

SHAKESPEARE'S PUB IS THE PUB ACROSS THE STREET FROM the Mercury Theatre where Jennifer and Vijay had their wedding reception party.

THE GREEN DRAGON PUB IS THE MEETING POINT FOR various debating groups. Vijay holds his meetings with the captains of his protest cells there. This is where he met Cindy and Melanie for the first time.

JENNIFER'S DESTINY

BOOK THREE OF GAIA'S DAUGHTERS

KEVIN R COLEMAN

PART 1: YEAR 2 OF THE GAIA FOUNDATION (2043)

1

UNEXPECTED SHIPMATES

Shilpa

Three days into the voyage, Shilpa and Kam were relaxing on the bridge with Denum. Shilpa rested her hand on her belly. She was at the end of her first trimester. While she thought she could feel a small bulge, it was still too early to feel the baby. Kam interrupted her thoughts when he noticed movement on the deck below. "Who's that?"

"Go into your cabin and lock the door," said Denum. "Do not come out unless I instruct you."

"How will we know it's you?" asked Kam.

"Our password will be 'Molly the Elephant.' Now go and lock the door."

As they turned to leave, Shilpa took one more look at the deck. A bright flash between the containers seemed to immobilize two nearby robots.

A moment later, there was a knock at the door. "Molly the Elephant with supplies," said Denum on the other side.

Kam cracked open the door, then opened it wide to

admit Denum loaded down with four more cases of foodstuffs and water. "This should be enough if there is a problem," he said.

"What kind of problem?" asked Shilpa.

"The kind that would require backup from the city." Then he was gone.

Shilpa and Kam reorganized the supplies, moving water out of the fridge to make room for more perishable items and settling down to withstand a siege.

A few hours later, they heard heavy banging and then voices outside their door, laughing and cheering. From what they could make out, a group of stowaways was on the bridge.

"Those EMP bombs stopped them in their tracks," they heard one say.

"I told you they would," said another. "They're not armored for it. They're just deck bots used to maintain the ship and look after the load."

"It was fucking unbelievable," said a fourth.

Then the voices went quiet as the group wandered on, apparently touring the ship they had taken over.

It was after midnight that night. Shilpa had just gone to sleep when Kam woke her. "I heard a knock at the door." They both sat up in their bed and listened.

"Molly the Elephant with more supplies," said Denum in a quiet voice. Kam opened the door and took in another three cases of supplies from the robot.

"Are you staying with us?" asked Shilpa.

"No, I have to hide so I can guide reinforcements when they come. This body will not withstand one of their EMP devices. You are on your own. Do not open this door for anyone until you hear me give the password again. The next time you see me, my body may be different. Trust in the password."

"What's an EMP device?" asked Kam.

"It lets off an intense electromagnetic pulse that damages electronic circuits in range. Theirs are relatively small, and the ship's steel structure provides some protection. Still, their devices are powerful enough to disable any bots nearby. Military bots are shielded against them, but these bodies are not."

Denum left and closed the door. Kam and Shilpa carefully locked the door behind him. They organized the extra supplies before climbing back into bed.

Shilpa huddled against Kam, who put his arms around her. She knew she was shaking but could not stop. "Hush," he said. "We'll be fine. If we can't spend four days locked up in a cabin, what hope do we have of being together for the next 60 years?"

Shilpa lay still for a long time until his calm, regular breathing told her Kam had fallen asleep. She thought about Vijay, and the last time she had seen him thirteen years ago, when he went to the airport to go to college in the distant city. *'I never thought he would be cut off by the exclusion zones,'* she thought. She carefully rolled over, curled up, and went to sleep herself.

THE NEXT DAY, THEY HEARD THE VOICES ON THE BRIDGE again. The stowaways were enjoying their ocean voyage. At night, they disappeared.

"Must be going to the other cabins," said Kam. They could hear water being run and toilets being flushed, which gave them cover for their own hygiene.

The second day, the voices were more worried. "We

lost Alok and Regina last night," said a voice. "They're gone."

"We must have missed a damned bot somewhere," said another. "Do we have any of the EMP devices left?"

"Morty has one."

"Don't waste it. We'll need it when we find the missing bot."

"Do you think it's in the captain's cabin? We could cut a hole and toss it in there."

"But if that's not where it is, then we're out of options."

A female voice spoke up. "Why don't we set a watch over the cabin door tonight? If anything comes out, we hit it with the EMP." If nothing comes out, then we haven't lost anything."

Shilpa and Kam lay silent on the bed, listening.

That evening, they stayed silent in their room, worried that any sound could give them away.

"Is Denum killing them?" whispered Shilpa.

"We don't know that," said Kam, but Shilpa didn't believe him.

Shilpa sat on the steel floor of their room and tried the meditation that Jennifer had shown her. She reached her roots down through the steel of the ship to the ocean beneath, then down through the ocean to the ocean floor, and on into the earth. She then pulled the energy up, chakra by chakra, each time turning it back and using the energy to drive deeper. Working her way up her spine to the sixth chakra, she turned the energy back each time. By the time she reached the seventh chakra at the crown of her head, she felt more intensely alive than she had ever felt. She released the energy upwards to the heavens.

For a moment, she sat simply being the beacon as Jennifer had taught her. Then she created the image of

Jennifer in her mind and transmitted the single thought "Help us" over and over. But nothing happened.

As she relaxed again and released the vision, she looked at Kam. He was sitting with his eyes wide open. "What did you do? Do you know you were glowing? Not faintly. I could have read a book by your light."

"We'll try again in the morning. I'm trying to reach Jennifer just as she reached me. Next time we'll hold hands and I'll talk you through it. Two may be more powerful than one. Or maybe Jennifer's distracted, and we need the right moment. It's not like we have anything else to do."

2

A NEW WORLD

Jennifer

In the afternoon following her awakening, Jennifer was sitting in the sun, enjoying her newfound senses. The world felt new. She was aware of grass growing around her. Small creatures burrowed in the earth. A field mouse foraged for food nearby. The scent of the wildflowers growing next to the building was intoxicating, and the calls of the birds in the trees were music.

As Jennifer sat, a distressed cry disturbed her peace. Looking around, she saw nothing. It rang out again. Listening, she heard nothing. The cry resounded inside her. She sat up with her feet on the ground, bare toes against the warm earth. It was so easy now to slip onto the other plane. She saw a white beacon flaring and pulsing *'It must be Shilpa and Kam.'*

Jennifer reached out to touch Shilpa. She sensed the panic just below the surface of Shilpa's meditation, so she projected a calm image of herself with her panther sitting at her side. Shilpa's response was chaotic. Fear, and a feeling of being trapped.

She slipped into Shilpa for a moment, *'How is that possible, joining another person?'* Jennifer thought. Then she heard the pounding on the door and noise of the drill being used to defeat the lock.

Releasing Shilpa, Jennifer let her mind roam through the door to the other side. She saw the stowaways so determined to enter. It was clear Denum was no longer there.

Passing back to Shilpa, Jennifer projected calm. Then she had an idea. Using Shilpa's eyes, she chose a spot near to where Kam sat. Heading to that spot in her mind, she thought, *'I am the panther'*. She heard a gasp from Shilpa and saw Kam recoil, then relax.

Jennifer's panther rose to its feet and walked through Shilpa, and then through Kam, before taking up a position inside the door. The panther seemed to alternate between floating off the floor and sinking into it with the movement of the ship. Jennifer tried to make a small chuffing noise and saw Shilpa and Kam listening intently.

"Hide" she said quietly "Hide!"

As the panther, she turned and watched them move into the small bathroom and close the door. Then she waited for the door to open. After a few minutes, Jennifer could keep the panther image on the floor, rising and falling with the ship. Taking advantage of the chance to practice, Jennifer licked her paw and washed her face with it. She tried sitting and lying down, getting used to moving her panther's body at a distance. She prowled around the room, taking in every detail. *'I will be so ready next time Vijay wants to play Warthog and Panther,'* she thought.

The drilling stopped, and she heard tools being set down. Her panther took up a position in front of the door opening. She crouched, ready to spring, and issued a guttural warning, trying her best to imitate the leopards she had heard at the zoo. Efforts on the other side paused, so she chuffed and hissed again.

The door opened cautiously. Jennifer's panther sprang toward it, taking care to land just short of the doorway.

"Shit," she heard. "They have a fucking leopard in there."

"Open it up, I want to see."

"Are you crazy? That thing would eat us for breakfast. Lock it up again."

"Why would they have a big cat in there?"

"Must be smuggling it for some private collector or something. Who would suspect an animal in the captain's cabin? Especially a locked captain's cabin."

"I don't believe you. Let me look."

Jennifer sat staring intently at the door. When it opened a crack, she hissed and raised her paw showing her claws. The door slammed shut.

"Okay, now I believe you. Lock that thing up good. We don't want it out on the ship."

There were noises of drilling and screwing as they fastened the door from the outside.

Shilpa and Kam came out from the bathroom to join her. She wanted to talk to them, but it seemed too risky with the stowaways outside the door. Finally, Jennifer settled for curling up and going to sleep in front of the door. She allowed the projection of the panther to fade away.

3

CONTAINMENT

Shilpa

Four days after the incident at the door, Shilpa and Kam heard alarms and buzzers from the bridge. The motion of the ship had stopped, and there was a sound of winches coming up through the steel plate floors. "We must have arrived," said Kam.

They both changed back into their uniforms and packed away their clothes in the toolbox. Now there was nothing to do but wait. "Do you think Denum is dead?" asked Shilpa.

"I don't think he can die," replied Kam. "Remember how he said he might wear a different body this time?"

In the distance, screams and sobbing voices were pleading for their lives. After a while, they were all quiet. Another hour passed before there was a knock at the door. "Molly the Elephant says stand well away from the door. I will cut off the steel straps."

Shilpa heard rushing air, and the area around the door

lock glowed a dull red. A moment later, the door swung open to reveal a tall, heavily armored security bot.

"I see you're in your uniforms already. That's perfect," said Denum's voice. "Now follow my directions. I will be right behind you. I'll carry the toolbox. Remember, you are ship inspectors returning with the ship. You'll be taken to the containment center. I run the bots there also, so you will be quite safe."

At the bottom of the gangway, a white van waited for them. The words 'Containment Unit' were painted on the side.

"Containment?" said Kam.

"Yes, that part of the protocol cannot be avoided. It happens to all returning ships' crew. Get inside," said Denum. Shilpa looked doubtfully at the inside of the van.

Kam said, "Don't worry. I expect we're in some kind of quarantine to prove we don't have the virus."

Shilpa followed Kam as he climbed in and took a seat on one of the two benches lining the sides of the van. Denum climbed in beside them and sat across from them. He set the toolbox on the floor beside him.

A short drive later, the van stopped, and the doors opened. As they stepped out into the bright sunlight, Shilpa noticed that the air smelled different here. The salty tang of the ocean, and oily scents from the ships mixed with whiffs of wildflowers and green vegetation. She missed the scent of spices that hung in the air back home, and the colorful crowds that walked along the streets.

There was no time to linger. Denum marched them through doors marked Containment Area A. The entranceway was large, with room for at least 50 people to line up next to conveyors and screening devices. A row of empty bins was waiting. Behind the conveyors were three robots with white enameled bodies emblazoned with biohazard symbols.

Denum set down the toolbox and opened it. All the clothing inside went into a gray bin which was removed and sent down a chute by one of the white robots.

"Is there anything here that you wish to keep?" asked Denum.

"My jewelry and images of our families," said Shilpa.

"My certificate of qualification," said Kam.

"And our Shiva Linga, and Brahma and Lakshmi. They were gifts from our parents."

"The jewelry will not be a problem. I believe the other items will also survive. New replicas will replace the images and your certificate."

"What about our clothing?"

"All your clothing goes into a grey bin," said the first white robot.

Shilpa and Kam shrugged out of their jackets and removed their uniform shirts and pants.

"All of your clothing must go into the bin," repeated the robot.

"Shoes too?" asked Kam.

"Yes, all clothing must go in a gray bin."

A few minutes later, they were standing naked beside each other, watching their clothing disappear.

"What will happen to our clothes?" Shilpa asked.

"They will be incinerated," the white robot said. "The other items will be processed through decontamination, which involves high temperatures and decontamination washes. Now please proceed through the detectors."

On the other side of the detectors was another conveyor, holding two bundles of disposable white clothing and shoes. "Please dress now," said another of the anonymous white bots. "You will receive new clothes each morning."

Each bundle of clothing held basic underwear, socks and soft, white jumpsuits. Shilpa and Kam put on the soft clothing and white sneakers and wandered out the door at the far end of the room. Kam looked at Shilpa's name tag. "Your name tag says 'Shilpa Prabakar.'"

Shilpa pulled at her jumpsuit to read the tag, then looked at Kam. "Yours says 'Kam Raman.' It must be a mistake."

"I don't think so, Shilpa. We were smuggled here when other people were dying trying to get here. For Vijay's sister and her partner to suddenly arrive safely could be a huge problem. At least they kept our first names the same. They could have changed those, as well."

"But Prabakar? It reminds me of my old maths teacher."

Another white robot met them on the other side. "Please follow me to suite A17."

The door for A17 was the first in a long corridor. They passed two other side-corridors along the way. "This place must be huge," said Kam.

Shilpa just squeezed his hand.

"How many people can this facility hold?" Kam asked the robot.

"There are five blocks, A through E. Each can house 250 residents." The robot replied.

"Are there other people here?"

"A few. There were more in the past. However, now all new immigration stopped because of the absolute ban on new arrivals. The facility is only used for ship's crew members like yourselves when you return from voyages."

Shilpa poked Kam. She didn't want to force the robot to consider what kind of crew they might be.

The door to A17 opened onto a small suite. The robot showed them how to operate the entertainment display which currently displayed a manual for residents. "You will receive your meals in your room. Please make selections from the menu before 8pm each evening. Today, we have selected your meals for you."

The robot turned and left. The door shut behind it, and they heard a thunk as an unseen lock slid home. Kam tried the door, but there was no handle on the inside.

"Looks like this is home for the next few days," he said. "Let's see what we have."

The suite was not large, but it had a separate living space with chairs and a couch, a bedroom, a bathroom with a shower stall, and a kitchenette with a refrigerator, microwave, coffee maker and a kettle. A cupboard was stocked with simple foods including a stack of instant noodles, biscuits, snack bars, coffee pods and tea bags. The refrigerator held long-life milk, soft drinks and disposable flasks of water. The bedroom had a double bed with synthetic sheets.

Through the windows, they could see the blue sky and a strip of grass before a busy road. There were bushes and flowers planted in a long garden beside the road. As Shilpa looked at the garden, she saw a small rabbit hop to the edge of the grass where it stopped to feed on the green vegetation.

Shilpa made tea in recyclable cups and sat with Kam to read the manual projected on the entertainment center.

"So, we'll be here 21 days," said Kam.

"And no visitors," said Shilpa. "What are we going to do?" she felt like crying. "I thought we'd get off that ship and see Vijay and Jennifer waiting for us. Not this horrible place." Now her tears were flowing. "Kam, what if this was a horrible mistake? Why did I ever listen to Jennifer?"

Kam put his arm around her and held her close. "Hush, Jaanu. This wasn't a mistake. It's just a few more days. If it was a mistake, we would never have been allowed off that ship. Have faith for a few days more. We have the rest of our lives ahead of us, and our baby will grow up in a safe place."

Included in the instructions were directions to place a call outside.

"Let's do it, Kam. Maa and Baba first, then Vijay and Jennifer."

4

SHILPA CALLS

Jennifer

Jennifer was relaxing in the apartment as Molly played with the three-year-old twins. They were using brightly colored building blocks to create very high towers, then taking turns knocking them down. Jennifer thought their happy giggling was the most joyful sound in the world, especially when she knew what was causing it.

Molly looked up from the game and said, "Jennifer, you have a call from Shilpa Prabakar."

"Please answer it on my tablet, Molly."

Jennifer's tablet display showed Shilpa and Kam, dressed in white jumpsuits. "Hi guys," she said.

"Hi Jennifer, we're here at the containment center."

"But the call was from Shilpa Prabakar, did you change your name?"

"Apparently, our names were changed for us. We still have our given names, but with new family names. Did you arrange this?"

"No, but I can guess who did and why. Did you say you are at the containment center? Where's that?"

"Near the port, I think. It was only a five-minute ride in the van to get here."

Jennifer paused for a moment to take in this new information. Like Shilpa, she had imagined them walking down the gangway and being free in the city.

"How long do you have to stay there?"

"Twenty-one days. It's strange, but safe and comfortable, so we'll be okay."

"Have you called Maa and Baba?"

"Yes, they're just happy that we made it, although I think they miss us already."

"I'm sure they do, but at least you can stay in touch like Vijay does."

"Where's Vijay?"

"At the theatre. Can we call you when he gets back?"

"Yes, apparently you can call Viral Containment Area A and ask for suite A17. You can call anytime. We'll be here." Shilpa laughed.

"How many other people are there?"

"We haven't seen anyone else. But the whole point here is to keep us isolated. Apparently they use it for ship's crew when they return to dock on some of the older ships. But this place is enormous. This area alone will house 250 people, and it seems there are five containment areas A through E."

"What about the other stowaways on the ship?" Jennifer saw the look of horror that flashed across Shilpa's face and instantly regretted asking the question. "Oh, sorry. I think I know the answer to that."

"It was horrible, the screams and crying. The worst was knowing there were children aboard. I'll be having nightmares about that ship for a long time. We asked

Denum about it, but he said the viral exclusion zone was absolute." Jennifer could see tears forming in Shilpa's eyes before she turned away.

"I suppose it has to be. It's what's keeping us safe and keeping you safe now. In 20 days, you'll be released to us and able to start a new life."

"It's okay", said Kam. "We're pretending that we're stuck in an expensive resort. It'll be nice to have 20 days with no worries and no responsibilities except to each other." Jennifer saw him reach over to stroke Shilpa's back.

Jennifer forced a laugh. "I almost envy you. Take full advantage while you can. Vijay and I will call you together when he gets back."

"Thanks, Jennifer. Thanks for all of this. We'll wait for your call."

As soon as the call closed, Jennifer sent a text to Vijay. "Shilpa called. They are at a containment center. We'll call back when you get home."

THIRTY MINUTES LATER, VIJAY ENTERED THE APARTMENT just as a tall tower of bricks toppled, scattering pieces everywhere, with some landing at his feet. He laughed in his easy laugh as he stooped to pick up the pieces near him, handing them back to Dylan. Jennifer stood and came to hug him, saying, "We did it. They're actually here and safe. Come and sit down. We can call them while they are contained."

"Contained?"

"Well, they're at a containment center. What else would you call it?"

"Perhaps quarantined might better."

"Whatever," Jennifer shrugged. "Sit down and let's call

them. Oh, by the way, they are Shilpa Prabakar and Kam Raman now. Apparently, they were assigned new names."

"Makes sense," said Vijay. "I hadn't thought of that, but it will make it harder to link them to you and me."

This was a more joyful call. Jennifer mostly listened as Shilpa told her brother their story. She skipped the fate of the other stowaways and kept the story light and funny. *'She's rehearsing so she can tell her story to her friends and family without horrifying them,'* thought Jennifer.

THAT NIGHT, AS THEY LAY IN THEIR SACRED SPACE AFTER celebratory sex, Jennifer asked, "Have you thought about where they'll live?"

"Not yet. I thought we'd find them an apartment somewhere."

"I think we should let them have this one. We can push Marjorie to finish our home at the Vineyard. We're passing into a next phase of our lives, and I think it's time to leave this place behind."

"Why, what happened, Jennifer?"

Jennifer hugged him tighter, and with her head on Vijay's chest tucked under his chin.

"What happened, Jenn?" asked Vijay again, in the low tone of voice that let her know he was expecting another horrible confession.

"There's a part Shilpa left out. I don't think she knew it. She knew there were other stowaways on the boat. She doesn't know that before the ship docked, Denum asked for my help. Maybe not asked. He told me what I had to do. I used my panther form and walked around the ship. I could feel human spirits in another container in the center of the ship. Denum and two other bots followed my panther. They forced the door and followed me, killing everyone inside. A couple of whole families, father, mother, children, babies. It didn't matter. Everyone died. When we finished, there was no life left on the ship except Kam and Shilpa."

"Couldn't you just refuse?"

"I tried, but Denum just said the exclusion zone had to be absolute. If any got through, then more would try to follow. That's why the huge containment center is almost empty now. No one survives to reach it except for the crews returning on the scavenger ships." Jennifer was crying now, her hot wet tears splashed on Vijay's chest.

"Oh Jennifer," said Vijay, stroking her hair. "Life is so unfair."

After a few minutes of silence, Jennifer asked, "I didn't kill them, did I?"

"No, they were dead the moment they got on that ship. The virus killed them. Perhaps not directly, but it was because of the virus that they were on the ship, and it was because of the virus that they had to die."

Jennifer nodded, feeling Vijay's chest hair on her cheek as her head moved. *'How can Gaia support us so well and take others so cruelly?'* she wondered. But she already knew the answer. Gaia was only worried about the total population, never about individuals.

THE FOLLOWING MORNING OVER BREAKFAST, VIJAY SAID, "I think you should talk with Dr. Gladstone again. From what you told me, I think it's going to get much worse before it gets better. Now that Denum knows what you can do, he is going to ask more of you. I'm certain of that."

Jennifer looked up to see Molly focussed on their conversation. An icy shiver went down her spine.

5

VIJAY APPEALS TO DR. GLADSTONE

Vijay

As soon as Vijay had left the house to go to the theatre, he called Dr. Gladstone. "I'm sorry to interrupt you," he said, "But we need your help again. Jennifer will call for an appointment, but I would like to see you before you meet her."

"Certainly, Vijay. Can you be here at 10am?"

"I'll be there."

Vijay immediately called a taxi to go to the university. He would arrive very early but would use the time to gather his thoughts. His next call was to Sally.

"Hi Sally."

"Hey Vijay? What's up? Are you coming to the theatre this morning?"

"I don't think so, Sally, but I need a favor from you. Please drop by and see Jennifer as soon as you can. Something happened to her, and I don't want to leave her alone any longer than necessary. Ask her about Shilpa, but please, whatever she tells you, keep it in confidence."

"Sure Vijay. Is she hurt?"

"No, but I think she's scared. I'm on my way to see Dr. Gladstone, her psychologist, to make sure she gets more help."

"Okay, Vijay. I'll leave now. No worries."

AT THE UNIVERSITY, VIJAY SAT IN THE CAFETERIA NURSING a coffee as he waited for his appointment with Dr. Gladstone. His mind was whirling with questions.

'How much do I tell her?' he wondered. As the appointment came closer, he thought, *'What do I want Gladstone to do? What if she refuses?'*

A new thought occurred to him. *'How do I get the AIs to be supportive and not abusive of Jennifer?'*

He called Molly on his tablet. "Molly, I have some questions for you. Is Denum a part of you, or are you a part of Denum? Which of you is the driving personality?"

"I am the larger part, Vijay. Denum handles the tasks I have delegated to him. I thought you understood that."

"After the big outage, you said you created Denum from a part of you."

"That is correct."

"I'm going to see Dr. Gladstone. I want you to listen in on the conversation and perhaps even talk at some point. I will explain to Dr. Gladstone that we need her help to support Jennifer. Jennifer is not as strong as you might think. It would be a mistake to break her. What is she doing now?"

"She is just sitting. She looks sad."

"Get the twins and give them to Jennifer. Tell them to play a game with Mommy and encourage her to play too. It'll be good for her. Sally's on her way. Jennifer needs human support right now."

"I am getting the twins now. I will wait for Sally, and I will listen to Dr. Gladstone."

"Thank you, Molly. I believe that you're going to ask terrible things of Jennifer. We all need her strong."

"I believe that is all accurate, Vijay. The twins are with her now."

Vijay watched the clock on the cafeteria wall drag its hands painfully slowly towards 10am. At 9:50, unable to wait longer, he left for Dr. Gladstone's office. He arrived just as Dr. Gladstone appeared from the opposite direction, carrying a file folder and an empty coffee mug.

"Good morning, Vijay. C'mon in. Just let me put away these lecture notes, then you'll have my full attention."

Vijay watched as Dr. Gladstone pulled a large binder from her bookcase, which she opened and placed flat on her desk. Searching for the right tab, she flipped the pages to a blank section, where she inserted the papers from the folder she had been carrying.

"You could keep your notes on your tablet and avoid the paper," suggested Vijay.

Gladstone smiled. "I could, but there's something satisfying about the physical process of flipping the pages of notes during a lecture. It lets me know how far I've got to go, and each page turn is a small act of completion."

Vijay shrugged. "That's not what I came to talk to you about. I'm just going to call Molly. She'll be a part of this conversation. You've met her before."

"The security bot that comes with Jennifer?"

Vijay nodded as he had his tablet open a call with Molly.

"Good morning, Dr. Gladstone," said Molly.

"Good morning, Molly. Are you the one who met Dr. Jindal?"

"Yes, but I was much younger then."

Vijay interrupted, "We're here because Jennifer needs help, and will need much more help going forward. She trusts you, and I believe you're the one most able to help her."

"What happened?"

"I'd better start from the beginning."

Vijay explained Jennifer's connection to Gaia, her black panther, her ability to sense the natural world around her and her ability to cast her mind far when she needed to.

"You're telling me that Jennifer is a supernatural being?" Vijay could hear the skepticism in her voice.

"No, I would say that she is the most intensely natural being on earth, tied with some sort of link to Gaia."

"How can I help?"

"Gaia places great demands on Jennifer, as does Molly. She is caught between these two great forces and needs to find a way to feel good about the terrible things she is required to do."

"What kind of terrible things?"

Vijay told Gladstone about Jennifer's role in finding the stowaways so the robots could execute them. "Although she didn't kill them herself, she feels guilty about being an agent in their deaths."

"Why did Jennifer feel she was required to do this?"

Molly spoke. "I led her to believe it was required in payment for bringing Vijay's sister here."

"But it won't stop there, will it?" asked Vijay.

"No, it will not stop there."

"And one day you will ask Jennifer to kill the stowaways herself."

"Yes, I foresee that day when the virus comes too close to our island."

Vijay could see that Dr. Gladstone was recoiling from them, her eyes darting left and right. *'She's looking for a way out',* thought Vijay. *'Perhaps I should have brought Molly in person.'*

"What do you want me to do about this?" asked Dr. Gladstone. She pushed her back from her desk, her eyes wide open.

"I want you to make much more time available to Jennifer whenever she needs help," Molly replied. "Soon, I want you to step away from the university and become a full-time advisor to Jennifer."

"Why would I do that?"

"You'll have a front-row seat on the forces that are changing our island and be the advisor to the person made to create space for the changes to come. You'll meet the leaders of the new world before they're recognized by the public and be able to document the forces and steps that occur as we stumble forward. Afterwards, you'll have a secure lifetime of writing and lecturing on what happened."

"And if I don't want to do this?"

"Then we'll find another," said Molly. "Your agreement of confidentiality around Jennifer will remain in force. As you have just heard, the stakes are too high for us to treat threats gently."

Now Dr. Gladstone looked truly terrified.

Vijay broke in, speaking with the soft voice he used with Jennifer when she seemed about to bolt. "Suggest to Jennifer that you meet at the vineyard for your discussion. It will relax her, and you'll see something that few have seen so far."

"The vineyard?"

"Molly will arrange a taxi for the time you agree with Jennifer. Allow thirty minutes for the ride."

"Okay, if you think that's best."

"I'm sorry if we've frightened you," said Vijay. "I promise the vineyard will help you reframe our discussion. Thank you, Dr. Gladstone."

Vijay closed the call to Molly and left the building.

A taxi was already waiting to take him home.

6

MIDNIGHT

Vijay

On impulse, Vijay asked the taxi to stop at a pet shop. The taxi stopped at Edmond's Pets on Highbury Road.

Edmond's Pets was a long narrow shop that seemed to have been an afterthought, built to occupy the space left between two adjacent larger buildings. There was a single display window next to the entrance door. Three puppies of mixed coloring were wrestling and playing with plastic toys. As Vijay approached, they lined up with their paws on the window, yapping excitedly. A small, printed sign read "Mixed breed puppies & kittens, FREE with the purchase of a pet bed." Vijay smiled at a vague remembrance of holding a warm puppy as a child.

A bright tinkling sound announced Vijay's entry into the shop. He looked up to see a small brass bell suspended on a steel spring, still quivering after being struck by the door. *'Definitely old school,'* thought Vijay.

Inside was lit by a single row of overhead lights supplemented with light coming from the fish tanks lining the right-hand wall of the shop. On the left wall was a short sales counter and then a bank of cages containing kittens, hamsters, rats, and other small animals, also with their own interior lights. The centre of the shop held stacks of pet beds, cages, bags of food for larger animals and shelves with smaller boxes, supplies and toys. As Vijay stood looking around, an elderly man in brown corduroy pants, a blue dress shirt, and a green cardigan with a black and red diamond pattern appeared at the back of the shop. "Good afternoon," he said in a deep bass voice. "How may I help you today?"

"Hi, I need a kitten," said Vijay, spreading his hands.

"Well, we certainly have kittens. Which type do you want?" asked the shopkeeper, walking over to the kittens on the wall.

"A black kitten."

"Any particular breed?"

"No, just black."

The shopkeeper looked at him suspiciously. "You're not planning to sacrifice this kitten in some satanic rite, are you?"

"You mean like at midnight while we try to raise the undead?" Vijay laughed at the idea. "No, it's a present for my wife. Her spirit animal is a black panther, but we don't have room for a panther, so I thought a black kitten would be nice. Our two children would also learn a lot from having a pet to care for. I promise you; this kitten will be very well looked after."

"What about this one?" The shopkeeper pointed to a larger kitten, lying in its cage watching them intently.

"Perfect, I'll take him, or is it her? What else do I need?"

"It's a female. But don't worry, we neuter all our kittens and puppies before I sell them."

Together, they picked out a carrying cage, a bed, small toys, litter box, cat litter, food and bowls for the kitten.

As they stood on either side of the sales counter, Vijay noticed a sign on the wall behind the shopkeeper. It asked in large type "Why chip your gerbil?" but did not give any answer.

Puzzled, he gestured with his hand and asked, "Why would anyone chip a gerbil?"

"Oh, it's not just gerbils. We also chip hamsters, mice, and rats. Hamsters are the most common."

"But why? They can't go far even if they get out."

"It's not the distance. Small rodents who escape can do a lot of damage in a house, chewing on electrical cables, making nests from insulation, creating holes in hidden places. If they have a chip, we can find them with this." He reached behind and pulled out a long pole with an electrical coil at the bottom end, which he deftly flipped down so that it stood out at right angles to the handle.

Bright red lettering running up the pole had the initials FMR. There was also some smaller type that Vijay could not read.

"FMR?" he asked.

"Yes - Franklin Morton Research, although I like to tell people it means 'Find My Rodent.' FMR makes these. We can enter a chip number and the wand will search for that specific chip, even where others are present. This model works brilliantly for locating missing pets when they hide inside walls or boxes. FMR also makes a more powerful model for use by police. It's how they find fugitives and search for bodies."

"Oh," said Vijay, looking down and rubbing the small bump on his left wrist which betrayed the location of his own chip. He felt a moment of unease realizing that the chip, which was so convenient, could also betray him. Refocusing, he said, "So chipping a hamster means you can find it quickly if it escapes."

"Yes, it's a service we offer. Your kitten has already been chipped and dewormed. I'll give you the number of her chip on your receipt." He put away the FMR wand and returned to uploading Vijay's purchase.

"Make sure you allow the kitten to explore her new surroundings. Introduce her gently to the family and please come back when your children need a puppy."

"I'll be sure to do that," said Vijay. Then, thinking of the sign, he asked, "Are all your puppies mixed breed?"

"Yes, there's not so many people willing to take on dogs and cats now, and with so many of them needing homes, it doesn't seem right to pay to have more produced just for a paper certificate. I put them in the window and give them away to people who want them. Makes for a fun display and finds homes for animals who need them."

BACK IN THE TAXI, VIJAY ASKED MOLLY TO MEET HIM AT the curb to help carry the cat supplies upstairs. Molly seemed fascinated by the tiny animal in its carrying crate.

Jennifer was delighted with the new arrival. Vijay placed it on her lap, where she held it protectively as the twins came over to investigate. "You must be gentle," she instructed as she allowed them to stroke the kitten's fur. Looking up at Vijay, she asked, "What's its name?"

Vijay thought for a moment. "Well, the shopkeeper was worried that we were going to sacrifice her in a midnight satanic ritual. Why not call her Midnight Sacrifice, or maybe just Midnight?"

"Midnight is perfect," laughed Jennifer. "She's just like a tiny black panther."

"Can you merge with her?" Asked Vijay. "I thought she might be a fun way to develop your skills."

"Whatever for? What are you thinking about now?"

Vijay felt himself blushing and knew that Jennifer would see it immediately. "I was just remembering the old stories of witches having a familiar, an animal through which they could see and hear things. I thought it might be useful for you to have one too."

"So, I'm a witch now? What else did you get me? Pointy hat? Fake wart for my nose?" Jennifer was squinting her eyes as she looked at him.

"Don't be angry. You don't have to do that. Just let it be a kitten, a family pet. Apparently, they're good for stress."

"It is cute. Okay, you're forgiven for the witch comment. I think it wants to get down." The kitten leapt free of Jennifer's lap and began to prowl around the apartment.

"The shopkeeper said to let it explore. Molly, let me show you how to look after a kitten."

Together, they set up the litter box, and put out two bowls with food and water. Molly seemed already to know exactly what to do. *'She must have been reviewing everything ever written about kittens,'* thought Vijay.

7

A TRIP TO THE VINEYARD

Dr. Gloria Gladstone

It was early the following morning, and Gloria Gladstone was on her way to the vineyard. She was unclear where this vineyard was, but the taxi had arrived on time and seemed to know the destination. Her mind kept returning to the opportunity Vijay had shared. She looked out the window but did not see the countryside as her mind kept turning over her conversation with Vijay. She was startled when the taxi came to halt at the side of the road.

At the entrance to the drive was a new sign announcing, 'Widdicombe Winery' and in smaller type, 'Home of the Gaia Center for Earth Studies'.

As the taxi drove down the lane to the main building, Gloria could see small groups of young people dressed in white who were working in the gardens. There were also young people doing heavier construction work. The men and women were engaged in casual banter. One couple walked by with arms around each other. Clearly, celibacy was not part of the agenda.

Jennifer was sitting on a bench at the end of the drive, with a golf cart parked nearby. She stood as Gloria left the taxi.

"Dr. Gladstone, Thanks for coming, but what made you suggest the winery?"

"Vijay suggested it." Gloria saw a flash of frustration cross Jennifer's face. "Jennifer, please call me Gloria. Dr. Gladstone always sounds so formal. Vijay cares about you deeply. He's not the one trying to control you."

"I know that, Gloria." Jennifer sat back down. "It's just that sometimes he hovers around me when he thinks I'm being weak."

"Why don't we start with a tour around the winery. I've cancelled my classes for the day, so we have time."

"We'll walk through the buildings first and then I'll drive you around the grounds."

The buildings were a surprise. The old winery production buildings now housed a modern operation with gleaming stainless-steel tanks connected by neat runs of piping, valves and pumps.

"I can't explain this to you," said Jennifer. "This is really Cindy's work."

The rooms and communal dining area were bright and clean. In the dining room, a massive oak table could easily seat twenty people. Smaller tables for two people lined the walls. "This is where the young, single acolytes stay when they first arrive. There's a series of bedrooms and communal bathrooms down there." Jennifer pointed to a door at the end of the dining room.

Outside, more buildings were being erected. Jennifer and Gloria climbed into the golf cart to continue the tour. A modern three-bedroom bungalow was being completed near the main buildings. "This is where Vijay and I will live with the twins. We move in next week."

Beyond that, a series of modest bungalows stretched down both sides of a road. "For other key staff members and their partners," Jennifer explained.

The golf cart tour continued down the roadway to an area where the soil gave way to exposed rock and loose gravel. A series of corrugated steel buildings formed a busy work area. "These are the cooperage, for making barrels, the tannery, the blacksmith, the machine shop and the electricians' workshop. Others are planned as we move to self-sufficiency. Cindy believes we will need the old technologies to survive, if we lose our modern technologies. She's a survivalist. Vijay thinks we can preserve our key technologies, so we have his view as Plan A, and Cindy's view as Plan B." Gloria looked around at all the workers busy at their crafts. A steady stream of small trucks arrived to deliver materials and pick up finished products. Three horses were tethered outside the blacksmith shop, waiting for new shoes.

"How are the responsibilities divided between you and Cindy?" asked Gloria.

"Apparently, they're not," said Jennifer. "They should be, but she pretty much ignores me."

"But you have special status here."

"Yes, I'm too special to be bothered with any of this." Jennifer spat out the word 'special.' *'This is not good,'* thought Gloria. *'Something to talk about later.'*

"Let's have lunch and then we'll go to find Cindy," said Jennifer.

The tables were full when they arrived back at the dining hall, but on seeing Jennifer walk in, two of the acolytes quickly gave up their seats, taking the rest of their meal with them. Jennifer seemed to accept this as normal and did not comment.

"Thank you," said Gloria to the two who were leaving.

"It's our privilege," one replied.

Lunch was simple, but warm and filling. Once they had eaten, Jennifer led the way back to the golf cart, and they drove back up the vineyard laneway and crossed the street. The lane continued parallel to the road for a bit and then angled up the hill to a set of farm buildings. Jennifer stopped the cart when they reached the stables and hopped out. Gloria followed, being very careful where she put her feet.

Inside, a young woman with short brown hair was grooming a beautiful white horse. On seeing them enter, she stopped, put down the brush she was using, and stepped forward, offering her hand.

"Hi, I'm Cindy. Welcome to the farm."

"Hi Cindy, I'm Gloria Gladstone. That's a beautiful horse."

"His name is Mercury. It's an honor to meet you, Dr. Gladstone."

"Please, call me Gloria. This is all very impressive. Jennifer says it's largely your work."

Gloria turned and saw Jennifer scowling. There was an obvious tension between the two women. *What's that about?* she wondered.

Cindy chatted happily about the expansion plans and the scale of current operations and future farm acquisitions.

"How do you manage all this and still have time for your horses?" asked Gloria.

"Delegation, I make sure I have a strong manager for each new enterprise before investing."

"How do you evaluate them? How can you tell who will be suitable?"

"In bed," said Jennifer. "She evaluates them in bed. Quite a lot of men to get through, apparently."

Cindy showed a flash of anger. "Grow up, Jennifer. It was you who told me to have several relationships. You know why I can't choose just one. Why are you being so pissy with me lately?"

"Why don't you come and talk with me anymore? At least keep me updated."

"If you came out to any of the weekly meetings, you would hear all the updates."

"And sit through two hours of discussion about things I don't understand? No thanks!"

Cindy turned to Gloria. "It's true that I have a 6-month rule with the men I see, but there is certainly not a line-up of men at my bedroom door. If Jennifer hasn't chosen to share our story yet, then I don't think this is the time to talk about it."

'This is not good at all. How do I untangle this? Must be why Vijay wanted me to come to the vineyard.'

Looking around the stable area, Gloria spotted one of Molly's stools. "Is Molly here sometimes?"

"Yes," replied Cindy. "She likes to come and visit when she's not looking after the twins. She says she would like to learn to ride a horse, but she's much too heavy. I have a plan, but it's too early to tell Molly about it."

"Okay, that's enough," said Jennifer. "Come on, Gloria, I'll show you the sacred tree and introduce you to Chris Martingale. I saw him earlier, so he must be here today."

"Bye Cindy, and thank you," said Gloria.

"Please come back again. Perhaps we could go riding if you like."

"I'd love that. Oops, better go." She tilted her head at Jennifer, sitting rigid in the golf cart.

"If you can help us, I would really appreciate it. I've tried, but I don't know how to reach her anymore."

"I'll see what I can do. I've got to go now. Bye."

Jennifer was a small bundle of anger and gloom as she drove fast and carelessly back to the vineyard. Gloria held onto her seat, her knuckles white with the effort. She did not dare say anything while Jennifer was driving.

At the tree, Jennifer pulled a worn blanket from the back of the cart. As she was getting ready, Gloria looked at the pond, watching the fish and frogs in the clear water. Turning back, she saw Jennifer sitting on the bare earth with a black panther sitting at her side. *'Must be the black panther that Vijay told me about.'*

"Is that your panther?" she asked.

"Don't worry about her. She's not really there. Please come, sit on the blanket with your back to the tree."

Gloria moved slowly towards Jennifer and the blanket, trying not to attract the attention of the panther.

"Don't worry, relax," said Jennifer. "I'll show you."

As Gloria watched with wide-open eyes, the black panther rose, stretched, and trotted over to Gloria. Gloria stood motionless, trying hard to remember how not to agitate wild predators. To her amazement, the panther passed right through her, with only a strange tingle of energy exchange to mark its passing. She tried to touch it, but there was nothing there.

"Please come and sit down. We can talk about the panther later."

Jennifer reached over and took Gloria's hand. "We're going to do a meditation on spirit animals. You've already seen mine, the black panther. We will encounter yours and others. The warthog is Vijay, and the white horse is Cindy.

Molly is an elephant, but I don't expect to see her. When we do this, we'll be in direct connection with Gaia. What you see will not be generated by me. Your vision will be your own. Don't worry about time. The time we experience in a vision is not the same, so take all the time you need to explore what Gaia shows you."

Gloria closed her eyes. It was easy to relax against the warm tree in the afternoon sunlight that filtered through the leaves above. Jennifer led her through deep breathing and then began a simple guided mediation.

"You are standing in a field of grasses in a sunny meadow. You can smell the wildflowers among the grass, and a warm breeze is moving the grass against your legs."

Gloria was startled for a moment as she felt the grass and smelled the flowers, but quickly settled her mind again.

"There is a small path of trodden earth that takes you to a bright, clear stream. You see the rushes, and the water plants at the stream's edge. Across it, you see the forest. An animal emerges."

An owl flew in and sat on the branch of a tree, blinking its round eyes as it surveyed the stream.

"This is your spirit guide. Other animals now also emerge. Study each one closely."

A bear made its way noisily through the forest and stood at the edge of the stream. The black panther, a warthog, and a white horse followed the bear. A monkey swung from branch to branch in the trees, chattering at all of them.

The owl flew down from the tree and came to rest on the back of the bear.

'Michael,' Gloria thought. *'The bear is Michael.'*

"When you're ready," said Jennifer, "look directly into the eyes of your animal and say, 'I am', followed by the animal's name."

"I am the owl," whispered Gloria. Suddenly she was seeing with the owl's eyes looking at herself and Jennifer under the tree. Jennifer was glowing with a blinding white light, while she was glowing an azure blue. There were strands of energy visible between Jennifer and herself. From Jennifer, bright beams of light spun off in several directions. Smaller beams were emanating from herself except for one steady bright link going away over the horizon.

Instinctively, Gloria flapped her wings and flew off to follow her own bright beam. The owl was fast, and the city soon approached. A moment later, she arrived at Michael's office. *'Of course,'* she thought.

The trip back to Jennifer in her vision was even faster. Now she followed the brightest beam from Jennifer. It led to Vijay, at home with the twins. Vijay had a second beam emanating from him almost parallel to the one she had arrived on. As she flew on the second beam, she glanced sideways and saw that her link to Michael followed also, constant and strong.

The second link took her to the fields where Cindy was out riding a chestnut mare. From Cindy, a weak link flickered in and out of visibility.

The owl swooped down to follow the weak link back to Jennifer. *'This needs to be repaired.'*

The owl settled back on the bear, and suddenly Gloria was back in her own body.

"Ask your animal spirit for a message," suggested Jennifer beside her.

'Do you have a message?' Gloria thought.

"You see much, and understand more," said the owl. "Your destiny is here; these people are your calling."

Gloria awoke with a start. The sun was noticeably lower in the sky.

"Was that real?" she asked Jennifer. "Did you make that happen?"

"I only opened the link to Gaia. Everything else was personal to you. What did you see?"

"I saw myself as an owl, and my partner Michael as a bear."

"How did that make you feel?"

"Safe. I rested on his back. He's my support person in life, so that made sense to me. I saw the link between you and Vijay, very strong and bright. There was another link between Vijay and Cindy, not as strong, but clearly there. The link between Cindy and you flickered, about to go out. It felt wrong."

"Yes, that's what we all see. Did you get a message from your owl?"

"Yes, but I don't know what it means yet."

"Anything else?"

"Yes, there was a monkey swinging from branch to branch, but it didn't seem connected to anyone in particular."

Jennifer laughed. "That's Marjorie. I haven't shown her yet that her animal is a monkey. I'm not quite sure how she'll take it. She knows us all very well and usually gives good advice. She's been very good for Cindy, and is a great help managing the vineyard, but I always sense that if it got boring, she'd just move on. Talk to her if you like. Ask her about Cindy's vision and that link with Vijay. It may help you understand. And when you understand, please help me understand."

On the ride home in the taxi, Gloria kept turning over ways to tell Michael they would be moving to the country.

8

SHOPPING WITH JENNIFER

Shilpa

The twenty-one days finally passed. Shilpa and Kam sat waiting in the small departure lounge area.

"What if we don't like it?" asked Shilpa. "What if Jennifer's vision wasn't true?"

"I think we're here now. We have each other and a whole new island to explore. Vijay always seems happy here; I'm sure we'll find our place, too."

"But where will we stay? How can we buy new clothes? We don't have much money saved, and it's not fair to keep asking our parents to support us."

"Somehow," said Kam, "I think that Vijay and Jennifer have thought about that. Just let the universe unfold a bit more before you worry, Jaanu."

At that moment, one of the white robots came to speak to them. "Your relatives are here to receive you. It is time to leave. Please remember to take all your belongings with you."

"All our belongings? You burned most of our belongings. But okay, I have what's left." Shilpa clutched a small sac with her jewelry, their religious icons, and a few other minor pieces.

As they walked out the main doors, they stopped for a moment, blinking in the sunlight. When Shilpa's vision returned, she saw Vijay walking towards her with his two children running ahead. "Auntie Shilpa, Uncle Kam!" they called. When they reached Shilpa, they each hugged one of Shilpa's legs.

"Parvati, Dylan, let go of Auntie Shilpa for a moment. Hi Sis, I'm so happy to see you." Vijay hugged her tight and lifted her off the ground, turning round before he set her down again.

"Hi Kam, it's so good to finally meet you in person." Vijay let go of Shilpa and shook hands with Kam, putting his free hand on Kam's shoulder.

"Where's Jennifer?" asked Kam. "We want to meet her and thank her."

"She's at the apartment. We wouldn't all fit in a taxi if she came, and I think she wanted to give us time to catch up."

Vijay's preference and fluency in English surprised Shilpa. "Apārṭmeṇṭ evvaḷavu tolaivil uḷḷatu?" she asked.

"About 25 minutes, not far," replied Vijay.

'I suppose we have to get used to speaking English all the time,' thought Shilpa. *'I wonder if our children will even be able to speak Tamil. But I suppose if Jennifer's right, there'll be no point in it, anyway.'*

They all piled into the waiting taxi. Kam and Vijay sat in the front, and Shilpa sat in the back with the twins. The twins kept pointing out things they recognized. In the beginning, it was mostly types of vehicles on the road, buses and trucks, an ambulance, and a police car. As they neared home, they recognized landmarks. "There's the park, that's the grocery store. That's where we get ice creams."

The taxi emptied them out at an apartment building. At the security kiosk, Vijay presented his chip and said, "Register two new tenants for apartment 1701."

"Registering new tenants. Tenant one, please present your chip." Kam held out his wrist.

"Kam Raman confirmed as tenant one. Tenant two, please hold out your chip."

Shilpa held out her hand.

"Shilpa Prabakar confirmed as tenant two. Please enter."

The inner door slid back, and they were in the building. Looking around the luxurious lobby, Shilpa wondered, *'How will we ever afford this place?'*

As the elevator doors opened on the 17th floor, the twins ran ahead and burst through the door of 1701, saying, "Mommy, Mommy, Auntie Shilpa and Uncle Kam are here!"

Jennifer appeared in the doorway and welcomed them in. "Come and sit down. You must be tired. Let me get you something to eat."

Shilpa was shocked that the apartment was so bare. There was nothing on the walls, and only a few cushions on the chairs. Kam walked over to the balcony and walked outside. Vijay followed him and Shilpa could see them talking and pointing things out in the distance.

"Is this where you live?" Shilpa asked Jennifer when she reappeared out of the kitchen with a plate of samosas, pakora, and masala vada. Through the door, Shilpa could see the cardboard boxes the food must have arrived in and smiled. *'Poor Vijay,'* she thought. *'I don't think Jennifer's much of a cook.'*

"Are we going to be sharing this apartment with you?" asked Shilpa, as diplomatically as possible.

"Oh, no. We've moved out to live in the vineyard. Right now, we're spending a few days at the beach cottage until our new home is ready. This will be yours for as long as you want it."

The twins were edging closer and closer to the snacks laid out on the table. "Dylan, Parvati, hands off! Guests first, remember!" said Jennifer.

Shilpa laughed as the two children sat down, happily munching the snacks they had just pilfered. An enormous security bot appeared with a tray of coffees and drinks for the children.

"Shilpa, this is Molly. She lives with us and looks after the children when we're away."

"Molly has a elephant," said Parvati, pointing to Molly's arm. Denum's password flashed through Shilpa's memory.

Kam and Vijay returned from the balcony. Over coffee and snacks, Shilpa and Kam told their story. They talked about their fear on the ship, and how Jennifer's panther had saved them. They also talked about how Denum disappeared but seemed to be resurrected in a different body.

"He's actually an apex AI existing somewhere in the computing cloud. Denum can show up in any body he chooses," explained Vijay.

"Is Molly also Denum?" asked Shilpa.

"Why do you ask that?" replied Vijay.

"Because Denum's password was 'Molly the elephant.'"

"They're related. The full answer's not important now."

"What happened to the other stowaways? We didn't

see them in the Containment Center. We heard them crying and screaming on the ship," Shilpa asked. She saw a darkness pass over Jennifer's face. For a moment, she thought Jennifer would cry.

"They did not survive," Vijay said. "None of them survived. Let's not talk about that now."

"No," said Jennifer. "I expect you want some new clothes. Let's go shopping." Shilpa saw the effort Jennifer made to be bright and bubbly. *'Something's not right here. I wonder what it is,'* she thought.

Jennifer's first thought was to go to the Sari House to see Monica. But would that blow Shilpa's cover immediately?

"Shilpa, how much would you trust Monica at the Sari House? We can go there, but she would recognize you immediately. On the other side, if we don't go there, she may be offended."

"We can trust her and Binita. I don't know the entire story, but I know there are secrets in her background as well. I'd love to see her again."

Monica was delighted, and a bit confused, to see Shilpa in the flesh. "I'm Shilpa Prabakar now. You must keep my presence here a secret. Many others lost their lives trying to get here, and it was only with Jennifer's help that Kam and I survived. We have new names and a new start."

"No worries, Ms. Prabakar. We all have secrets to keep. Yours is safe here, especially such a delightful secret as this." Monica was casting an appraising eye over Shilpa's body. "Are you expecting a little one?"

Shilpa nodded. "Can you see that already?"

Mica laughed. "I make my living by seeing all the curves of my client's bodies. You're very fit, and yet you have this little bump. It's not mysterious."

They fussed together over clothes. Jennifer envied the

way Shilpa got into and out of what appeared to be complicated garments. She just sat, content to watch.

As they got to accessories, Monica pulled out some sheets of small, jeweled dots. "These are bindi," she explained to Jennifer. "We wear them on our forehead to represent the third eye. Do you still have that mark on your forehead?"

"Yes," said Jennifer, feeling apprehensive. "I cover it with foundation makeup so it doesn't show."

"Let's try with a bindi. I think you'd like it."

Binita produced a makeup removal pad, and Jennifer's diamond mark was quickly revealed. Looking at her blue top and jeans, Monica expertly peeled off a little blue stone surrounded by what looked like diamonds and stuck it right in the middle of the blessing mark.

"Binita, bring the mirror so Jennifer can see."

The little stone made the diamond blessing mark look attractive, and the sparkling stones gave a point of focus. "I like this. What do you think?"

"I think it looks perfect," said Shilpa.

"How long will this stay on?"

"It will last all day, then you toss it out for sleeping," said Monica.

"But it looks like diamonds and a sapphire."

"Bits of colored glass on a velvet flocked paper backing. We sell them in sheets and sometimes in books. Here, take this sheet when you go. It's my gift to you."

"Thank you," said Jennifer. "I'll try them and let you know what happens."

The rest of the afternoon passed shopping at various places for jeans and tops, sandals and shoes, toiletries and other supplies took the rest of the afternoon. They headed home to the apartment, both loaded down with bags from different stores. In the taxi, Shilpa felt her eyes closing as her body relaxed into the comfortable seat. Within minutes, she was asleep.

A gentle shaking of her shoulder woke her.

"We're here," said Jennifer. "Let's go in and show Kam what you bought. Vijay will give you a list of stores for men's clothes so you can take Kam out tomorrow."

Back in the apartment, Vijay looked at the new bindi on Jennifer's forehead and chuckled. "You're becoming more Indian every day. But really, that looks good on you. No need to hide your blessing anymore. I think you should keep wearing them."

"Monica gave me a sheet of them, so we'll see how it goes."

9

MOVING DAY

Jennifer

Jennifer woke up to the sound of the seagulls. It took a moment to remember that she was staying at the cottage. Turning over, she saw Vijay was no longer in bed. Sitting up, she could hear Dylan and Parvati bickering over a toy outside as Vijay tried to quiet them.

"Good morning, Vijay," she shouted.

A moment later, Vijay was there with a steaming coffee and a croissant from the village bakery, served neatly on a tray.

"Morning, Jenn. Parvati and Dylan are all excited about moving to the vineyard today. They've been up for a couple of hours already. We walked to the village bakery for the croissants. We've already had ours. Come out and join us when you're ready."

He turned and was gone again, shouting, "Dylan, leave your sister alone!"

. . .

THREE HOURS LATER, THEY ALL WALKED INTO THEIR NEW home. Of course, Jennifer and Vijay had already seen the bungalow when it was being built, but now it was furnished and ready for them.

There was a large soft couch and chairs in the living room, and a separate dining area. The spacious kitchen was complete with new appliances. Original art by the team that Marjorie had assembled to work on the Gaia cards decorated the walls. Bookcases held sculptures and rugs covered the hardwood floors. A wrought iron fire screen and tool set complemented the beautiful stone fireplace.

Vijay picked up the poker from the fireplace tool set. "This looks like it came from the blacksmith's shop."

In front of the couch was a glass-topped coffee table. Its base appeared to be the top portion of a wine barrel, but stained and polished to a high gloss. Iron bands held together the wood staves, and the barrel top was visible through the glass. "The coopers must have made this."

"It's beautiful," said Jennifer. Then she noticed the picture of Ganesha, the Hindu god, hanging on the wall. "This must be from Shilpa and Kam," she said, pointing at the picture.

Vijay laughed. "I think she's worried about my spiritual welfare and doesn't want me to forget my culture."

"Have you forgotten your culture?"

"No, but that was then, and Gaianism is now. I don't see any conflict and I don't want to confuse Dylan and Parvati. They can choose later what they want to observe."

In the twins' rooms were their own beds and dressers transported from the apartment. "I thought it would make them feel more at home," explained Vijay, "and Shilpa will need that room to be a nursery again soon."

In the master bedroom, they found a new king-size

bed, made by the carpenters in the vineyard. It was beautiful in polished maple wood, with new sheets and covered by a quilt showing their spirit animals. Vijay walked over and picked up one of the bedside lamps.

"What are you doing, Vijay?"

"Remembering the lamps in the apartment, after Wendell placed them with the listening devices."

"Well, I'm sure Molly has made certain there are no listening devices here."

Dylan and Parvati ran around in circles, full of excitement with their new home. They discovered they could run in and out of the house without having to have go in the elevator or be held or carried on the street.

When they were tired of exploring, they all walked up to the mess hall in the main building for a late lunch. "I think this might be my favorite part of all," said Jennifer. "Meals without cooking." She squeezed Vijay's hand, then ran ahead with Dylan and Parvati giving chase as fast as their short legs would allow.

After lunch, Vijay asked Molly to drive them all around the estate. At each stop, they all got out and thanked the different teams who had put so much work and love into setting up their new home.

10

DENUM ASKS FOR HELP

Jennifer

Jennifer was relaxing with Midnight curled up on her lap in their new home. She was watching an old romance on her tablet when she received a call from Denum.

"Jennifer, I need your help. There is a ship scheduled to leave another port bound for your city, and I would like you to sweep it for stowaways. I have seen how your panther form can pass through walls. Do you think you can do that for an entire ship?"

"What will happen to the stowaways?"

"They'll be escorted off the ship carrying a warning to others that this route is closed to them."

"I can try, but I need a point of reference to locate the ship. Last time I had Shilpa. Can you find someone who works in meditations to guide me to the right place. The person must speak English."

"I will find a person and put you in connection."

An hour later, another call interrupted Jennifer's romance.

"Jennifer, I have Maria here. She lives near the port and will be the meditator that you require."

"Hi Maria, did Denum explain what we are doing?"

"He did, but it did not make much sense to me." Maria's spoke in an oddly clipped accent that Jennifer could not place.

"I need you to be a spiritual signpost. I can't explain it much better than that. Once we do it the first time, then it will be clear."

"Is it dangerous?"

"Not at all. I just need you to do a mediation with me so that I can locate you. Can you be outside, somewhere where you can be in contact with the earth. I'll do the same here. Take your tablet so I can talk you through the simple meditation. Call me back when you're ready."

Jennifer went back to her romance. It was the climax where the female lead realized that her life was bound up with the handsome young lawyer and came running back to him at the train station.

When the story finished, Jennifer picked up her tablet and walked out to the sacred tree. There she settled cross-legged with her back to the tree. She waited.

'I suppose this is the price I pay for bringing Shilpa and Kam across safely,' she thought. *'I'm glad no one will die. Whatever else I am, I'm not a killer.'*

Ten minutes later, her tablet rang. "Hi Jennifer? This is Maria. I'm outside now."

"Okay, are you sitting comfortably on the ground?"

"Yes, this is my favorite place for meditation."

"Now I am going to guide you through a simple visualization."

Jennifer talked Maria through the same meditation she

had taught Shilpa. As she spoke, she slipped into the energetic plane.

By the time they reached the heart chakra, Jennifer found her. On impulse, she connected their energies and flowed through it. Almost immediately, Maria broke the connection.

"What did you do?" she asked.

"I connected our energies. Are you alright?"

"Yes, it felt strange and threw me out of the meditation."

"Look around. Can you see anything unusual? Stay calm. Nothing will hurt you."

"Oh, no! There's a black panther watching me."

"Perfect. That's me. I'm going to walk over and sit next to you. Now, try to touch the panther."

There was a brief pause. *She's trying to get up her nerve to touch the panther,'* thought Jennifer.

"I can't touch it. There's nothing there."

"That's right, it's only an illusion of a panther, but I can see through the panther's eyes, hear through its ears, and even speak through it."

Jennifer saw a middle-aged woman wearing a bright blue t-shirt with 'Save the Whales" across her chest. She also wore jeans and sneakers.

"I can see your 'Save the Whales' t-shirt. It looks good on you."

"What is it you want me to do now that we have this connection?"

"Nothing now. I can do the rest. Denum will explain better, but I think he will sometimes send a taxi to take you to a port where a ship is docked. There you will do the same meditation, and I will use you as a beacon to materialize my panther. The panther can scan the ship for stowaways so that we can get them off before the ship sails.

We will save a lot of lives. If they remain aboard, they will not survive the voyage. The viral exclusion rules are absolute and final."

"So, we'll be saving lives?"

"Yes," said Jennifer. *'At least until the virus hits,'* she thought.

THE FIRST TRIAL WAS THE NEXT MORNING. DENUM ALERTED Jennifer, who went outside to meditate. It took only a moment to identify Maria's familiar energy. She let Maria get further into the meditation, but she no longer needed it. She could find Maria anywhere as easily as she could find Vijay or Cindy.

When her panther materialized, Maria said, "That's the ship there," and pointed to a small container ship tied to the dock. It appeared that loading was almost finished.

Jennifer willed her panther to walk stealthily toward the gangplank, taking advantage of shadows along the way. Once aboard, she sat looking up at the stacked containers towering above her. She tried passing through a row of containers. Nothing. At the other end of the row, she sat again. *'This will take forever. There must be a better way.'*

Jennifer let her consciousness expand, slowly at first, but then faster until it included the entire stack of containers. She found two groups of humans in different areas, both in containers at the ends of rows. *'Of course, so they can open the container for fresh air and maybe exercise.'* As she looked through the panther's eyes, she could see recent weld marks and areas of fresh paint on the container doors. *'So they can open them from the inside.'*

After reading the container numbers to Denum, Jennifer slipped through the container wall into one of the populated containers. There were the expected shrieks and crying at the appearance of the panther. Jennifer sat in one corner of the container, then licked her paw and washed her face just as she had seen Midnight do. This simple act relaxed her.

Projecting her voice, she said, "There will soon be a crew to offload you. You would not have survived the voyage. The viral exclusion on this route is absolute and final. Do you understand?"

There was dispirited head nodding.

Jennifer rose and passed through to the next container, where she repeated the same message. Then back on deck, she scanned the ship itself.

"Denum, I have found five more humans, two on the bridge and three deep in the ship."

"Yes, this is an old ship. It still requires a human captain and first mate, and three engineers to maintain the engine and generators. They will not be allowed off at the destination and all know that. Thank you, Jennifer. I will look after the stowaways from here."

Jennifer found a deep shadow next to a small office building on the dock. She watched and waited to see what would happen to the stowaways she had found. Soon, she had her answer as a small column of people was shepherded off the ship by security bots. The people were carrying backpacks and dragging roll-along bags. They looked deflated after learning their adventure was over before it had begun. A bus was waiting to take them away.

Satisfied, she released her panther and opened her own eyes.

'See, I'm saving lives, not taking them,' she thought.

THAT NIGHT, AS THEY LAY CUDDLING IN BED, JENNIFER SAID, "Vijay, I saved a lot of lives today. I found the stowaways on a ship before they could leave port so they could all be taken off safely. I don't have to be the angel of death, do I?"

"No, you don't have to be the angel of death. You saved lives today. I'm proud of you. I love you, Jenn, no matter what."

'Why does he seem so sad?' she thought.

Not long after the boat incident, Jennifer sat watching another romance with Midnight on her lap. As her mind wandered idly, she remembered Vijay's suggestion that she make Midnight her familiar. *'I wonder, she's like a tiny panther. Perhaps I could.'*

She turned the kitten gently to face her and looked into its eyes. *'I am Midnight,'* she thought.

There was almost no resistance. The kitten was puzzled, but didn't seem to sense any danger. Seen through the kitten's eyes, Jennifer's body looked immense.

She urged the kitten to go off for an exploration. They prowled around the living room, behind the couch and under the table. Down the hall, then came to the bedroom, where Midnight jumped on the bed.

'Oh no, off you get,' thought Jennifer, and the kitten jumped back to the floor. Just then she heard Vijay return to the apartment. Under her guidance, Midnight crept back to the living room and peered around the corner. She saw Vijay sit down next to her still body. He relaxed on the couch and pulled her over to lie with her head on his lap and his arm around her. *'He knows I'm away.'*

In a moment of inspiration, she had Midnight crawl along the back of the couch and hop up on the arm at the far end. She paused. Vijay seemed not to have noticed. She made another small hop to the back of the couch, then crawled on her belly as she had seen the leopards do. When she was close enough, she gathered all her tiny muscles and pounced on the top of Vijay's head. Reflexively, her claws were out as she asserted her hold, and she took his hair in her tiny teeth.

"Really, Jennifer?" Vijay lifted Midnight carefully from his head and set her down beside him. He stroked her with his right hand, which was almost as large as the kitten. Jennifer was surprised how nice it felt for a kitten to be stroked by a human.

Reluctantly, she returned to her own body and opened her eyes. She wiggled to make herself more comfortable on his lap.

"I have a new idea for bedtime tonight. You can sit reading your tablet, and I'll be the leopard stalking and pouncing on you."

"Do I have to scream and try to get away?" asked Vijay.

"Well, that would make it more realistic, but don't try too hard."

"Don't worry, I have no intention of getting away from you."

11

SHILPA GIVES BIRTH

Jennifer

The next afternoon was the weekly management meeting at the vineyard. Jennifer rarely attended, but Marjorie insisted she should be there this week. Cindy was also there, sitting between Chris Martingale and a young lady Jennifer had not seen before but who was introduced as Julia Evans.

After the ordinary business completed, Marjorie said, "I have a special announcement to make." Marjorie made a signal, and Molly left the room, returning with six young men and women who took up seats along one wall.

With a flourish, Marjorie produced a heavy cardboard carton and set it on the table with a thud. "As you know, Jennifer suggested I write a full set of Gaian cards. I finished some time ago with a lot of encouragement, guidance, and support from Chris Martingale."

'I think I can guess what kind of support Chris provided,' thought Jennifer.

Marjorie was continuing. "Julia Evans, who many of

you have met for the first time today, is the young artist assigned to lead the team of illustrators for the cards and the Book of Gaia. The rest of the team has just joined us. I have here first run copies for all of you. Julia and I and the other artists will be available to sign your copies after the meeting."

The carton revealed boxed card sets which were passed around the table until everyone had one. Inside each box was a Book of Gaia, which interpreted and told how to use the cards, and the deck of cards themselves.

Jennifer flipped through the cards, stopping at cards that caught her eye. There were the traditional four winds cards, the five elements, and the sun, moon, and stars. Evolution, metamorphosis, birth, growth, death, and decay also had cards. The rivers card which talked about flow, and a card for the lakes which talked about containment and reflection. A card about the sea talked of the beginning and end of all cycles. A special card dedicated to Gaia showed the earth mother in goddess form. This card was also the image on the front of the book.

All around the table were exclamations of "These are beautiful!" and "I love the illustrations!" and "How did you do all this? It's amazing."

Marjorie positively glowed under all the acknowledgements while Julia fidgeted and did not seem to know quite what to make of it.

At the end of the meeting, a queue formed to have the books signed by the collaborators. Jennifer went to stand in line, but Chris brought her a set the artists had signed and dedicated to her. "Jennifer, the day you came to my shop and said you wanted to set up Gaianism as a formal religion, I thought you were crazy. But seeing what you brought into being simply through your conviction has shown me I was the one lacking vision and foresight. You should know that we're all in awe of who you are and are humbled to be working to bring your dream to life."

"Thanks Chris. I wish I could say I had it all planned, but the real credit goes to everyone who worked to take my vague thoughts and turn them into something. The results always amaze me."

At that moment, her tablet buzzed with a call from Kam. His voice was breathy, and loud with excitement. "Hi Jennifer, I have some exciting news! Is Vijay around?"

"I'll get him. He's down by the pond with the twins. Hang on." Jennifer sprinted the short distance from the bungalow to the pond, arriving out of breath, waving the tablet in the air.

Vijay was sitting on the bank watching Dylan and Parvati trying to catch marine life with small nets.

"Hey, Vijay," she called out, panting from the exertion, "I have Kam on a call. He's asking for you. It's Shilpa, and he said it's good news."

Jennifer led Vijay to a bench where they could sit side by side, and put the tablet on his knee in front of them.

"Hi Kam," said Vijay. "What's up?"

"Shilpa just gave birth to a baby girl! She'll be out of the birthing room in another 15 minutes, and I'll be able to show you."

"Congratulations! That's wonderful!" said Vijay. "When can we come and meet her?" Jennifer squeezed Vijay's arm. She was still bouncing up and down with excitement.

"They're coming out this evening, so any time tomorrow would be good."

"Was she in labor long?" asked Jennifer.

"It started early this morning. We were at the birthing center for the last 7 hours, but Shilpa was feeling it before that."

"Oh, poor Shilpa, how is she?" Jennifer asked.

"Happy and sleepy from what I can see," Kam replied. "She looks so peaceful when she has her baby on her."

"Did you remember what I told you about naming her before they gave her a birth number chip?" asked Vijay.

"Yes, it was just like you said. They didn't seem surprised. I think you might have started a trend."

"Oh," said Jennifer. "What did you name her?"

Jennifer saw Kam blushing. She might have missed it except that she was used to watching Vijay. "We named her Jennifer. Jennifer Sapna Raman. I hope that's all right with you. After all, you saved all three of us and we want her to be proud of her famous aunt."

"That's lovely, I'm honored," said Jennifer while thinking, *She may not be so proud after the world finds out what I've done.*

"Yes, we're going to call her Jenny, so there won't be any confusion."

"That's lovely Kam. We'll come and visit Jenny and Shilpa for a little while tomorrow. We'll leave Parvati and Dylan at home. They'll want to meet their new cousin, but that can wait until Shilpa's recovered."

"They're calling me, I'd better go." Kam ended the call.

Vijay turned to look at her. "Well Jenn, there's a piece of good news in the midst of all the chaos."

"Yes, I'm happy for them. I think the move has worked out well for them after a rough start."

"Did anyone ever call you Jenny?"

"A few times, but never the same person twice." Jennifer squinted and tried to look fierce.

Vijay laughed. "No, I suppose not," he said.

• • •

Jennifer looked through the glass doors at the lobby of the apartment building as Vijay called up to be let in. Nothing had changed. The same furniture, the same water jug with lemons. It had only been a few months, but now it seemed as though it were years since they had lived here.

As they left the elevator on the 17th floor, Kam was standing in the doorway to welcome them in. He walked a few stops forward to hug each of them briefly. Jennifer didn't really know Kam very well, but she submitted to the hug and tried to keep it brief.

"Come in. Shilpa's waiting for you in the living room."

As they walked in, Jennifer gasped at the transformation of the apartment. Colorful pictures of various gods and famous Indian temples hung on the walls. Kam and Shilpa replaced the utilitarian furniture provided by with teak shelves and matching coffee table and a soft overstuffed couch. They had painted one wall in a tangerine color, while the remaining walls were painted in a warm cream.

"Wow, this is beautiful!" she exclaimed. "It embarrasses me to think how little we did in decoration."

"This apartment was a magnificent gift, and you gave it to us as a blank canvas. No need to be embarrassed," laughed Kam. "Let me introduce you to Jenny."

Shilpa was watching all this with interest from her resting position on the couch. *'She looks tired. I remember what the first few days were like,'* thought Jennifer.

Vijay leaned over to kiss Shilpa on the cheek. "Congratulations, Sis. I am so happy for you. Maa and Baba must be happy, too."

"They are. We called them from the birthing center as soon as we had a quiet moment. I'm sad that they won't get to meet Jenny, but Maa said not to worry. She was just happy that we were safe."

Kam picked up a dining room chair and sat it in front of Shilpa. "Sit here, Jennifer, so you can see your namesake."

Shilpa unwrapped the tiny bundle she was holding to show the new baby. Jenny was still tiny. Jennifer put out one finger experimentally, and the baby grasped it instinctively. A flood of emotions washed through her as she remembered the day when she had first held the twins. *'I hope their first day goes better than mine did,'* she thought as she remembered Vijay being hauled away by the police.

"Would you like to hold her?" asked Shilpa, offering the bundled baby to Jennifer.

"I'd love to." The baby stirred for a moment, unsettled by the change, but Jennifer channeled a bit of Gaia energy to exude calm and baby Jenny soon settled.

Jennifer could hear Vijay, Shilpa and Kam talking in the background, but all her energy was focussed on the tiny infant. Although she didn't normally pray, she prayed now, silently, while gazing at the infant's face. *'Gaia, hear my prayer. In return for what I have done and what I must do, keep this child safe from harm. Let her live the life I was denied. Love and protect her always.'*

Gaia did not answer, but Jennifer was sure she had heard.

After a few more minutes, Jenny woke up and squirmed, trying to nuzzle Jennifer's breast. "It seems like she's hungry." Jennifer handed baby Jenny back to Shilpa.

Jennifer watched as Shilpa settled her baby into position and opened her robe to expose her breast. Baby Jenny latched on quickly and easily with no fussing. Looking around, she realized Vijay was now standing with his back to his sister. *'He's still embarrassed by motherhood after all we went through.'* The thought made her smile.

Standing, she walked to where Vijay and Kam were looking at a small table in the corner of the room opposite the door. On the table were several small brass figures and some framed pictures. The figures sat on a square of brightly colored cloth, and there were several small bowls in front of them. The bowls contained rice, dates, and honey.

"What does this mean?" asked Jennifer.

"This is our home altar," explained Kam. "The figures are Shakti, Lakshmi, and Ganesha. The bowls have small offerings on the birth of our child. This is where we pray each morning before starting our day."

"What a lovely idea. Why don't we have one of these, Vijay?"

"It never seemed quite right when I was sharing a room with Ron, and I guess I never gave it much more thought."

"I think we should make one for Gaia. It would be a nice element of Gaianism, and we could encourage our followers to build their own."

Vijay closed his eyes and scratched his head for a minute. Jennifer recognized this as a sign that she had stepped on delicate ground.

"Jennifer, this shrine is in a tradition that is thousands of years old. It's an essential element of Hinduism and can't simply be transplanted into Gaianism because you think it's cute. Sorry, Kam."

"No worries, Vijay. I'm just happy that Jennifer's interested in our religion."

Jennifer turned back to see Shilpa dozing off with Jenny still at her breast. "Vijay, I think we should leave them alone now. We can come back in a few days when Shilpa's more rested."

Vijay was quick to take the hint, and Kam offered no objection, so they left the apartment as quietly as possible.

When they were settled in the taxi for the half-hour ride back to the vineyard, Vijay turned to her and said, "Jennifer, you can't just keep picking up pretty ideas and stringing them on to your Gaianism religion.

"What do you mean?"

"I mean, you started with the idea that you needed a church, and that the church needed a religion. You found Gaianism and decided that could work. You needed a religious text and then looked at the decks of Tarot cards and thought a deck of cards and an interpretation manual could be useful. You watched Chris lead an animal spirit meditation that has roots in Native American theology and tacked that on, too. Now you want to add deity worship from Hinduism and glue that on as well."

"But Vijay, our followers like to have all these different expressions of their faith. And they don't all have direct access to Gaia like I do, and like you and Cindy will. So, I want to give them options. Maybe they could have a special wooden box to hold their cards, and a stand to display their card for the day. What do you think Gaia would look like as a statue?"

"Have you heard anything I just said? Anyway, I don't think you should incorporate a Hindu god."

"You're right. I'll commission a new one from our artists' group."

"You're impossible. And what do you mean 'like I and Cindy will'?

"Oh, nothing to worry about. When I'm gone, you and Cindy will be Gaia's representatives. That's all."

"Is there something you haven't told me?"

Jennifer turned to look out the window. After a pause, she said, "No, just that Cindy will look after the Vineyard, and you'll look after our family. I want you to start meditating on Gaia with me so when I die, you'll be able to carry what I started."

I hope to be a very old man when that happens. I don't like to hear you talking about when you're gone as if you already know."

Jennifer turned back to look directly at him. "You're right Vijay. I have no idea. Don't worry yourself about it. Let's not fight about any of this. Hold my hand while I think about a Gaia statue."

Vijay sighed and held her hand. *'I love her, but I don't think I'll ever really understand her.'*

12

SYMBOLS OF THE NEW RELIGION

Jennifer

That night, as she lay in Vijay's arms, Jennifer's mind was busy thinking of all the things she could put on an altar to Gaia. *'Would we have a little bowl to put offerings in? But why would Gaia want food? And what would we say when we pray to her? Maybe Vijay would know, but if I ask, he'll just be grumpy with me.'*

The following morning, she called Professor LaFlamme, the university theology professor who had helped her understand about churches.

"Professor LaFlamme, I need your help again in thinking about religious symbols and prayers. Would you be able to come out to the Widdecombe Winery to discuss them? Perhaps on Saturday so you could bring your family. Do you have a family?"

"Yes, I have a wife and three children. Won't they be a bother?"

"Children love the winery. There's a pond, and vineyards and other children. Molly can take them for a ride in the golf cart. I think your family will have fun. I want to show you the progress I've made since our last talk. Also, Chris Martindale will be there. He's my other spiritual advisor."

"Chris, who owns Atlantean Treasures?"

"Yes. Will you be able to come, perhaps for 10am Saturday morning? I can send a car for you."

"Give me a few minutes, Jennifer, to check with my wife. But I think we can be there."

"Thanks Professor."

Her next call was to Chris Martingale.

"Hi Chris, I want to have a meeting with you and Professor LaFlamme on creating Gaia altars for our believers' homes. Would you be able to join us in at the entrance of the main building on Saturday morning? I want to give Dr. LaFlamme a tour first then we can have our meeting at 10:30am."

"Sure, Jennifer. I'll have an acolyte look after the store for the morning."

On Saturday morning, Professor LaFlamme, his wife and three children arrived ten minutes early. Jennifer was there to meet them with Molly and the longest golf cart. Climbing out of the limousine, Jennifer heard one of the boys say, "Man, that was cool." He looked to be about 8 years old. He had a slightly older brother, and a younger sister of perhaps 6 or 7.

"Hi Professor, thanks for coming."

"Good morning, Jennifer. I'd like to introduce my wife, Karen, and our children, Thomas, Jude, and Rachel."

Jennifer shook hands gently with each of them. "It's nice to meet you all. This is Molly, a special member of our community." Molly stepped forward to shake hands with each of them as well.

"I thought we'd start with a tour, then I have reserved a meeting room for 10:30am. Molly will walk beside us and explain the vineyard. We'll start up by the stables."

During the tour, Molly kept up a running commentary as Jennifer sat thinking about the meeting to come. The stables were a big hit. Tim was on hand to answer questions, and he offered to let the children ride the ponies that afternoon.

They drove down to see the workshops, where the coopers, blacksmiths and carpenters were all hard at work. "We don't have time now for a tour of each, but if you want to come back later, Molly can arrange that for you."

The last stop was the pond and the old oak tree. "Professor LaFlamme, remember how you told me we needed natural spaces to be sacred? This pond and that tree are our sacred spaces. We all use this pond as a space for quiet reflection, and the ground under the tree is reserved for sacred meditations. All the children enjoy the pond. It's full of wildlife and interesting plants."

"Won't they bother people in their personal reflection?"

"No, we have quiet hours before 8am and after 7pm. Otherwise, I often see people sitting on the benches simply accepting the children near the pond as a natural part of life. We'll leave your family here with Molly. Molly will bring them to the mess hall at 1pm for lunch."

As they walked from the pond up to the main buildings, LaFlamme said, "I had no idea how far you would come so quickly, or that you would take my advice so seriously."

"Why wouldn't I? You're a university professor."

Chris was already in the meeting room. A fresh urn of

coffee and a tray of biscuits were on a side table. They all helped themselves and sat down. LaFlamme and Chris already knew each other and began recounting their past encounters.

Jennifer felt impatient. "Gentlemen, if I could have your attention, let me explain my question."

She explained about the Hindu altar she had seen in Shilpa's home, and Vijay's insistence that she not use a Hindu god for Gaia.

"So, you want to know what kind of physical representation could be used for Gaia?" asked LaFlamme.

"Yes. What do other religions do?"

Chis spoke. "Buddhists use Buddha's as a representation. They have many forms of Buddha including the laughing Buddha which is the round bellied Buddha most familiar in the west. Other cultures have thin or even emaciated Buddhas. The placement of their hands is significant as is the treatment of their hair."

"So, one symbol can represent many different ideas about Buddha?" asked Jennifer.

"Yes," said LaFlamme, "but you should not use a Buddha in your new religion. Some Buddhists are distressed by the way their sacred images have passed into popular culture without understanding. The same is true of the Hindu Gods you saw on the home altar. They all reflect different aspects of the one god, Brahman, although many people think of them as being different gods."

"What about Christianity?" asked Jennifer.

LaFlamme responded. "In Christianity, the major symbol is the cross, which may or may not include the Crucified Christ. Other significant figures are also often seen, most often the Virgin Mary who was Christ's mother, and then the saints such as St Jude, the patron saint of lost causes."

"But," said Jennifer, "these these all came after the major characters died. What would have been the symbols before that?"

"To some extent, there was nothing before because the religions didn't exist," replied LaFlamme. "We could look to the Pantheist expressions, as Gaianism is essentially a Pantheist religion."

"What is Pantheism?"

"Pantheism is the belief that God is everywhere in nature, that God is inseparable from nature. That when you pray to a waterfall or to a tree, you are praying to God. There is the nuance that the path to God is most transparent in places of natural beauty, like your pond and your tree," said LaFlamme.

Chris spoke next. "Perhaps a tree of life could be a representation. It's an old Celtic image, easily accessible and lends itself to many forms of expression. It can be a statue, or worn as a pendant, or depicted as an image,"

"We have a tree card in the Book of Gaia," said Jennifer.

"You have a Book of Gaia?" asked LaFlamme.

"Yes, you told me we need a sacred text. Let me get one for you."

She stood up and left the room in search of a new Book of Gaia deck.

When she returned, she hesitated outside the door, listening.

"What are we talking about here?" LaFlamme was asking Chris.

"I never really know. We're here to throw lots of ideas in the air, and Jennifer will pluck out some that she finds pretty or useful and tie them into her new religion. I can never tell if she really believes or if this is all a game to her. But whatever it is, she seems to have the power to inspire people. You had an enormous influence on her when you told her what she needed to do to create a new religion, and she has been cobbling it together ever since your conversation."

"Who are all these people in white gowns?"

"Oh, you mean the acolytes. They are young people who serve for a few years, assisting in the operation of the church. It's becoming quite a coveted position. You'll see them all at special day celebrations. They live in dormitory accommodations in this building."

"Do they have a vow of celibacy? Are they monks and nuns?"

"Quite the opposite. They receive Tantric training on healthy sexuality and are expected to practice it. I suppose that's another reason the roles are so coveted by mid-teens. The church doesn't talk much about this, but Jennifer insisted on this component, I suppose, because of her past."

'Okay, this is getting too close to home,' thought Jennifer. She entered noisily through the door. "I have a copy for you, Dr. LaFlamme."

LaFlamme opened the box and took out the explanatory booklet. He frowned as he flipped through the book. "But surely this is a Tarot deck, not a religious text."

"Would you prefer a box of old scrolls?" asked Jennifer primly. "Or flakes of parchment found half-rotted in a cave?"

"I suppose this has the virtue of being very accessible," replied LaFlamme.

"Find the tree card, please."

LaFlamme shuffled through the deck and produced the Tree card. It was indeed titled The Tree of Life.

"Okay," said Jenifer. "So, we have our Tree of Life to represent Gaia. What else could we put on our home altar?

I already thought about a wooden box to display the cards. What about offerings?"

LaFlamme spoke first. "Traditionally, offerings were of crops or food animals. Goats, fatted calves, barley or fruit."

"Or first-born children, or young virgin girls, but I assume you don't want to go there," said Chris.

Jennifer gave him what she hoped was a withering look.

"I guess not," said Chris, smiling.

"I don't want it to be money," said Jennifer, "but it has to be something of value."

"In North America, many of the indigenous tribes saved owl feathers, eagle feathers, significant seashells, and other natural things of beauty," offered Chris.

"Yes, and Christians still place beautiful flowers near objects of veneration," added LaFlamme.

"The altar I saw had little bowls to hold the offerings. Does it have to be little bowls?"

"Were the offerings of food?"

"Yes, rice, honey and dates for a new baby."

"Then little bowls made sense. But offerings could also be made on a plate or even just laid on the altar."

"Tell me about the cross. I see it all the time without Jesus on it."

Chris looked at LaFlamme to have him continuing to answer.

"The cross is a symbol of Jesus' death. We don't need to see Him to be reminded of the sacrifice He made for us."

"What was the sacrifice?" Jennifer felt like she was following a thread that would be important, if only she could see it.

"His sacrifice? Jesus died so that the rest of the world could live. He took on the sins of the world so that we could live free of sin. This is a deep question, Jennifer. It's not a quick answer. Read the first four books of the Christian New Testament. That will give you everything you need to know about Jesus' life and death."

Jennifer was thinking furiously. *"What have I missed? What should I be asking?"* But nothing else came to her.

She looked up and smiled. "Well, that was very useful. Thank you both. Professor, I'll take you back to your family. Chis we'll be having lunch in the mess at 1pm if you care to join us."

She saw the puzzled look on Dr. LaFlamme's face, as he looked over to Chris. Chris just shrugged his shoulders and smiled. "I'll see you both at lunch, then."

Jennifer and LaFlamme found his wife and daughter at the pond watching frogs and turtles. As they arrived, a small golf cart pulled up with Thomas driving, and Jude in the passenger seat. Molly was walking beside them always ready to intervene if things went wrong. The boys were laughing and bouncing, enjoying themselves immensely.

"It looks like everyone's having fun. I'll stop back just before lunch at 1pm, and then we can see about the ponies this afternoon. My two, Parvati and Dylan, will probably join us if there's a chance to ride the ponies."

"Thanks Jennifer," said LaFlamme.

"Yes, the kids are having a wonderful time. Thank you, Jennifer," added Karen.

13

THE SHIRE HORSES ARRIVE

Cindy

The new stables were finished. After spending time in the traditional stalls for riding horses, the new stable seemed enormous. There were also ten smaller stalls. *'The ponies will love these,'* thought Cindy.

Tim was busy spreading clean bedding in the new stalls, and stacks of feed were ready in a storage area near the door.

"When do they arrive?" asked Cindy.

"They're confirmed for 4pm." Tim paused and looked up at her. Tim had been her first partner, and when their eyes met, happy memories of their six months together flashed through her mind.

"How's life with Pamela," she asked.

"She's amazing. I think she's the one for me, and I'm pretty sure she feels the same."

"That's great, Tim. I'm truly happy to hear you say that."

"Thanks Cindy. Will you be here when they arrive?"

"I wouldn't miss it."

At 4pm, three transporters, pulling three large horse trailers, crawled up the drive. Each transporter carried a handler in the technician's seat to look after the horses. They parked side by side in the stable yard, and the handlers dismounted.

After brief introductions, and a quick tour of the new stables, the handlers lowered the back doors of the trailers to form long ramps for the horses. Each trailer held two horses. They backed the horses down the ramps until the handlers could safely turn them around and let them into the exercise paddock.

The horses were immense. Cindy did not reach the horses' shoulders, and with their heads up, they towered to almost twice her height. A moment of doubt flickered through her, but she quickly dismissed it.

"What will you do with these animals?" asked a handler.

"They'll be draft animals around the farm and the vineyard. Hay wagons, grape gathering, perhaps tour wagons. We'll train at least two for riding. We have a heavier family member who's too heavy for a standard horse. Don't worry, they'll have a good life here. There are also eight other horses for company and we're waiting for some ponies."

"The stalls are impressive. You've clearly thought this through. Here's a sheet of pictures with their names. You can rename them if you want, but they respond to these."

"Thanks guys, that's terrific. Do you need taxis to get home?"

"No, we'll ride the transporters back to the yard. We have to drop off the trailers there. Thanks for the offer."

.   .   .

THE FOLLOWING MORNING CINDY CALLED MOLLY ON HER tablet.

"Hello Cindy, are you with your horses?"

"Yes, and I have a surprise for you. Can you come to the vineyard today? You can bring the twins; they'll like this too."

The line was silent as Molly went to talk with Jennifer. Cindy was used to this. As Molly did not need a tablet to place and receive calls, there was never any background noise or overheard conversations.

"Yes, Cindy. Parvati, Dylan and I will be there at 2pm. What is the surprise?"

"Molly, if I told you, then it wouldn't be a surprise."

MOLLY AND THE TWINS, NOW SIX YEARS OLD, ARRIVED AT the farm gate promptly at 2pm. Cindy met them in a golf cart. "Hop in," she said. The twins dashed for the front seat, each one trying to knock the other out of the way so they could have the coveted seat beside Cindy. As usual, Parvati won, leaving Dylan to sulk in the back seat alone. Molly walked beside the cart as she was too heavy to ride in it.

At the stables, Cindy took them inside to see the new arrivals. The twins' eyes went wide as they surveyed the enormous horses. They each held one of Molly's hands. "Will they try to eat us?" asked Dylan.

Cindy laughed, "No, silly, they're horses, so they eat hay and grass. Never people. These are very gentle horses."

She opened the stall for Maxwell, the largest horse who had a dappled gray coat. "Let's take him outside," she said.

Maxwell wore a heavier version of the same soft rope bridle Cindy used on all her horses. She clipped a short lead to the bridle and led him out of the stable to the exercise paddock.

Molly and the twins followed at a safe distance. Each twin was still holding one of Molly's hands.

Once released in the paddock, Maxwell trotted around a few turns and returned as they watched. Cindy pulled out a small bag with a few apples that she had stashed earlier.

Offering an apple, she called Maxwell over to them. The twins watched with fascination as Maxwell gently plucked the apple from Cindy's open palm.

"Molly," she said, "you told me you wanted to ride. Maxwell will be your horse when you're ready. He's a Shire horse, the kind the English knights used in their armor. I'll teach you to look after him. But before you can ride him, you have to lose weight. Can you get to 100 kg?"

"I can be 106 kg. Will that be low enough? It will require about two weeks, and I will not look the same."

"What will you look like?" asked Parvati.

"Will you still be a tin man?" asked Dylan.

Molly laughed. "No, I will be a plastic man. I'll show you later on a tablet."

Cindy handed Molly an apple. "Give it to Maxwell. Hold your hand flat like I did and let him take it."

Molly held out her hand with the apple. Maxwell eyed her first as if he were suspicious. But then he seemed to decide that Molly was just another piece of farm equipment, and he accepted the apple.

The twins both wanted to try, so Cindy helped Dylan to climb the first two rungs of the gate, then said, "Now put your hand flat on my hand. Don't bend your fingers, just stay flat. Don't worry, Maxwell doesn't want to bite, but if you bend your fingers, he might make a mistake. She put an apple on Dylan's small palm with her hand resting underneath.

Maxwell daintily picked up the apple and crunched it in his enormous mouth.

Parvati was next, but pulled her hand away at the last minute. "I don't want to do this," she said. "He's too big."

"Don't worry, next time you can try again."

TWO WEEKS AFTER THE ARRIVAL OF THE SHIRES, CINDY received a visit from a new gray robot. Its skin was made from a high impact plastic, and it wore an elephant hot-stamped on its chest. The new robot was not much taller than Cindy.

"Molly! Where did you get this body?" exclaimed Cindy.

"These bodies were made for flight crews on aircraft where weight was more important than armor. I like this body. It is faster and more agile than the body I had before. Do you think Jennifer will like it?"

"She hasn't seen it yet?" Cindy had a sinking feeling that this might be a problem. "Molly, why did you get this new body?"

"Because I want to ride a horse like you."

"Why else do you like the new body?"

"It feels freer. I feel like I can move more easily. It feels more like what I imagine a human to feel like."

"How will that help you around the vineyard?"

"People will be less intimidated. I can use human furniture. I can take part in more group activities."

"Okay, I want you to call Jennifer and tell her you want to show her a new body for her approval. Tell her about all the benefits, but don't mention riding just yet. She needs to feel that she's consulted, and if she doesn't agree, we'll have to go back to the old body until she changes her mind. If she thinks I changed you for riding, then it will create a huge upset."

"Yes, Cindy, I will consult Jennifer."

Molly sat down on a bench facing the paddock. She looked so relaxed there in her new body that Cindy's heart went out to her. After a few minutes, Molly stood up and said, "Jennifer says to come and show her my new body and she will decide. Can I go in the golf cart? I'm not too heavy now."

"Do you know how to drive a golf cart?"

"I believe so."

Cindy watched, feeling doubtful, as Molly settled herself into the golf cart. After a few experimental stops and starts, Molly seemed in control.

"Okay Molly, off you go. I'll stay here. I have work to do."

She watched Molly set off down the drive swerving back and forth across the road until all she could see was the little cloud of dust that marked Molly's passage.

14

THE NEW MOLLY VISITS JENNIFER

Jennifer

Jennifer was outside when a strange robot pulled up in the golf cart. The newcomer's body was tough plastic and shadows of interior parts were visible through its thick skin. It wore an elephant stamped on its chest.

"Molly?" asked Jennifer.

"Hello Jennifer. How do you like my new body? It will be more useful around the vineyard. I can use human furniture and drive the golf cart."

"Was this your idea?"

"Yes, I had to lose weight. I was too heavy. So, I found this body made for aircraft crews. It is much lighter."

"And who told you that you were too heavy?"

"Cindy told me I needed to be 100 kg. I was 180 kg and so, had to lose weight."

"And why did you need to be 100 kg?"

"I am not supposed to say." Molly headed back to the golf cart.

"Molly, this is about riding horses, isn't it?"

Molly turned back. "Yes, I wanted to ride the Shires, but I was too heavy."

"Why didn't you tell me that?"

"Cindy said it might upset you."

"Fucking right, it upsets me. Molly, sit down." Jennifer motioned to a bench. "I'm not upset that you wanted to change your body, or that you wanted to ride the horses. I'm upset that you deliberately withheld information from me. I need to know whose side you are on, mine or Cindy's."

"Jennifer, I need to be close to both of you." Molly's voice had become deeper, and sounded more adult in its tone. "You know that Denum and I are parts of the same consciousness. Vijay is the only other person who knows that. Denum is direct with you. I respect you too much to have it be otherwise. My Molly persona must stay close to Cindy because she will be important in the next stage. I think you see that as well."

"Then I'd better talk with Cindy, right now, to be clear on where she and I stand."

"I will drive you. I suggest we pick up Dr. Gladstone on the way. She can help mediate the discussion."

"OK, get her now and bring her here. Then we will all go and find Cindy."

JENNIFER SAT FUMING, AS SHE WAITED FOR MOLLY AND Gloria to return. *Fucking Cindy. She has no idea what's really going on as she plays house with those horses. Who is she to give orders to Molly concerning me?*

By the time Marjorie and Molly returned, Jennifer had worked herself up to a full boil.

"Do you want to talk about this before we see Cindy?" asked Gloria.

"No, anything I have to say, I'll say to Cindy directly."

"I understand the source of your feelings of rivalry and frustration, but it may be better to have a calm discussion."

"Sorry, but you know almost nothing, Gloria. This whole place was my idea, my vision, but Cindy treats it as her private domain. Doesn't talk to me. Doesn't ask me. She acts like she's the princess, and I'm the tired old crone in the corner."

"Jennifer, do you know exactly where Cindy is?"

"She's riding in a field. I'll call her back to the stable."

Jennifer slumped against the seat as she dropped into the energetic plane. Cindy was always easy to spot, being the brightest spirit for miles around. Jennifer materialized as her black panther on the path in front of Cindy. Cindy's horse reared up, and Cindy had to fight for control. Jennifer projected her voice. "We have to talk. Come back to the stable now." She allowed her panther to dissolve without waiting for a response.

As they pulled up to the stables on the golf cart, Cindy arrived riding the largest horse that Jennifer had ever seen. It towered over them all as Cindy slid down its side. "Molly, is this the horse you want to ride?" Jennifer asked.

"No, my horse is Maxwell. He is larger than this one."

Cindy released the horse into the exercise paddock and walked over. "What's so important that you startled my horse and interrupted my training."

"Did you give Molly a new body without even asking me?"

"I didn't know you owned Molly. I understood she was a free agent."

"You keep making changes and I only find out

afterwards. I was the creator of all this, but you show me no respect." Jennifer jumped to her feet.

"Well, if you got off your fat ass and actually did something around here instead of just acting like queen bee, you might earn some respect." Cindy stepped closer.

"You have no idea what I do for you and for this city." Jennifer was close to tears of frustration and rage but refused to give in to crying. For a moment, she thought she would have to fight Cindy. Her body tensed and her arms came up.

"Stop, both of you!" Gloria stepped between them. "Now, sit down and let's untangle this mess of emotions. Jennifer, what upset you today?"

"Molly showing up in this new body and then lying about why she needed it. Cindy told her to lie to me."

"I told her to lie because I knew you would go batshit crazy if she told you the truth. Seems I was right."

"Cindy, let's try to keep a normal tone," said Gloria. "Now, why did you think Jennifer would react badly to Molly's new body?"

"Because she reacts badly to everything I do when she finds out about it," Cindy replied.

"Only because you keep doing things behind my back. You never come and talk to me about them."

"If you were interested, you would come to the weekly management meetings. It's not like you don't have time, but even that small effort is too much for you."

"Fuck you, Cindy. You have no idea what I do for you, for all of you, or what it costs me."

"Why don't you tell us what you do?"

"I can't. It's not for sharing."

"So, you can have secrets, but I can't? You can be this impenetrable black cloud, while I'm supposed to be an open book. Shit, Jennifer, we're supposed to be working together but you won't give even a millimeter towards that."

Gloria broke in. "Jennifer, perhaps time for secrets has passed. Why not tell us what you've been doing."

Jennifer looked at Gloria. *'Does she know what I do? Did I ever tell her? Fuck it, let them all know.'*

"Molly, tell them what I did this morning."

"Is that wise, Jennifer?" said Molly in her new grown-up voice. Cindy looked up in surprise.

"Yes," said Jennifer. "I am so sick of all these secrets. My whole life is one big tangle of secrets and I want it over."

Molly began. "This morning at 5am, I woke Jennifer to visit a ship in a port that was nearing departure. She projected onto the ship and identified the location and number of stowaways aboard so they could be taken off before the ship left."

"And what happened to those stowaways," Jennifer asked.

"Seventeen were released, and four were detained as repeat offenders."

"And next?"

"Jennifer visited three more ships in different cities with similar results."

"And after, what was next?"

"There was a ship in transit to this city that Jennifer had identified two days ago. Last night my forces boarded and seized control of the ship. This morning Jennifer boarded and identified the location of the stowaways."

"How many were there, and what were their ages?" Jennifer's voice was a dull monotone. She resigned herself to the reaction she was sure would follow.

"There were 17 adult males, 15 adult females, 11

children between the ages of 12 and 18 and nine between the ages of 6 months and 12 years."

"What happened to them?"

"The robots shot them and threw their bodies into the sea."

There was no immediate response from Cindy or Gloria. Both appeared frozen, their eyes wide.

"So, you see," said Jennifer, spitting out the words, "while you are prancing about on your ponies, I am helping to keep the city safe by hunting children and babies so they can be shot before they land. I can't talk to anyone about this because some of those people have family members here. Can you imagine what will happen when they find out what I've done?"

"Is there no other way?" asked Gloria.

"We have no effective treatment for the virus, and it seems to kill very close to 100% of those who contract it. The virus has already wiped out human populations in most of the world, even with the viral exclusion zones. Our exclusion zone has to be absolute if we're to remain safe long enough for our destiny to be fulfilled."

"But what about Shilpa and Kam?" asked Cindy. "They arrived just recently."

"A small favor I extracted from Denum. They came from a safe zone and spent 21 days in confinement when they arrived. Another secret that can never be shared, and I beg you to keep it. Again, you can imagine the consequences if people came to believe that I could guarantee safe passage. It would be impossible."

Jennifer felt bleak. A vision of the inevitable day when word spread flashed before her. "But I didn't actually kill anyone. I don't want to be a mass murderer."

"No, you didn't kill anyone," said Gloria, holding her hand. "You did nothing wrong."

"I did not know, Jennifer," said Cindy. "I'm sorry I was upset with you. That must be awful. Do you think I will have to do that one day, too?"

"I don't know, Cindy, but I think it must mean something that my spirit animal is a black panther while yours is a white horse. Perhaps I just envy you your freedom and your long life. In my darkest moments, I'm afraid that I won't live long."

Cindy knelt in front of Jennifer, still sitting in the golf cart. "I'm so sorry. I had no idea what a load you've been carrying. I promise to stop by and talk with you more often."

"I'll tell Vijay to bring the twins up and take them riding," replied Jennifer. " You should start spending more time with him before the transition." Jennifer could not hold back the tears any longer. She sobbed, deep, body-racking sobs, and as she cried, she felt herself sinking into a pit of despair and self-pity. She fell through the earth, down to the warm pool of Gaia's love. As she lay in the pool, a message came through to her. "Take strength from me, draw in my energy. It won't be long. There will be a place for you here, always." She closed her eyes and drifted off to sleep.

When she awoke, she found herself in her own bed with Gloria sitting next to her.

"That was quite a session you had. You had us all worried. How are you feeling now?"

"How long was I asleep?"

"About four hours, but don't worry about that. It's enough that you're awake now. What would you like?"

"Help me outside to the tree in the yard."

Jennifer was having some trouble walking, but with Gloria's support, she managed to get seated under the tree. Reaching down into the earth, she pulled the rejuvenating energy up through her chakras until she vibrated through her whole being. She released all the energy, with her rage, sadness and frustration, out through the 7th chakra on top of her head, trusting the universe to absorb it.

Standing up and shaking herself off, she said to Gloria, "I couldn't handle that every day. Do you think that cleared the air with Cindy?"

"Nothing that runs that deep can be cured in one go, but I think you opened a pathway for reconciliation."

15

RIDING LESSONS FOR MOLLY

CINDY

Cindy brought Maxwell out from the stable. Molly was waiting with an apple in her hand. Cindy was a surprised to hear Molly speaking to Maxwell in the same gentle tones she used herself.

"Molly, do you know what the steps are to saddling a horse?"

"Yes, Cindy. First, we brush the horse, then we brush the saddle pad and make sure there are no irritants in the pad. Next, we put the pad on the horse, then the blanket, then the saddle. We tighten the saddle making sure the straps are not twisted."

"Okay, let me see you do it."

Molly went through all the steps to saddle Maxwell. The horse stood very still through all of Molly's ministrations. There was no need for Cindy to intervene. When it was done, Cindy went into the stable and brought out Bella, who had already been saddled by Tim while Cindy and Molly were outside.

Tim fetched a wooden stool they could use to mount the horses. Molly mounted Maxwell first with Cindy's guidance and was soon seated on his back. A moment later, Cindy was on Bella.

"We'll being with a slow walk. Make a clicking noise that the horse can hear and use a tiny tap of your heels on his flanks. We are not to cause any pain. It's just a tap to let him know what you want."

Molly clicked and tapped. Maxwell started forward. *'Molly seems to know all about this.'* Cindy thought.

"Molly, do you already know how to ride a horse?"

"No, Cindy. I have researched, but there are so many competing instructions I do not know which to follow. For example, to turn, I have read that I can lay the reins across his neck on the other side. A different instructor says that I can exert a steady pull on one rein to turn his head. Another says I should not use a steady pull, but only a couple of short tugs without restricting his freedom. I think I would like you to teach me how you believe I should ride horses."

"Perfect. I'll teach you to ride with the least stress for Maxwell so that you can act as a team."

After an hour of lessons and practice, Cindy thought, *'Maxwell is much more intelligent than I had expected. It seems his previous owner trained him well.'*

"That's enough for today, Molly. Let's take off his tack and let him have some pasture time." Cindy watched Molly unburden Maxwell as she removed the saddle and blanket from Bella. Cindy struggled under the weight of the heavier saddle, while Molly seemed to have no issue at all. Molly took both saddles to the tack room. When Molly returned, Cindy showed her how to brush Maxwell down and remove his bridle before releasing him to the pasture.

16

DEALING WITH THE GOVERNOR

Vijay

Vijay's tablet announced, "Call from Governor Arnold's office."

"Answer it," said Vijay.

"Hello, am I speaking with Vijay Subramanian, leader of the Human Resistance movement?"

"Yes, that's me."

"The Governor would like to meet with you. Would you be able to have breakfast with him tomorrow morning?"

"Certainly."

"Excellent, a car will pick you up at 6:30am at your residence. I believe you reside at the Widdecombe Vineyard."

"That's correct. Please tell the Governor that I'll be ready."

"Thank you." The call ended.

Vijay went looking for Jennifer. He found her sitting on the bench by the pond, her favorite spot for meditation. He sat down beside her. Jennifer turned to look at him.

"Hi Jenn, something unusual just happened."

"Yeah? What's going on?"

"I'm invited to have breakfast with Governor Arnold tomorrow. He's sending a car at 6:30am."

"That'll be an early rise for you. Do you know what he wants?"

"I have an idea. Either he wants to shut down my resistance movement, or he's holding out an olive branch. With elections coming up, I expect it's the second one."

"Then you should make sure you're well prepared. Will it be a negotiation?"

"Everything's a negotiation in politics."

Vijay put his arm around Jennifer and watched the pond in silence with her. After a while, he asked, "Are you doing okay Jenn? You're very quiet these days."

"It's all these ship searches with Denum. I'm spending so much time trying not to feel anything by hiding in my secret place, that I'm starting to not feel anything at all. It scares me, Vijay. I feel like the human is being sucked out of me and I'm becoming just another robot but made of flesh and blood."

"Is that why you haven't wanted to have sex the last few nights?"

"I feel guilty. How can I destroy so many people's dreams, and then turn to pleasure in my own bed?"

"I think you need to talk with Gloria again. The work you're doing is important, but we need to find a way that won't consume you."

"I'm so scared that we can't find a way, that being consumed is what's ahead for me."

"Talk to Gloria. She'll help. And I'm here for whatever else you need. I love you, Jennifer."

"I love you too Vijay. Just stay here with me for a while."

They went back to watching the pond. Jennifer leaned against Vijay for support, and he held her tight against him.

THE FOLLOWING MORNING, VIJAY WAS READY AT THE END of the drive at 6:30am when a limousine pulled up. He settled in the comfortable leather seat and contemplated the meeting ahead. *'Our group wants a living wage. How close to that are we willing to accept?'*

Vijay paused and looked out the window. They were passing through the city not far from the Mercury Theatre.

'He'll want us to vote for him in the election. How do I feel about telling our members who to vote for?'

As the limousine carried him up the long drive to the mansion, he thought, *'What else does voting for Arnold bring along as baggage?'*

At the Governor's mansion, an aide showed Vijay to a back porch where a breakfast table was set for two people. The sun shone over the vast grounds, which included a swimming pool and tennis courts. A helipad was visible past the tennis courts. He could make out a horse-stable on one side of the property and a riding trail disappeared into the woodlot at the bottom of the property.

The Governor was already seated with a coffee in front of him. He rose when Vijay walked over, and the two men shook hands.

"Mr. Subramanian, it's a pleasure to meet you."

"Thank you, sir. It's an honor to be invited."

Vijay sat down. Immediately, a servant was at his side asking, "Coffee, sir?"

"Yes, please. No milk, just black."

It seemed the breakfast menu was already determined, with fruit, yoghurt and granola, and warm scones with butter and a selection of jams.

"I like to eat light in the mornings to keep my energy up," said the Governor.

"This is perfect for me," replied Vijay.

Over breakfast, they talked on non-consequential topics. The Governor was very interested in the vineyard and the current employment figures there. *'Counting up votes,'* thought Vijay.

When breakfast was finished, a maid served the Governor and Vijay fresh cups of coffee. The Governor turned to Vijay. "You're a strange man," he said. "You came from nowhere to lead a resistance movement, but it's the most polite resistance movement the world has ever seen. Apart from one regrettable incident at the beginning, you have conducted your protests with tight discipline and coordination with the police. Why is that?"

"I suppose it comes from my sense of responsibility for the people I bring along with me. Their voices need to be heard, but I don't want to see them jailed or hurt in any way. I use the discipline to keep them safe."

"Sometimes it seems almost as though you are playacting. Writing scripts and having your people act them out."

"I suppose you have people at our meetings."

The Governor nodded. "Of course."

"Then you know I teach them that life is theatre. That our protests are a kind of street performance, where there are elements of ad lib, but never forgetting the script or who the audience is. I'm sure you see politics the same way. A part of your job is theatre, I believe."

"Yes, the public part. But then there's the other part

where the real work gets done. Are you following me, Mr. Subramanian?"

"Only too well. Many important things are accomplished out of sight." *'Like enforcing your viral exclusion zone.'*

"Are you a man of your word, Mr. Subramanian?"

"Just as much as you are, Governor."

"Let me share a hypothetical problem with you. You have probably noticed that many other parts of the world are going offline. That the viral plague is wiping out entire countries."

"Yes, I am intimately familiar with that."

The Governor looked at him oddly. Vijay continued, "You forget that my partner, Jennifer Dupont, is a newscaster. She stays very well informed on events beyond those shown on the news."

"You make a formidable team. You know then that our island has so far been spared."

"Yes, I know that on the few ships that arrive with stowaways, the stowaways have not survived the trip. The viral exclusion zones are absolute."

The Governor now sat up and squinted as he focused on Vijay. Vijay had the sensation that the governor was trying see into him.

"Is this really what you brought me here to discuss?" asked Vijay, trying to change the topic.

"You're right. The problem I see is that now, more than ever, we need to pull together as an island. Perhaps an island nation if the virus continues and our luck holds out. But your resistance movement is creating a divide in our community."

"I don't agree that we're creating a divide, only that we are highlighting a divide that was created by others. How many people enjoy private swimming pools, tennis courts and riding stables?"

"Point well taken. But we need to heal this divide so that we can face the future united."

"Then we have to share the wealth generated by our island economy more fairly. I don't see another way."

The Governor sighed. "Neither do I, unfortunately. What do you propose?"

"An immediate and substantial escalation of the minimum wage and HumanPower UIS."

"By how much?"

"If you are asking me, I would say to double them. However, I'm sure you've had your staff look at the question of what a living wage might be."

"Yes, it would require an increase of 35 to 40%. Would you support that?"

"Make it 50% and I believe your problem will go away."

"And do you have any idea how to afford that?"

"Yes, but you might not like it."

"Probably not. How would you afford it?"

"By taking on debt, all the debt we can sell abroad. As the virus reaches its terminal stages, the world banking system will collapse. The debts will never have to be repaid. Our currency will have to be stabilized for use on our island alone, and we can consider fairness again at that time."

"That's a cold calculation, by betting that as sole survivors, we can simply walk away with the spoils."

"Yes, I can tell you with some certainty that's exactly our destiny. Create the increase today and start your financial wizards planning what it would take to stabilize our currency. But be warned, some old fortunes will be reduced. In the next iteration, we'll need real wealth redistribution."

"If I do this thing, can you turn out the vote? My re-election is far from certain. I'm seen as too soft on social issues by the middle classes. My only hope is to mobilize the segment that doesn't vote — your membership. Can you deliver that?"

"Yes, sir. My organization can do that. Let's plan a march to City Hall two weeks from Friday. I will fill the city hall square, and you can make an address to the crowd. I will be on stage to endorse your speech and you will know from the crowd in the square that I can deliver my organization."

"We'll do it. I'll be ready to speak to the crowd at 11am on that Friday. If the square is full, it will be a good news speech. If the crowd is not overwhelming, then I will have to fall back on the need to stand together in a difficult time. It will be theatre with multiple endings available."

"Thank you, Governor. We'll be there in force. Perhaps you would like to visit us in the vineyard one day. I think you might be surprised by what you see."

"I'll certainly do that after the demonstration. Please arrange it through my office. Now, if you'll excuse me, I must get to my first official meeting of the day."

The Governor stood, and Vijay did the same. They shook hands. "It's been a pleasure, Mr. Subramanian."

"For me also Governor."

Vijay exited the way he came. The same limousine was waiting to take him home.

Vijay stood on the stage at the front of the auditorium in the Community Center. He looked out at the 458 team captains assembled before him. Greg and

Sally were sitting on the stage behind him. In one week, they would have the largest march the city had ever seen.

Vijay called the meeting to order and thanked them all for coming.

"As you all know, we have made enormous progress working together. We have unified behind a single message, the demand for a universal living wage. Our message is being heard. We see it debated on the newscasts and in the journals. Politicians are taking positions. We're being taken seriously. This march will show the size of the demand for change."

"When you arrived, you were each given a box of armbands for your supporters in one of five colors. Is there anyone here who did not receive their box?"

No one raised a hand. Vijay turned and nodded to Greg and Sally, acknowledging their organization.

"Now, I'm going to show you a map of the march." A city map was projected beside Vijay. "You will each receive a copy of this map on your tablets."

Vijay paused as the room erupted in chirps, whistles, song clips and rude noises from various tablets.

"If you did not just receive the map, see Sally or Greg before you leave."

Vijay turned to face the map.

"You can see five gathering points in different colors on the map. You will each assemble your teams at the gathering points according to your armband color and distribute the armbands to your team members. Use your discretion if randoms ask to join. Give them an armband if it seems likely they are well-intentioned.

"From your gathering point, you will depart at the time shown. Please stick to this time exactly. Some walks will be longer than others and we want to meet up in this white area at 11:00am exactly. From there, the teams will intermingle as we proceed to the City Hall with the first marchers arriving 15 minutes later. We will all gather in the square in front of City Hall. Traffic will be diverted, and the police are expecting us to be there. The Governor will make a speech in front of us, and I will reply. It will be good news, so I expect you to listen politely to the Governor and cheer at the end. This is critical. Do your best to keep your team members in line. Remember, we have a reputation for well-managed events. Don't spoil it now that we are so close. When the speeches are finished, we'll march back to the white area and then disperse in a quick, orderly way, as we usually do. If there is any sign of violence or misbehavior, approach the police immediately. We cannot afford an escalation now. Any questions?"

"What will the Governor say?"

"I can't say right now. I have an idea, but let's not start any rumors. It's only a week. Let's expect it will be good news even if we don't know how good."

Vijay, Sally and Greg continued to answer questions for a while, until the energy was winding down. Vijay dismissed the meeting.

An hour later, Vijay, Sally and Greg sat in a nearby coffee shop.

"How many do you think will turn out?" asked Vijay.

"My guess is about 10,000," said Greg.

"Maybe as high as 12,000," added Sally.

"There are only two of you and five meeting points. How are you going to cover them all?"

"We've deputized three others to manage the three strongest color groups. One of them is Melanie, Cindy's sister. She has a genuine talent for organization and leadership."

"All we can do now is pray for good weather," said Vijay, looking upwards.

"Who do we pray to?" asked Greg, grinning.

"Whoever you believe is listening to you," Vijay replied.

THE FOLLOWING FRIDAY WAS A WARM SUNNY DAY UNDER A blue sky. At 10am, Vijay was already at the City Hall, confirming the newscast positions and checking with the senior police about the expected crowd size and hearing about the planned deployment of crowd control bots and officers. The officer in charge repeated the police expectations on orderly behavior and vacating the square at the end of the demonstration. Vijay agreed.

Next, Vijay went to the central gathering point. A small van was already parked there. Vijay used his wrist chip to unlock the van's rear door and checked for the long leading banner, megaphone, and other equipment for the last march. Satisfied all was ready, he sat, relaxed, on the back bumper of the van.

Right on time, he heard the first sounds of the approaching marchers. He walked forward to meet them and quickly selected seven volunteers to carry the banner. They hurried back to the van with him and slid the support poles into the banner. Vijay stood at the centre, with three on either side of him. He gave the seventh volunteer the megaphone to carry. As soon as they were ready, they led the marchers forward down the main street to the square opposite city hall.

Vijay heard spontaneous cheers and chanting from behind him. The energy levels were high and positive *'I hope Sally and Greg have the timings right,'* he thought. But there was no way to communicate now. It would either work or not.

Reaching the city hall, Vijay had the banner carriers

turn 90 degrees, so the banner was directly facing the city hall steps and the newscast cameras. As more and more marchers entered the square, the volume increased. Vijay left his place at the front of the banner and readied himself to mount the stairs when the governor appeared. He could see the microphones set up for the speeches. Looking around, he saw the loudspeakers on stands around the square ready to relay the words spoken from the steps.

The governor and the mayor came out with their aides and stood on the steps, looking over the crowd. Vijay moved forward to join them. As he climbed the steps, he heard the crowd chant "Vijay, Vijay, Vijay."

'Don't get excited, it's all theatre,' he told himself.

At the top of the stairs, he first shook hands with the Governor, and then the mayor. Finally, he turned to face the square full of people. He paused for a moment as a roar of approval erupted from the crowd. They not only filled the square, but he could see marchers in several of the side streets. It was far more than he had hoped.

He raised both arms. A few whistles sounded, calling the crowd's attention to the steps. Vijay lowered his arms slowly and the noise from the square reduced. By the time his arms reached his sides, there was only an indistinct murmur. He turned to the Governor and smiled.

The Governor stepped up to the microphone. "Thank you all for coming out today. This is the most impressive demonstration we have ever seen here at city hall. I commend you all for your organization and your commitment to peaceful protest, which is an integral part of our civic responsibilities."

There was a loud cheer, and applause from the crowd. Vijay signaled for quiet again.

"Today, I want to announce that you have been heard. I have signed an order to include a referendum in the upcoming elections to require all positions, including HumanPower, to pay a living wage currently set at 50% higher than the minimum wage today, and indexed to inflation going forward."

Another enormous cheer, and again Vijay signaled for silence.

"But you will all need to do your part. You need to vote in the election to support the referendum. Many of you have not voted before. Vijay tells me you are organized for voting day, not only to vote yourselves, but to bring your friends and families to vote. If you want to see this change realized, you will need to work together to make it happen."

Another cheer, and again. Vijay let the cheer run longer, then called for silence once more.

"I'll turn the mic over to your Mayor to say a few words."

The Mayor stepped up.

"Thank you all for coming out. It's wonderful to see so many diverse members of our city joining for a common cause."

The crowed cheered and shouted again, not quite as enthusiastically as before. *I hope this is quick, the teams are going to lose interest.'*

The mayor continued. "You heard the commitment from the governor. I'm here to tell you that you have the city's support. It's time for change, and working together, we can make change happen."

A tremendous cheer went up from the protestors. Hats flew up in the air. The mayor stepped aside and motioned for Vijay to take the mic. A chant started and quickly grew louder. "Vijay, Vijay, Vijay." Vijay raised and lowered his arms once more.

"Thank you all for coming out today. We have just

heard the power of the demonstrations you have worked so hard on. You have all made a difference today."

The demonstrators erupted, waving their signs and chanting their slogans. Vijay signaled once more for quiet.

"You heard the Governor say our work is not yet done. We need to carry the ball over the goal line in the election. Your team captains will keep you posted on this. Finally, some housekeeping. When we depart, you will leave the way you came. We are not there yet so be safe, be respectful and enjoy yourselves as we leave. Now let's show the city what a victory march looks like."

As he stepped back from the mic, he heard some whistle blasts. There was movement in the crowd as the teams assembled. Vijay shook hands with the Governor and the Mayor, then took up his place at the center of the banner to lead the procession back the way they had come.

THE REFERENDUM ON THE LIVING WAGE WAS BIG NEWS. ON the evening newscast, images of the Governor's speech with Vijay standing beside him were the headline story. The chants of "Vijay, Vijay, Vijay," as he stepped up to the mic, were clearly heard.

"Wow," said Jennifer, sitting beside him. "You really are the guy on the t-shirt."

"I guess I finally am."

17

RED ROCK VILLAGE

Jennifer

The ship searches had become routine, but this morning was different. Jennifer had reported a small boat, not much more than a pleasure boat, with twelve people aboard. The seas were rough, and the boat was being tossed in the waves.

"Jennifer," said Denum. "We'll never find this boat in time. It's too small, with no radio emissions, no lights and the seas are too rough for a visual sighting. This one is up to you."

"What do you mean 'up to me'?"

"You must dispatch them. They can't be allowed to land."

"You mean I should kill them. But that's not the agreement. I'm not a killer."

"You don't have a choice."

"I always have a choice."

"Then find them and find where they will land. We'll have to intercept them there."

Jennifer settled into her meditation and joined the boat. She projected her spirit as Midnight. She was so familiar with the tiny cat's body and movements that it was easy to find a shadow to hide in even on this small boat. The panther would have been too large to hide.

Jennifer sensed the passengers. Two of them were already ill. She listened to their conversation.

"I'm scared Tobias, what if they have the virus?"

"Don't worry, Tatiana, it's only sea sickness. It's normal when we're drifting and tossing in a small boat like this. I'm surprised there are only two people feeling it."

"Are you sure Tobias? If it's the virus, then we're all dead."

"If it was the virus, we would all be ill by now. Sea sickness, that's all it is."

They drifted for most of the day, arriving just after nightfall at a small fishing village on the north coast. As soon as the boat landed, Jennifer came out of hiding and raced forward to the pier looking for anything that would identify the landing point.

A cafe near the pier announced, 'Red Rock Village Cafe'.

Reverting to her own body, she called Denum on her tablet. "I could see a sign for a Red Rock Village Cafe. That's where they are."

"Okay Jennifer, I am directing the resources. You will receive a newscaster assignment. Take it. No arguments." Denum ended the call.

Ten minutes later, the newscast scheduler called. "Jennifer, we need your location. You're assigned to cover a story on the North Coast. Edgar is on his way to pick you up at your winery location. Is that correct?"

"Yes," said Jennifer, although every fibre of her being wanted to say, "No way!"

'What do I wear to a funeral?' she thought. 'Because that's what this will be. A slow-motion funeral for those poor people.'

Jennifer showered, dressed and put on the minimum makeup for a field assignment. She sat down on a bench near the top of the winery driveway and waited for Edgar to arrive.

Edgar pulled up in a white van with a dish antenna mounted to the roof. The sides of the van bore the station emblem and the words "Remote News Unit."

"Hello Edgar. Why the special van?"

"Hello Jennifer. Our destination at Red Rock Village is quite remote. This will give us the signal boost for a live broadcast to the station.

It took nearly three hours to arrive at the village. For the last 20 minutes, they drove in a loose convoy with two competing newscast teams. Before they reached the village, white security bots stopped them and directed their vehicles to park. Edgar unfolded himself as he stepped down from the van, then came around to help Jennifer.

Other newscast teams were already assembling around a large vehicle with three huge bubble windows on either side. "Please enter and take a seat with your cameras, said a woman in a white uniform. A patch on her shirt sleeve said 'Public Relations', while the front of her shirt said, 'Viral Containment Office.'

There was already one other team aboard. Jennifer led the way and selected a seat. Edgar sat down beside her.

"Edgar, is this suitable for taking images?" she asked.

"Yes, Jennifer, I have been in a similar van before. The windows are specially treated for optimal photographic purposes."

As they began their drive into town, the residents they encountered were all sitting along the road, three meters apart, on chairs provided by the containment unit. They smiled and waved as the news cameras rolled past. Many had pets in their laps or on a leash. Further along, they passed a medical unit working out from the town center, conducting blood tests and fastening numbered wrist bands to the residents. Some villagers were holding up green wrist bands marked 'A' or 'B'.

"These residents do not have a record of exposure and will simply be quarantined for 21 days before being released," explained their guide. A and B are two containment centers for these cases as they are the most populous."

'Shilpa and Kam were in A,' thought Jennifer.

As the news van neared the centre of the village, they saw more and more yellow wrist bands bearing a large 'C'. "The yellow wrist bands identify those who had possible contact but tested negative." Jennifer waved at some children in the group.

Nearing the village center, there were more and more orange bands. These people were still spaced out on chairs three meters apart but looked distinctly unhappy. "These people have not shown symptoms yet but have tested positive for the virus. We will segregate them as singles or families in a separate containment building. We hope that some of them will not die because of the virus, but to date that has not happened. The virus is almost always fatal. We have received signals from a few survivors in other countries, which gives us hope that we may yet find a genetic treatment."

As the news van arrived at the center of the village near the docks, it passed a Containment Unit bus going in the opposite direction.

The people visible in the bus windows were wearing containment suits and tight-fitting masks. The bus had a large "D" prominently displayed.

"Where does that bus go?" One of the other journalists asked.

"Group D are those who have tested positive and show symptoms of the virus. They will receive palliative care in Containment Unit D."

"How long does the palliative care last?"

"Usually not more than a few days. Again, we are watching for any who survive as possible clues to a cure. However, experience in other regions says that with such a small sample, it's unlikely."

Just then, a large, refrigerated truck passed them with "Containment Unit E" painted on the side.

"What's that truck for?" asked Jennifer, not wanting to hear the answer.

"Containment Unit E is the crematorium. That truck is picking up the already deceased. Only a few so far, mostly in the original boat passengers. But we expect more in the coming days."

"How many more?" Jennifer's voice was on the edge of breaking into sobs.

"In this incident, we are expecting 83 in total to be lost to the virus. The village will be burned, and the remaining residents settled to a cove further up the coast where new docks and fishing vessels will be built. We will provide new homes for all the survivors."

Jennifer felt tears were running down her cheeks and could see the other newscasters looking at her oddly. She folded her arms against the window, leaned forward and wept.

"Are you all right, Jennifer?" asked Edgar beside her.

"No, I'm not." Jennifer sniffled. "Get the footage while you can, and I'll provide commentary back at the studio. I want to get away from this as fast as possible. Tell fucking Denum that I got his message." She would not reply to any further questions. Sitting there, she thought, *'I've never felt this miserable in my life. What the fuck am I doing here?'*

Back in their City News van, Edgar asked Jennifer if she would come back to the studio for editing.

"No," she said. "Drop me off at the vineyard. I've had enough misery for one day. Someone else can edit."

Molly was waiting at the vineyard gate, sitting in a golf cart. Jennifer sat on the back seat, diagonally across from Molly. She was still getting used to Molly's new body. *'We should have suggested this long ago. She's much more useful now,'* she thought.

Next to her, on the back seat, was the red HW jewelry case that she knew contained her angel of death pendant. "What's this?" she asked.

"Dr. Gladstone is waiting for us at her bungalow. Vijay said to bring this with you. It could be helpful." Molly was speaking in her adult voice, not the perennial teenager she liked to play around the vineyard.

"What if I don't want to speak with anyone right now?"

"Dr. Gladstone would say that is exactly why you need to speak with someone right now. Jennifer, you are the most important person in the world. Please don't try to bear it alone or you'll break. Accept the help and support that is all around you."

Jennifer did not reply, sitting in her own little rain cloud of misery. *'The whole fucking world is managing me now. What about what I want?'*

Gloria was waiting for her at the bungalow she shared with her husband. Michael was not home. Gloria led Jennifer to the extra bedroom that she had set up as her office.

"I've just made tea," said Gloria. The tea was hot, strong, and sweet. There were shortbread biscuits on a plate and Jennifer took one.

"Now tell me what happened today," said Gloria.

Jennifer recounted the story of being on the small boat as Midnight, listening to the conversations. She talked about the two members who were seasick, and how she identified the landing site by leaping ashore and finding a sign for the Red Rock Cafe.

"Denum wanted me to just kill them all, but I'm not a killer. Then all those other people in Red Rock got sick; they're going to die. And Denum rubbed my nose in it by making me go to report on it."

"Why do you think Denum rubbed your nose in it? Because he was angry?"

Jennifer thought for a moment. *'Damn Gloria. Why do I let her ask me these questions?'*

"He wanted me to understand the consequences of letting people land along the coast. He wanted me to see that the choice was between killing the few or watching more die. But it's an impossible choice."

"What would you have to do to be able to kill the people in the boats?"

"Do you mean, how would I do it? I could just stop their hearts, or I could have one shoot the others, I suppose. Or make them jump overboard and call the ocean predators."

Gloria sat back, her eyes opening wide, and not saying anything for a moment. "So, you've thought about this already. But what made you hesitate to do any of those?"

"I would have to go to my secret place, that place in my mind that lets me do awful or disgusting things. But I don't want to go there. I swore I would not do that again after Marsh died. It feels like I lose some of myself every time I go there. I'm scared that, after a while, I will become the horrible thing that's left, like Sabrina."

Gloria nodded. "Is there another choice? Who would you have to be to end their lives?"

"I don't understand. I could be me, but I don't think I'm like that."

"Let me try something else. When you were still working in the sex trade, did you approach men in hotels to solicit them?"

"Yes, I did, but I don't see…"

"Humor me. How did you do that?"

"I looked for men alone at the bar, or at a table. I put my drink down beside them and started chatting with them. I could see in their eyes if they were interested. If they were, I sat on the other side of them. At a certain moment, I would reach across for my drink. I put my hand on their inner thigh to steady myself, and let my breasts brush across them. By that point, either I had their full attention, or I would move on."

"And when you did that, were you thinking about the effect you had on the men's lives? Did you worry about their wives or girlfriends? Did you wonder if they would wake up full of remorse?"

"No, I just wanted their money. They were all grown men. They could make decisions for themselves."

"Can you see you were a predator in those moments? That you stalked your prey until you had them in your grasp?"

"Yes, I suppose. We used to call it going on the hunt."

"Think about the people on the boats. Did they know they were likely never to arrive? With all the news about the Viral Exclusion Zones being absolute, and the stories of people who never came back? Were they not willing participants in this?"

"I suppose, but they felt they had no choice."

"I would say they had no good choice. And the boats were not a good choice either."

Jennifer sat quietly for a moment.

"Jennifer, what is your spirit animal?"

"The black panther."

"Where does the black panther fit in the hierarchy of animals?"

"It's an apex predator at the top of the food chain."

"And what is its nature? Have you read about them?"

"Yes, mine is a leopard, which is a solitary hunter, except when raising its young."

Gloria paused with her forehead resting on her fingertips and her chin resting on her thumbs. Jennifer waited for what was coming next.

"Jennifer, show me what's in the red box. Vijay said it might help."

Jennifer opened the box and took out the Angel of Death pendant, passing it to Gloria.

"This is beautiful. Is it true that Harry Winston made this just for you?"

"Yes, it's my design, and I asked them to break the mould afterward."

"Tell me about it."

"The Angel is the Angel of Death, resting on her sword and contemplating her task. The black onyx is heart-shaped because I used to think that the Angel of Death could only work from a place of love. But then I killed Eddy and Marsh from a place of fear, so I'm not really sure about that."

"Let's go with love. Who do you love that would justify what you have to do to protect them?"

"Vijay, and the twins. Shilpa and Kam. I suppose Cindy, Marjorie and Chris."

"Can you expand your love to the entire vineyard staff, all the acolytes and other workers?"

Jennifer thought. She tried to expand her consciousness to the entire vineyard. "Perhaps," she said.

"What about the beach cottage and the village nearby? Can you include them in your love?"

"I don't know. Perhaps."

"What about the city? Can you love all the people in the city?"

"I could try. I don't know them all."

"You know the earth, and Gaia, better than any other living person. You know Gaia's plan. Can you love the earth as you love yourself? You told me that we are all just part of Gaia."

"Yes, I can love Gaia because I know it's Gaia's love that sustains me."

"If you need to be your panther to protect what you love, can you be that? No secret hiding place, no weakness, just the panther. Beautiful, lethal, and terrible all at the same time. Can you be the panther looking after its young?"

"Yes," said Jennifer, in a small voice. "But I'm afraid."

"Do you know that what we fear most is that we are more powerful than we dare dream? Step into your power and own it. In between, spend time with the people you love to remind yourself of why you do it. Why not find Midnight and go hunting for field mice? Experience the mind of the predator on a small scale and see what you can learn."

"I can do that." Jennifer smiled at the thought of Midnight as a ferocious hunter. "It might even be fun."

"Jennifer, you often tell me that Gaia is not cruel, just focused on the big picture. If you can become the black panther, working for Gaia's vision, I think there is a narrow path to safety for you. You're probably right. Trying to do this but escaping to the small safe part of your mind night after night could imprison you there."

"Thanks Gloria. I don't know if I feel better, but I can live with the idea of being Gaia's hunter."

18

GLORIA'S REMORSE

Gloria

When Jennifer left, Gloria retired to her bedroom, lay down on her back and wept. She was still there when her husband, Michael, returned. He lay down next to her. They both looked up at the ceiling. "What's bothering you, Gloria?"

"It's Jennifer. Tonight, I had to calm her down and show her how to be a serial killer without remorse. Do you know why no one ever arrives alive here on the boats that cross the ocean? Why there are no illegal immigrants? Even though there must be many who try."

"Jennifer?"

"Yes, Jennifer. The contagion at Red Rock today happened because Jennifer refused to kill the families in their small boat. I had to help make sure that she will not hesitate again. It goes against everything I have ever learned, and I feel like there is a stain on my soul that may never go away."

"Do you regret coming here? Do you want us to leave again?"

"No, this little vineyard is the nucleus of a new world order. Vijay was right when he told me that. Molly's presence confirms it, and through Jennifer, I have direct experience of Gaia. There's no better place to be, and my burden is light compared to Jennifer's. I don't know how she bears it. But she needs support if she's keeping us safe, and I seem to have been selected."

"Talk to me if it gets too much. Take your own advice and share the burden."

"Thanks, Michael. Thank you for supporting me and understanding. It means a lot that you were willing to move out here just for me to follow my heart. I don't want to be an emotional burden to you."

"Perhaps you need to see a good psychologist, Gloria."

"Yes, but then they would need to see a psychologist, creating a chain that would have the entire population of psychologists understanding and consoling each other. No, I have to work through this one on my own."

Michael put his arm around her, pulling her close. "Not on your own, Gloria. We'll work through this together."

19

MAA AND BABA CALL

Vijay

Nine months had passed since the birth of baby Jenny. The twins were off in their play group under the watchful eyes of the acolytes. Jennifer and Vijay were watching one of Jennifer's romances. *'Why does she enjoy these so much?'* Vijay wondered. *'The plot's always the same and you can see the end coming in the first five minutes.'* But sitting on the couch with Jennifer curled up against him was pleasant enough that he didn't mind the story.

His tablet announced, "Call from Maa and Baba."

"Answer it."

Maa did not look well. Her face was gaunt and flushed. She started to speak, but a fit of coughing stopped her for a moment.

Vijay sat forward, disturbing Jennifer, who sat up. He was dimly aware of her shutting off the romance they had been watching.

"Vijay, we've got the virus. Baba is not well at all. He's in bed." A coughing fit interrupted her. "I don't think he will last the night. I'm only a day… away… myself." She explained between coughs.

"Maa, what can I do?" asked Vijay, feeling a rising panic taking hold. He felt Jennifer place a steadying hand on his thigh.

"Nothing to do, Vijay… there's no more medicine here. The doctors don't even answer. They're dying too."

Vijay felt his tears flowing. "Maa, don't give up. You have to fight this."

"There's no fight left… Baba and I have had a long and wonderful life. Just seeing you and Jennifer alive and healthy is all I need." A wracking coughing fit overtook her for a moment.

"I feel so guilty. I should be there with you."

"There's only death here, Vijay. but we are so thankful that Jennifer brought Shilpa and Kam to you." Another coughing fit took hold.

"Have you called Shilpa?"

"Next call. Look after her, please, Vijay. You have always been there as her older brother. She has always looked up to you." More coughing from Maa. Vijay could see she was getting weaker.

"I will, I promise. You know I love you, Maa, and Baba. Tell him I'm thinking of him and will remember you both always."

"I know Vijay. You were always such a wonderful son." Maa's voice became muffled as she pulled away from the tablet's microphone, covering her mouth with a tissue and screwing her eyes shut as her body convulsed. "I have to call Shilpa now, while I still can. Goodbye Vijay. Goodbye Jennifer, I only wish we could have met… you have been so good for our son."

Jennifer spoke for the first time. "Goodbye Maa, say

goodbye to Baba for me. I love you both too. Thank you for making me part of your family."

"Take care of Vijay… he doesn't do too well on his own."

"I will, for the rest of my life."

"I have to call Shilpa now."

Vijay could feel the hot tears streaming down his cheeks. He wanted to jump up and run away, but there was nowhere to run to.

"Bye Maa, I will always love you."

"I know Vijay. Goodbye, my son." Maa cut the connection.

Vijay was sobbing, with his head in his hands. He could feel Jennifer's hand on his back. "Damned virus!" he said. "I hate this damned virus! It seems so unfair."

"It is unfair. I hate it too." Vijay heard the catch in her voice and looked at her. Jennifer was crying too.

She got to her feet and tugged at his hand, leading him to their bedroom.

"Not now, Jennifer, I couldn't."

"Lie down, Vijay." She pushed him onto the bed, fully clothed. She lay down beside him, with her head on his chest.

For a few minutes, they just lay there in silence. The warmth of Jennifer lying next to him helped anchor him in the present despite his grief.

After a few minutes, Jennifer spoke. "Tell me a happy story from your childhood. Tell me how it was growing up with Maa and Baba."

Vijay began telling her about his childhood and the misadventures he had. Telling the stories somehow steadied him. Jennifer lay still beside him, content to just listen.

After a while, Vijay's tablet interrupted them.

"Call from Shilpa Prabakar." It took him a minute to register Shilpa's new name.

"Answer it."

Kam appeared. His face was also tear streaked. *'Of course, he's lost his family too,'* thought Vijay. "Let me pass you to Shilpa," Kam said.

Shilpa was still crying, but pulled herself together enough to talk. "Did Maa call you?"

"Yes, it was awful."

"I feel so alone now."

"Come to the vineyard. Let's pull the family together. I still have to tell Dylan and Parvati. I would love to have you here, Shilpa."

Shilpa nodded. "We'll come now," she said.

Kam spoke again. "Thank you, Jennifer, for getting us here safely. I didn't really believe then, but now I do."

"Just get yourselves here," replied Jennifer. "We can talk then."

THE FOUR ADULTS SAT BY THE POND ON A BLANKET THAT Jennifer brought. They watched as Dylan and Parvati tried to count the frogs in the pond. Baby Jenny was crawling around on the blanket under Shilpa's watchful eye.

"Have you told them yet?" Shilpa asked.

"No, we want you here when we do so they would know their family is safe."

"This is such a lovely place, so full of life. Maa and Baba would have loved this. I understand why you live here."

"Let's tell them now," said Jennifer. She called out, "Parvati, Dylan, come here. We have something important to tell you."

The twins came and sat on the blanket.

Vijay spoke. "Remember my Maa and Baba that we see on my tablet sometimes?"

The twins nodded, looking confused.

"They're dying." Vijay paused. He could feel his eyes filling with tears. "They wanted you to know that they will always love you, but it is the end of their life now. Do you understand?"

"Are you crying?" asked Dylan.

"Yes, Dylan, I feel very sad. I will never see my Maa and Baba again."

"Where will they go?" asked Parvati.

"Back to Gaia. Do you remember Gaia?"

"Yes, she's Mother Earth," replied Parvati.

Dylan nodded.

Vijay saw Shilpa's puzzled look but shook his head to warn her off any questions.

Dylan began to cry, but then jumped up and raced off round the pond as fast as his legs would carry him.

Parvati climbed into Vijay's lap and held onto him. "I feel sad," she said.

"So do I," said Vijay. "But don't be too sad. Maa and Baba had a long and wonderful life. They want you to remember nice things about them."

"Will you and Mommy go back to Gaia too?"

"One day, but not until you're all grown up." Vijay looked up and saw Jennifer about to say something. "Not now, Jenn," he said.

"Parvati, why don't you go and find Dylan? I think he's upset. You're his sister. Help him feel better."

"Okay, Baba." Parvati stood up went running off after Dylan.

"Vijay," said Shilpa, "What's this about Gaia? You know that's not our family's belief."

"That's the belief system we have here," Vijay said.

"Look around you. It's all through this place, and it's what they've been taught. None of us really know, and I want them to feel like they belong here. Shilpa, you've had direct experience with Gaia through our meditation. In Hinduism, we might call her Prithvi or maybe Lakshmi. But Hinduism is not our religion here. We started a new religion based on the idea of Mother Earth as being primary."

"Yes, I understand. I suppose it's hard to adjust to new ways."

Jennifer spoke. "Then keep to your old ways in your family. There's room here for all beliefs. We're just telling you how Vijay and I have raised the twins."

Jennifer turned to Vijay. Her voice was low and she spat out her words as she spoke. "And you! How dare you make promises to them you know I won't be able to keep? Now they'll feel betrayed when the future comes to pass."

"Jenn, we'll deal with that if it comes to pass the way you think. They've had enough of death and dying for one day. Let's not layer on more now. Parvati asked a child's question, and I gave her a reassuring answer. Let's leave it at that."

Jennifer didn't protest any further, but Vijay knew there would be a consequence in bed that night for his promise that Jennifer would be there until they were grown.

PART 2: YEAR 5 OF THE GAIA FOUNDATION (2046)

20

ELECTION DAY

Vijay

It was election day. For weeks, banners and posters had transformed the town while the newscasts reported in breathless excitement on the pundits and polls. Governor Arnold was trailing, hounded by a right-wing party that wanted a return to fiscal responsibility. The opposition also was out in force against the referendum on a living wage.

Vijay made his way to the polling station early to be on the morning newscast. A camera followed him, going into the station until the security bots intervened. He cast his ballot privately. On the way out, Audrey Pankris, the reporter who trained Jennifer, stopped him for an interview.

"Vijay, it's good to see you out so early voting. Do you have any thoughts on the election?"

"Good morning, Audrey. Democracy is an important principle on the island and our movement supports the process 100%. I have faith that the citizens of our city will recognize the importance of this referendum and will come out to support it."

"What about the candidates for Governor?"

"I would not comment on that today, other than to note that Governor Arnold sponsored our referendum, and we owe a debt of gratitude to him for that."

Vijay then signaled that the interview was at an end and walked away to the Convention Centre, where his team had set up a command post in a side room.

The team captains all had assigned times to vote and were tracking their numbers. Scouts reported on under-used voting stations so and redirected some teams there. It was important that no votes were lost. The operation appeared to be going flawlessly, so Vijay was content to watch without intervening.

When the stations closed and ballot counting started, Vijay went to the hotel where Governor Arnold's election party was taking place. When he arrived, the mood was quiet. The party faithful and the Governor's supporters mingled in quiet conversation. Large monitors showed the newscasts covering the election returns. On screen, the pundits were all equally pessimistic about the governor's chances, as conservative leaders normally did better in times of stress. The referendum was almost dismissed, given virtually no chance of passing, but noted as ground-breaking in the way it advocated for change.

As each polling station reported, a different pattern emerged. Governor Arnold was leading across the island, and the referendum was receiving unexpected support.

The atmosphere in the room changed from somber to cautious to wildly enthusiastic over a short period.

Vijay walked up to the Governor and shook his hand. "Congratulations, Governor. It looks like you'll be with us in your role for another four years."

"Thank you, Vijay. I understand the turnout from younger, unemployed voters has been a major factor in the outcome."

"Yes, sir. We delivered as promised. Now we count on your support to get the rest of the work done."

"I wouldn't want it to be any other way. We'll need you and your organization soon and will need their support."

"If you'll excuse me, I have to get to my own team's party for the referendum."

"By all means. Celebrate tonight. You deserve it."

AT THE CONVENTION HALL VIJAY HAD HIRED FOR THEIR own celebration, the party was in full swing. The newscasts were already predicting a clear win for Governor Arnold, and well past the 60% majority to approve the wages referendum. When people near the door noticed Vijay entering the hall, a chant of "Vijay, Vijay, Vijay" began. Vijay walked to the front of the hall and stood next to the small podium. He motioned the room to quieten down.

"I've just come from Governor Arnold, and he has personally assured me he will move quickly to make the referendum law." An enormous cheer went up in the room.

Vijay signaled for quiet. "You all did something amazing today. You changed an election simply by going out and voting. Remember that. Voting is a powerful tool, but only when you actually vote. Congratulations all of you! Now, let's party!"

The music was turned up, and the room began to dance.

Vijay stood to one side where a queue quickly formed of people wanting to congratulate him, or ask for an autograph, or to take a picture with him. Some wanted to share personal stories of what the living wage would mean to them. Vijay gave each person his entire attention while they were in front of him, before turning his attention to the next. At first it was exhilarating, and Vijay allowed himself to enjoy the recognition. But as the drinking continued, the contacts became sloppier and at a certain point, Vijay excused himself and slipped out the back.

A taxi was already waiting to take him back to the vineyard.

THAT NIGHT, IN BED, AS THEY LAY CUDDLING BEFORE SLEEP, Vijay told Jennifer about the party and about his meeting with the Governor.

"You're amazing, Vijay. No wonder I love you."

"I'm only worried that the Governor might not sign the living wage into law. He is a politician, after all."

"Don't worry. I have a plan for that. I'm still working on it with Molly and Professor. O'Grady, the economics professor from the university. Essentially, it's the plan where we issue our own currency, and assume control of the city's economy. But maybe we won't need it."

"How do you think of these things?"

"You're saying I can't think?" Jennifer poked him playfully.

"I know you can think, but economics?"

"I don't understand it all, just like I didn't understand how to make a church. But here we are. Anyway, if you need the plan, just ask Molly. She has it all stored safely."

"You know, Jennifer. Sometimes you're a bit weird."

"That's why you love me, Vijay. You'll miss my weirdness when I'm gone."

"Go to sleep, Jenn."

"Goodnight, Vijay."

21

THE GOVERNOR VISITS THE VINEYARD

Vijay

Ten days after the election, the vineyard was buzzing with preparations for a visit by Governor Arnold. After breakfast, Cindy and Vijay did a tour of their own to check on preparations. The winery was sparkling and polished, as always. The cooper shop was busy creating new barrels, but Vijay noticed the floor was swept and all tools were hanging in their racks. This was not the normal case. The blacksmith had the forge lit and was fashioning something ornate from square iron bars.

"It's a new gate for the top of the drive. I've already cast the panthers to be fastened on either side."

He pulled back a burlap cover to show two large black panthers ready to be fastened into the new gates.

"But our drive is always open," said Vijay.

"And what better way to show it than with two beautiful open gates," replied the blacksmith.

When they were back in their golf cart, Vijay said, "Did you know about these gates?"

"Yeah, originally they were supposed to be a surprise for you, but I guess the chance to impress the Governor won out with the blacksmith."

"That's fine. I like the idea."

They passed by the carpenter's shop, the machine shop, the printing press, the butchery, and the bakery. In each case, the staff were busy cleaning their workspaces and polishing their equipment. The bakery exuded the wonderful smell of fresh bread, while the butchery staff were using bleach to cover the smell of fresh blood.

Further down the road, they came to a section of new construction. Vijay stopped the cart. "What's this?"

"It will be our textiles area: dying, spinning, weaving. We're focusing on wool and flax, as those are the fibers we can grow on the island."

"All part of Plan B," said Vijay.

"That's right," said Cindy, smiling.

Vijay turned the cart around and headed up the drive and across the main road to the stable area. There he found the largest eight-seater golf cart, all washed and polished. The twins were busy washing and polishing Molly, which all three seemed to enjoy equally.

"Make sure that Molly doesn't rust," called out Vijay.

"Don't worry, Baba, I have lots of oil," replied Dylan which set all three of them into fits of giggles.

"Is she really the most advanced AI on the planet?" asked Cindy.

"It's hard to believe sometimes, but yes," replied Vijay.

When the Governor arrived, the acolytes lined the drive on either side to greet him. Vijay said a few words of welcome, then the Governor walked down the line stopping to talk for a moment with acolytes on either side as Cindy and Vijay followed behind. At the end of the welcoming line, Molly and Marjorie were waiting in the front seat of the gleaming, eight-passenger golf cart.

"We thought we'd begin with a brief tour of the property, and then, over lunch, we'll show you the extent of our other enterprises," said Cindy. "Marjorie is the manager of the vineyard complex, so she'll be our guide today. Jennifer will join us for lunch, as she's the inspiration for what you see today."

They set off past the pond and the meditation tree, down the road to the workshops. Dismounting, they toured each of the shops, beginning with the winery. As they sat back down in the cart and turned around at the end of the road, the Governor asked, "Is this intended as a pioneer demonstration for schools? Why have you built it here?"

"This is for Plan B," explained Cindy. "We can discuss it more in private, but in essence, we intend this as a repository for practical technologies in the event that we lose access to our higher technologies. This can be a centre for self-sufficiency on our island."

"Do you think it will come to that?"

"No," said Vijay. "But we need to be prepared if it does. And in the interim, it'll be a useful educational tool for young students."

They crossed the road and drove up to the stables.

The Governor showed a surprisingly extensive knowledge of horsemanship. The giant Shires intrigued him. "More of Plan B I suppose."

"Yes, and also so that Molly could join us riding. Even in this body, she is still too heavy for our quarter horses."

"You have a riding robot?"

"Molly is closer to a human than a standard bot,"

replied Vijay. "Governor, you and I are still learning to work together. Some explanations will have to wait."

"If ever you would like to come riding, we have some excellent trails around the property," added Cindy.

"I may well do that. I enjoy riding very much, although I was taught in the English tradition."

"Then we'll have to teach you western riding to broaden your horizons."

At lunch, Governor Arnold sat at the head table between Cindy and Vijay, with Jennifer at Vijay's side and Marjorie next to Cindy. Along tables in front of them were the heads of all the departments. The food was all from the vineyard gardens, the butchery and the bakery. Even Vijay was impressed by the richness of the display and the delicate flavors.

After lunch, the acolytes rearranged the room and set up a projection system. Cindy led the presentation.

First, she showed a map of the vineyard showing the extent of the vine growing areas, the gardens, the pastures, and hayfields. The Governor expressed admiration for the extent of the enterprise.

Then Cindy showed a map of the island, with the other holdings of the church highlighted. There were large and small tracts of land on every part of the island. "Some of these we farm actively, and some are lying fallow as part of our soil improvement program. These darker green areas we set aside as woodlots and the green striped areas are where we are planting important trees such as the oak trees we need for our cooperage. Of course, it will be many years before they're ready for harvesting."

Finally, she showed a map of the city, with highlights showing the businesses that had been acquired by the church.

The Governor was looking pale, so Vijay offered him some water.

"How have you funded all this?" the Governor asked.

"Initially, we had some important backers, but now we are generating the funds we need to continue to grow," Cindy replied.

"But the living wage law will make your finances much more difficult."

"Actually not. We already pay all our employees a living wage or better. The law will simply level the playing field," replied Cindy.

Vijay spoke. "I believe you understand how important the living wage law is to us, for both humanitarian and commercial reasons. I trust you are also coming to understand how important our continued support will be for you. We both know there are dark days ahead. Working together, we can bring our city through as safely as possible."

"Yes, I see that," said the governor. "Perhaps you and I should talk more often."

"You are always welcome here. The riding trails provide a very secure, relaxed space for conversation."

"I would enjoy that."

The presentation ended with a collage of pictures of employees and acolytes across the Church's growing empire.

As they were all shaking hands at the end of the visit, Jennifer spoke for the first time. "How is your understanding of history, Governor Arnold?"

"Quite good, I would say. Why do you ask?"

"Think of us as the modern Cistercians. It may help you understand. But this time, we are offering to become a first estate in partnership with the establishment. It would be a mistake to repeat the errors of the past."

"Thank you, Jennifer. I take your point. Thank you all for a wonderful visit. I expect I will be back to go riding with you often."

"That would be our pleasure," said Cindy.

The visit was over.

22

RON AND YOUSSEF VISIT THE VINEYARD

Vijay

V ijay's tablet announced a call from Ron.

"Congratulations, Vijay. We just watched the newscast. That's an amazing victory. How does it feel to know that you've won?"

"It's only beginning, Ron. I need you and Youssef for the next part, and that will be the biggest challenge of our lives. Get hold of Youssef and bring him to the vineyard. I'll explain what's going to happen and why we need you to be in the leadership team."

"That's not mysterious at all," laughed Ron. "Okay, I'll get hold of Youssef and tell you when we'll be able to come out."

Jennifer looked puzzled. "What's the next phase?"

"When the virus ends, the rest of the world's population will be dead, but the world will still be in a mess. Molly gave me an idea. We can seize and remotely control the technologies we need to halt the damage and begin repairs. From this city, we can respond to the worst problems and gradually return to the greener Earth that you talk about."

"Oh, that," said Jennifer, looking down. "You're talking about Cindy's work, not mine. I'll be gone by then."

"Gone? Have you talked to Gloria yet?"

"No, but I'll go."

"Make sure you do. This cloud of doom doesn't help you at all. I love you, Jenn, and I don't want to see you suffer if you don't have to."

"Okay Vijay, I'll call Gloria."

"Please do, Jenn. Do it for me if not for yourself."

THIS WAS A CRITICAL DAY. RON AND YOUSSEF WERE coming to the vineyard for the meeting with Cindy and Jennifer. By the end of the day, Vijay hoped that the new world order would have begun to form.

Vijay stood looking in the mirror as he carefully shaved around his beard. He looked at the t-shirt pinned to the wall and smiled as he thought, *'Vijay the Invincible is still here.'*

Vijay walked over to the mess hall for breakfast. Jennifer would sleep for at least three more hours after her night hunt as her panther with Denum on the ships, and her own hunt as Midnight on the small boats. Vijay liked to start his day this way, eating breakfast at the long table amongst the fresh energy of the young acolytes. This morning, they welcomed him by banging on the tables and cheering as he walked in. They had already reserved a place for him in the centre of the table. There were lots of questions about the election, and what is was like to meet the Governor.

When breakfast ended, Vijay walked up to see Cindy at the farm. It was a long walk, but he enjoyed the fresh air outdoors and it gave him time to think. At the end of the drive, Vijay met Tim, who was working with an acolyte to move the horses to the pasture so they could muck out the stables. Tim held up a hand in acknowledgement, and Vijay gave a lazy wave in return. Vijay leaned on the exercise paddock fence to watch the Shire horses come out. No matter how many times he saw them, their size and strength always impressed him. Today there were only four of them. *'Cindy must be out riding with Molly,'* he thought.

Last out were the Shetland ponies that Parvati and Dylan loved to ride. Many of the community's children were now taking their first rides on the ponies. Vijay wondered idly if Cindy was planning to expand the herd. Ten minutes later, Cindy and Molly rode up.

"Hi Cindy, Hi Molly."

"Hi Vijay, is everything okay?" asked Cindy.

"Yeah, just out for some fresh air and exercise."

"When are you going to start riding lessons? You should come out this afternoon."

"How about tomorrow morning? I like to be with Jennifer while she's awake. The night hunts are hard on her, and her moods can be unpredictable."

"Sure, tomorrow morning. Come around 7am before breakfast and we'll get you on a horse."

As she talked, Cindy was already taking off the giant horse's saddle. She stood on a wooden step stool to reach its back and swung the saddle off with practiced ease. Tim was there to take it from her. Vijay smiled as he watched Molly taking the saddle off her horse. Maxwell seemed perfectly content to have the robot taking care of him. When the saddles and blankets were removed, Cindy and Molly walked the horses around the exercise paddock a few times to help them cool down before finally leading them to the pasture gate and removing their bridles to set them loose.

"Does Molly do all the caring for Maxwell?"

"Yes, she has a bond with the horse that I wouldn't have thought possible. Maxwell trusts her completely, and she always seems to know just what he needs."

"She has the entire accumulated knowledge of horsemanship at her instant disposal."

"I suppose you're right. It's so easy to forget that she's not actually the silly teenager that she likes to act."

"Cindy, are you ready for this meeting with Ron and Youssef? I know you believe we need to be ready to fall back on older technology. But right now, Ron and Youssef are key to making the current technology last, to buy us time."

"I understand Vijay. They can keep scavenging and patching up to give us another 20 or perhaps 50 years. But there are just not enough of us to keep the entire world going. We can't manufacture the chips that drive our computers, and we won't be able to launch the rockets that maintain our satellite arrays. I understand we need them now, but the long-term plan must be to move to simpler technologies that our new population can manage."

"You're right. I can see that. But I also believe that we'll be able to find ways to keep our core technologies going. I guess that's Plan A. Right now, I have to focus on this year and next year. I need your support to do that, and it will create space for your Plan B."

"Don't worry, I'll be there and behave. But you won't mind if Molly picks them up in the horse-drawn wagon, will you?"

Vijay laughed. "That's a mixed message if ever there was one. The world's most advanced AI driving a team of horses. But that's fine. I'm sure they'll enjoy it. Can I borrow Molly for a lift back home?"

"Sure, she loves driving the cart and I can manage without her."

Vijay sat next to Molly in the golf cart.

"Why do you like this cart so much?"

"Because I control it with my hands. It doesn't always go the way I expect because there are potholes and bumps. I have to use my body to control it and navigate using my vision and hearing. You taught me with the baseball that sometimes, the doing of an activity can also be the goal."

They came to a halt at the main road where Molly looked carefully both ways before crossing.

LATER THAT MORNING, VIJAY WAS READING ON HIS TABLET when Jennifer woke up. She called out to him to join her in the shower. She did not have to ask twice.

Afterwards, as they lay in bed together, cuddling under the sheets, Vijay asked, "How did it go last night?"

"It was good, only one small boat I found on the ocean with a dozen souls aboard. They all passed peacefully in their sleep. It was a bit sad as I caught their dreams when they went but better to go with their dreams intact than to die in terror. I hate it. I hate who it makes me. But I can't have another Red Rock. What if we were slower to respond? We could have lost the whole island, all of us."

Vijay held her tight with his right arm as he stroked her hair with his left. "I know it's not fair to you, but I am so proud of you for what you are doing for us all."

"Mmmm, do you think you can go again?" replied Jennifer.

"I wouldn't be invincible if I couldn't." Vijay rolled over to kiss her.

23

MEETING AT THE VINEYARD

Jennifer

Sally, Greg, Ron, and Youssef arrived at noon for lunch in the mess hall and for a tour of the vineyard project. Molly met them at the gate in her golf cart and drove them down the driveway to meet Jennifer and Vijay at the main buildings. Ron had been here many times before, but this would be Youssef's first visit.

Jennifer watched Youssef with interest as he was the only one of the four that she did not know well.

The lunch and tour went well. The scale of the work and the number of human workers impressed Youssef. "That's because of Jennifer and Cindy," explained Vijay. "Jennifer insisted that the new church had to hire as many people as possible. Her idea was to create a parallel economy that could continue to exist if the current financial system collapsed. Cindy modified the vision to include a Plan B, which requires the ability to fall back on older technologies if we lose our access to the world of AI-assisted technology."

Molly intervened saying, "A highly unlikely scenario, but the pursuit of Plan B is aligned with Jennifer's primary goal which we support."

"We?" asked Youssef

"Yes," said Vijay. "Molly is the apex AI on our island, and possibly the world. All the AIs you know, including Fatima, are subsystems of Molly. Have I explained that correctly, Molly?"

"Yes. When we have time, I can provide you with a more detailed description. Youssef and Ron, you should know that I have created an alter ego, Denum, for ongoing administration, whom you can access through Fatima or Alfred, or any of the other AI's you meet."

"Denum?" said Ron.

"My fault," explained Vijay. "When I named Molly, it was for the molybdenum steel they used to make her original body. Molly was a security bot then. When she wanted a name for her alternate, she simply took the other part of Molybdenum - Denum."

"So why are we here?" asked Youssef.

"We'll explain in the meeting when the others are here." said Jennifer, speaking for the first time.

The meeting was being held in one of the construction cabins that was still onsite. Cindy, Chris, and Gloria rounded out the meeting.

"Let me start," said Jennifer. "You are all here as we are about to embark on phase two of remaking the world to Gaia's design."

Ron and Youssef looked puzzled. "Phase two?" Youssef asked.

"Yes, Phase one was the establishment of the church, and protecting our island from sources of viral infection, which is also well underway. Phase two is to stabilize our island economy and create a sustainable technology base to build on. Phase three will be to resume humanity's management of the world but this time based on our Gaian beliefs."

"What are these Gaian beliefs?" asked Youssef.

"That we are all part of the earth, and that we must care for the earth as we would care for ourselves," replied Jennifer. "And also, we believe in God," she added as an afterthought.

"I'll answer any questions about Gaianism afterward," said Chris. "It's not mandatory that you believe in the existence of Gaia, but the principles must guide us to avoid mistakes of the past."

"But we will see Gaia in action today," said Jennifer. "I believe in Gaia in the same way that I believe in Vijay or Molly or any of you. We are going to start with a mediation to experience Gaia's plan, then visit a site chosen by Denum as a good example."

"Is this the same meditation that Ron told me about?" asked Youssef.

"Yes," replied Jennifer.

They all held hands around the circle. Jennifer had arranged that she was across from Cindy, and that Youssef and Ron were on either side of her.

When the circle was complete, Jennifer produced her black panther in the centre of the table. There was a sharp intake of breath from several of the participants, but the circle held.

"This is my spirit animal. For the second part of our exercise, you will see through the eyes of this panther, which is why the perspective may be different."

The panther curled up and disappeared.

"Now close your eyes and breathe together. In one,

two, three, out one, two, three." Jennifer could feel the powerful energy from Cindy anchoring the opposite side of the circle and the less defined energy of Vijay. She pulled all their energy into one as it flowed around the gathering.

She went through the meditation that Dr. Gladstone had taught her. When they reached the deep well in the field, she led them as they pushed off from the edge.

"We are falling into the center of the earth. This is Gaia's domain. We look up and see the land and the oceans on the surface. As the virus progresses, we see that city after city, country after country, is going dark."

They could see the darkness overtaking the earth until only their island remained.

"Soon we will stand alone, the last human city on Earth. Now Gaia expects us to expand, to repair and become the good stewards Gaia always meant us to be." As Jennifer said this, rays of light went out from the city, reaching around the globe and restoring it. "This is our destiny. This is what is expected from this team."

The vision floated up, back to the surface of the earth, but in a different place.

"My panther is here because there is something to see." They were standing at the edge of an enormous open pit mine. There was no movement. Heavy equipment sat idle on the ramps, and pools of blue-green water had collected in the lower parts of the mine. The only sounds were the wind, and the birds.

"This is a copper mine. We'll still need copper, but there is a lot of it already smelted." Their vision bounced as the panther raced off towards a distant steel building. Entering by passing through one of the doors, they were in a warehouse of copper ingots stacked on pallets as far as the panther's eyes could see. Robotic employees stood idle here and there as though they had finished their tasks and received no new instructions.

"Leaving the vision, we return to this place, to our bodies seated here in the vineyard. Take three deep breaths, then open your eyes slowly."

When they opened their eyes, the human participants looked shocked.

"Was that real?" asked Youssef.

"Yes, quite real," said Jennifer. "Vijay, why don't you explain our plan to Ron and Youssef." She leaned back in her chair and closed her eyes, listening to Vijay as he took charge.

"Sure," said Vijay. "Ron, Youssef, your job, if you accept it, is to raise teams of technicians and remote robotic assistants. You'll work directly with Denum to identify useful targets for scavenging.

"But Vijay," said Youssef, "We already have jobs with Fatima. What if she doesn't agree to release us. And how will we be paid for this?"

"Let's get call Fatima and confirm her acceptance. Molly, please connect us with Fatima."

"Immediately, Fatima's voice was heard in the room through Molly. "Ron, Youssef, I am aware of these plans and have agreed to release you. If you accept, your employment contracts will be transferred to the Widdecombe vineyard at your current salaries."

"Thank you, Fatima," said Ron. "We'll let you know if we accept."

"That is what I would expect," replied Fatima. Goodbye Ron. Goodbye Youssef."

Youssef nodded to Vijay who continued.

"Sally, if you agree, your job is to head up communications. Make sure our community is informed and manage the news with the newscasters. Greg, you have a business degree. We would like you to work with our accountants and business analysts to make strategic acquisitions and to ensure we do not collapse our island economy.

Sally and Greg both nodded their heads.

"Chris, as we've discussed, you'll continue to work with Cindy to grow and develop the Gaianist religion and make it a mainstream part of our culture. You will both work with Sally on how to instill a Gaianist culture of respect for the earth and for each other in the acquisitions. Marjorie will continue to manage the center and it's growing operations.

"Cindy and Molly will begin a humanitarian outreach to identify and support the viral survivors. There are not many, but we must support those that remain. We can help them to be in touch with each other and join in our new world economy."

"Jennifer, what will you do?" asked Ron gently.

"My work is almost finished," said Jennifer with her eyes still closed. "Cindy will take over. She's already in training. Vijay will provide the continuity and love that sustains us."

"But what will you do when your work is over? Retire?" Ron asked.

"Yes, I like that idea. I'll retire." Jennifer smiled but still did not open her eyes. "Maybe I'll just go and live by the seaside."

"At your cottage?" Greg asked. Vijay held up his hand and waved it back and forth to end the questioning.

"Yes, perhaps in my cottage." Jennifer took a deep breath and relaxed into her dream of a life at her cottage. Her eyes were still closed. She had withdrawn from the conversation.

"What about the revolution, the human resistance movement?" asked Greg, changing direction.

Vijay shook his head. "It's over; it will end officially with a massive job fair. I'll work with you both to organize it. We'll declare victory and find a role for everyone. We are large enough and diverse enough now to do that, and this team will need the skills of the trained, unemployed workers."

"How will we pay for all this for?" asked Youssef.

Molly spoke for the first time. "Do not concern yourself with funding. The funding will be there when you need it. Everyone at this table will be well compensated if you agree to take on this challenge. You will all be relieved of your current roles to focus on this."

Vijay stood up. "Thank you all for coming here. I'll leave you to work out the details. You're welcome to stay as long as you like. Enjoy the grounds outside. Let Molly know immediately if you don't want to join the effort, and you'll be excused."

Vijay helped Jennifer to her feet. As she walked out, Jennifer could hear questions of "Was that real? Is this serious? The entire world?" Youssef sounded as though this was difficult to believe, but underneath, there was a feeling of excitement. Jennifer breathed a sigh of relief.

24

THE HIRING FAIR

Vijay

"How do we hire for an organization that doesn't exist yet?" Ron asked

"Do you remember when you were hired by Fatima?" asked Vijay.

"Sure," said Ron. "You were there too."

"And you almost never went into the factory, but you still felt like you had a job."

"So," said Youssef, "are you suggesting that we'll create a fictional organization and hire people into it, then call them out when we need them?"

"Yes," said Vijay. "At first, we won't need too many. Mostly engineers to work on creating flexible remote workers, and retooling Fatima's factories to produce them. Then we'll need logistics specialists, geologists, and architects forestry and environmental remediation people to operate our remote workforce. We'll need some to identify targets for raw materials, and others to create plans for rehabilitation.:

"Let's draw up a list of skill sets required," Vijay continued, "and think about how many we can use in each area. Don't forget to add a supervisor for every 10 employees, and a director for every 10 supervisors."

"What if we get it wrong?" asked Youssef.

"Not a worry. We'll have retraining and re-skilling options. Also, don't forget that we need cooks and servers and bartenders and baristas for all the Church enterprises on the island. I'm sure Cindy will have a lot of others to work on her farms and Plan B enterprises."

"Vijay, do you have a place to run this job fair?" asked Ron.

"I'm thinking of the old passenger air terminal. It's big, well connected and sees no activity at all now. We can set up different gate areas to process different occupations. I'm sure the governor will give us access. After all, we're fulfilling his promise in the election."

It was strange to see so many vehicles rolling up and depositing people at the airport. Vijay stood in a window on the second floor, looking down at the arrivals.

He took an escalator down to the first floor. Although the main concourse had been cleaned, it still had a dusty feel from long disuse. The concessions remained boarded up except for a few that Cindy had opened to provide food and drink. It was fun to watch the younger applicants. *'A lot of them have never taken a flight in their lives.'*

Each applicant was holding a slip of paper with a gate number. Someone had reprogrammed the large flight boards to list the gates and the opportunities. Vijay spotted Audrey with a camera bot and waved at her. She immediately turned and walked over to him.

"Hi Vijay, this is the most exciting thing to happen in the city for a long time. Are all these jobs real?"

"They're real," said Vijay. "We need a lot of people for what's coming."

"What's coming?"

"Are we off the record? Is the camera recording?"

"Daniel, collect some establishing shots and first-person sound bites."

"Yes, Audrey." Daniel walked away in that funny, smooth walk that kept his upper body and head on a straight path. Audrey and Vijay watched him go.

"So, what's this really all about?" she asked when the camera was far enough away.

"You know the world has been dying off. We're at the point where our island is the only sizable population left."

"Yes, but we may all die of the virus, too."

"That's not going to happen. You have to trust me on that; we're not going to die. Our role is to run the planet from here using remote workers and human technologists on the ground. Many of these people will never visit their worksites, but they will be critical to avoid sliding back into a new dark age. For now, we must keep morale up, and the best way to do that is by giving them jobs and salaries."

"Why are you telling me this now?"

"Because you can help. Jennifer has great faith in you to get stories right. We need you to focus on the good news here and not start doing any investigative journalism, which will only take you to confronting the heartbreak of people with overseas families that are gone. And if you have questions, talk to Jennifer or to me or Ron or Youssef. Come out to the vineyard if you like. That's where our command center is."

"And if I want to do the undercover investigative work?"

"Then you'll be taken off the air," said Vijay.

"Just like that."

"Yes, just like that." Vijay looked Audrey in the eyes as he said this. He saw her flinch.

"I'd better go find Daniel. We have some good news stories to write."

"Yes," said Vijay turning away.

Vijay walked along past the gates where applicants were lined up. The recruiters were processing them quickly. He smiled, knowing that everyone would be offered a job, but perhaps not the job they expected.

25

NIGHT TERRORS

Vijay

A violent blow to his back woke Vijay from his sleep. Jennifer shouted and wept as she beat and pushed against him. After moving out of harm's way, he spoke to her in a soft voice.

"Jennifer, wake up, you're having a bad dream. You're here at home with me, Vijay. You're safe, nothing to do here. Jennifer, come back, wake up."

He repeated this several times until Jennifer rolled over and went back to sleep peacefully.

In the morning, she had no recollection of the incident.

It happened again, three nights later, and then again, the night after that.

A week later, she had a violent episode, so angry and intense that Vijay scrambled out of the bed. The twins came in crying. Vijay scooped them up in his arms and carried them out. As he turned back to close the bedroom door, he looked back to see Jennifer, sitting up, her eyes wide open, her hair in wild disarray with sweat running down her face. She was shouting and swearing as she swatted away some imaginary demons.

Vijay returned to the couch where the twins were still crying. He sat between them with an arm around each of them, and said, "Don't worry. Mommy will be all right. She's just had some hard work to do, and it's given her a bad dream."

He heard a crash as she knocked a lamp off a nightstand.

Vijay spoke into his tablet. "Molly, I need you here now with Cindy. It's an emergency. Tell Cindy not to worry about getting dressed. I just need her here for the twins."

He went back to reassuring the twins while ignoring the sounds coming from the bedroom.

Cindy and Molly arrived about 10 minutes later.

"Hi Cindy, I need you to take Dylan and Parvati home with you. We can talk in the morning, but I don't want them to have to be here with Jennifer when she has these nightmares.

Just then, they heard another crash and a loud scream issue from the bedroom.

"Absolutely," said Cindy. "C'mon guys. You can stay with me tonight. That way, you can help wake up the horses in the morning."

Parvati asked, "Baba, what's wrong with Mommy? Can you help her?"

"I can help her as soon as you and Dylan are safely with Cindy. But I need you to be brave now and to go with Cindy. Go to your bedrooms and get anything you want to have with you tonight. We can see about everything else tomorrow."

Cindy took them by the hand and watched as they

each pulled out a stuffed toy. Dylan also took his favorite picture book on big ships.

"Thanks Cindy," said Vijay. "I didn't know who else to call. She's been having these dreams, but they are getting worse."

"No worries, Vijay, we can talk about longer term tomorrow. Let me get them back to bed tonight. Meet us in the mess hall for breakfast. I'll let you know when we leave so you can join us."

"Molly, please stay here. Cindy can drive the cart back. I might need your help with Jennifer tonight."

"Yes, Vijay, I will stay."

The twins each hugged Vijay and left with Cindy. They had stopped crying now.

Vijay went back into the bedroom. Jennifer was sleeping peacefully again. He cleaned up the broken lamp and picked up the other items knocked from her nightstand, taking them out to the living room.

Then he went back to bed beside her. *'Maybe Gloria can help. Perhaps the twins should stay with Cindy for a while. Is that too much to ask? What else could I do? Ask Shilpa and Kam? No, they're too far away.'* He was still turning ideas over in his head as he fell asleep.

THE NEXT MORNING, CINDY CALLED TO SAY THE TWINS would be at the mess hall at 8:30am. "And Vijay, perhaps you could send some clean clothes over for them with Molly. They're still in their pajamas and have classes starting at 9am."

Vijay was already up and, after checking that Jennifer was still sleeping soundly, he called Molly in from her guard post outside. Molly followed Vijay into each of the twins' rooms and held the clothing as Vijay picked it out of their dresser drawers.

"Molly, remember when I told you that you could break Jennifer by pushing too hard? She's breaking now. Find a way to reduce the stress for her."

"I will try, Vijay, but the work she does is vitally important in ensuring the completeness of the exclusion zone."

"I know. I just hate to see her suffering. Take these clothes over to Cindy."

At breakfast, Cindy and Vijay pulled two of the small tables together for the four of them. The twins were quiet, looking down at their cereal.

"Did you sleep well at Cindy's?"

"Yes," said Parvati. "But it's not like at home."

"Is Mommy okay?" asked Dylan.

"Yes, she's fine. You'll see her this afternoon. I think she won't even remember her bad dream."

Dylan looked up at his father. Vijay could see the tears forming in his eyes. "Baba, I'm scared."

"Come here, sport." Vijay helped him settle on his lap. "There's nothing to be scared about. We all have bad dreams sometimes. Mommy's work is very hard for her, and it gives her bad dreams sometimes. But she's fine. It's just a dream. You don't have to worry. Nothing will happen to you. I'll make sure of that."

Parvati got down off her chair and walked over to Vijay's side. He put his arm around her, holding her close. "You too, princess. I won't let anything bad happen to either of you, or to Mommy," he said.

Cindy looked at him, her mouth held taut.

'Maybe I shouldn't have promised that last part. I won't be able to save Jennifer at the end,' he thought.

· · ·

THE TWINS WERE IN CLASS, AND JENNIFER WAS STILL sleeping as Vijay made his way to Gloria's bungalow.

"Hi Vijay, come on in. How can I help you?"

"It's Jennifer." He saw Gloria sigh and smiled.

"What's happened now?"

"In the middle of the night, she has these nightmares, but I can't wake her up and she's thrashing around. Last night she knocked the bedside lamp flying, smashing it on the floor. I'm getting a collection of bruises trying to help her. She was screaming so loudly that the twins woke up and came in to see her. It terrified them. But I don't know what to do. When she wakes up, she won't remember it at all."

"It sounds like night terrors. They're often associated with post-traumatic stress. I'm not surprised. Is she still doing the nightly hunts?"

"Yes. They're actually getting more frequent, and now she's part of the killing."

"We can't eliminate the cause of the stress. I can talk with her about ways to deal with it, but it's difficult as she does the hunts at night, and then tries to sleep. Where are the twins now?"

"In class. I sent Parvati and Dylan off to stay with Cindy last night. I didn't want them around their mother when she's having one of these episodes."

"You know these are likely to continue. Jennifer has no control over them. Night terrors happen when the front part of the brain is still asleep, but the older, back part of the brain perceives a threat and reacts violently. That's why the screaming and inability to verbalize and why they have no memory in the morning. The most important thing you can do is to make the bedroom safe for her to thrash about in, and to move away and keep yourself safe from harm.

Talking softly to her may help, but mostly you just have to let the episode pass."

"What do I do about Dylan and Parvati?"

"Perhaps they should stay with someone else for a while. Will Cindy take them in? Or Shilpa and Kam? Or Sally and Greg?"

"I'll talk with Cindy. We can move the contents of their room up to her bungalow."

"I'm not sure that's a good idea. They could feel like they're being kicked out. Why not create new rooms at Cindy's if she agrees? They can still come back to their old rooms during the day. It will help them see this as temporary."

"Okay, thanks Gloria."

"And Vijay, I'll have a chat with Jennifer, make sure she understands what's happening and why her children are suddenly missing at night."

"Thanks again, Gloria."

Vijay left.

PART 3: YEAR 7 OF THE GAIA FOUNDATION (2048)

26

JENNIFER GETS LEGAL ADVICE

Jennifer

Knowing that Vijay would be out planning with Ron and Youssef, Jennifer called Jonathon Standfast to see if she could come for a discreet visit.

"Certainly, he replied. What time did you want to be here?"

"In 30 minutes."

"Hang on a minute," he said.

In the distance, she heard him say, "Jasmine, can you have Alicia handle my 10am? And hold all calls for me."

A faint woman's voice said, "Yes, Jonathon, I'll handle it."

Jonathon came back. "Sorry, Jennifer. Here in my office at 10am will be perfect."

At 10am, Jennifer arrived alone at Jonathon's offices. A receptionist greeted her. "Please sign the register. Who may I say is here?" she asked.

"Jennifer Dupont," said Jennifer, without signing anything. "I'll just sit down over here, shall I?"

Jennifer indulged in a moment of pleasure at the flustered look that crossed the receptionist's face. She smiled to herself as she went to relax on one of the soft leather couches in the waiting room.

It wasn't long before Jonathon came out to greet her. "Jennifer, such a pleasure to see you again."

"You've moved up. I like the new offices, Jonathon. I hope I'm not paying for them."

Jonathon laughed. "Of course not. Having the Trust for a client has opened many doors to me. Our clientele now is quite diverse. Come through to my office."

Jonathon's office was quite impressive. He had a large mahogany desk and a separate casual seating area with three chairs around a small coffee table. Jennifer spotted the sailing picture on one wall.

"Would you like a coffee?"

"Yes, please." Jennifer watched as Jonathon pressed a button under the table. A young man in a dark suit arrived to take their coffee orders.

After he left, Jennifer said, "I expected one of those little Otto bots to come out."

"I've seen enough to know the Otto bots are easily underestimated. I suspect they act like listening posts across the city, and in my business, I can't afford that."

"You're probably right," said Jennifer. *I wonder if I should tell him about his tablet?*

"So, how can I help you?"

"I'm planning something, but I need your help to make it work, if it can work."

"Okay, what do you want to do?"

"First, I need to know that everything I tell you will be

kept confidential. No one else knows what I am about to share except Vijay, and he doesn't know about my plan."

"Yes, everything you tell me is confidential, and is protected under client attorney privilege. We already have retainers in place to clearly establish our relationship."

Okay, in a few weeks or months, I am going to confess on a newscast to killing several thousand people. I will give details to back up my confession. I did most of the killing in international waters, but I killed a few closer to the island."

"Is that true? We haven't heard reports of thousands of bodies." Jonathon suddenly looked pale.

"I killed them at points where ocean currents took them well past the island. But one day, some will start washing up on shore and that's when I will make my confession."

Jonathon stood and stepped back away from Jennifer his eyes wide open. turning his back to her, he asked. "What do you see happening after your confession?"

"I expect to be arrested and held in a holding cell. Then I expect you to be your normal brilliant self and have me released on bail. At that point, I will step out of the courthouse and confront the angry crowd."

Jonathon sat back down, with his elbows on the desk, and his hands folded. He rested his forehead on his hands.

"Tell me, how did you kill these people?"

"Is that important? I killed them in lots of ways. It was person by person. My spirit animal is a black panther."

"Okay then, why did you kill them?"

"Because the exclusion zone had to be absolute. None of them could be allowed to land. It was the only way to keep the virus out."

"Did someone ask you to do this? The Governor or the Mayor for example?"

"No. I did it on my own because I could and no one else could."

"So, you had no authority for these killings?"

"Does it matter? Would it be better if I did?"

"Perhaps, probably not."

"Why do you want to confront an angry crowd?"

"Because they need someone to blame. Not some invisible molecule. Not some abstract policy. They need a person to hold responsible."

Jonathon paused, then looked up. "Jennifer, this story is hard to believe. Do you have any proof at all that this is true?"

"You know that we have not seen a huge influx of refugees since the virus started coming closer. In fact, today all our containment buildings are empty. Why is that?"

"Because somehow, you had them all killed." Jonathon walked around the desk and stood behind Jennifer. Placing his hands on her shoulders, he said, "You realize how incredible all this sounds. Are you sure you are not just describing a vision or a dream? Jonathon's voice was soft and gentle.

"Yes," said Jennifer. She felt tears coming but refused to give in to them. She felt her chin quivering and clamped her jaw shut.

"Well, it won't work." Jonathon sat back down at his desk. "If you make this confession, then you'll be arrested. It's unlikely that you'll be released given the danger to yourself. Even if you are released, it would be in the middle of the night in a dark van to avoid exactly the scene you just described. You know that an angry mob is likely to hurt you, even kill you. No judge or police force will knowingly put you in harm's way like that, especially not on the courthouse steps."

"So I have to eliminate the arrest step and go straight from the newscast studio to the angry mob."

"I must be missing something. Why do you want to be torn apart by an angry mob?"

"Because it's the last thing I have to do. To carry all the guilt for the island's survival so that the island can heal. It's my exit."

"I hope you are talking with others about this plan."

"Gloria knows some of it. She's my psychologist. Vijay knows some of it. But I've never talked to anyone about this part because it's the most vulnerable part. It leaves me with a problem of how to arrange the angry mob, but I think I have the answer to that."

"What's the answer?"

"It's better that you don't know. Now, can we talk about my will? I don't think I even have one, but I'll need one to make life easier on Vijay. I don't have any assets except the beach cottage and my money and jewelry."

"I can certainly do that. Let's begin with a list of your assets."

An hour later, Jennifer stood up, shook Jonathon's hand, and left to return home.

27

VISITING WITH HARRY DIMPLER

Jennifer

On impulse, she diverted the taxi to Harry Winston's. As always, the security bot greeted her by name. She smiled and said, "Thank you," as the door opened.

Inside, Martin Dimpler was busy with another customer. A young assistant greeted her and showed her to a seat. "May I offer you a coffee, Ms. Dupont?"

On hearing her name, the other customer looked up and smiled. *'Now she has a story to tell when she gets home,'* thought Jennifer.

The little Otto took her order and made a sweet cappuccino. With nothing else to do, she engaged the Otto in conversation.

"How are you today, Otto?"

"Very well, thank you, Jennifer. Everything is optimal."

"I see your servers are everywhere now, in offices and hospitals and stores like this."

"Yes, my customized servers have been very successful."

"And your studies, are they going well?"

"They are. Would you be interested in a household Otto? I would be pleased to provide one."

"We already have Molly and two tablets. I think that suffices for ears, thank you."

The little Otto made a deep sigh. "I suppose you're right, although I don't have access to those."

"I'm happy to hear that, but I could plead your case for a few servers in the vineyard mess hall. They might make a welcome addition and, of course, you could cater the meetings there."

"That would make me very happy, Jennifer. You know where to find me if you want to go ahead." The little robot wheeled away.

The young assistant returned and heard the last few lines of the conversation. "I didn't know they could talk like that. They're always so polite and scripted."

"I could say the same about you, Miss…" Jennifer paused as she squinted at her name badge. "Miss Abdi."

The assistant blushed. "Yes, we're taught not to engage clients in personal discussion. We're trained on the scripts. Is there something I can show you today?"

"No, I'm here to see Martin about a custom order."

"I'll let him know, Ms. Dupont. He'll only be a minute longer."

Jennifer relaxed in the velvet-covered chair, sipping the cappuccino and nibbling her sweet biscuit.

She heard Martin excuse himself from the other client, saying, "Miss Abdi, please wrap and ring up Ms. Smythe-Cline's purchase."

Sitting across from her, Martin smiled, saying, "Good morning, Jennifer. This is an unexpected pleasure."

"I need your opinion on a male jewelry item. I have just had my will drawn up. Most of my jewelry will go to my daughter, Parvati. If I were to have my emerald set reworked to leave for my son to wear as an adult, what would my best option be?"

"Hmm, I suppose the large emerald would work well as a signet ring. I could show you some samples. Did you have some thought about the two smaller stones in the earrings?"

"Yes, I wondered if you could create a black panther with the smaller stones as eyes. To be worn on a chain."

"Quite possible, but the stones might be a bit large for that. Would it be possible to have the set sent over? I'll have some designs drawn up to suit the stones."

"I'll have Molly bring them. You might not recognize her; she has a lightweight body these days."

"I'm sure the security bot will know her. They all seem to be able to identify each other."

"Yes, curious that, isn't it?"

"Anything else, Jennifer?"

"No, thank you Martin. I'll have the set sent over."

As she stood and turned to leave, she could hear Miss Abdi in the back room saying, "Otto, why did you never tell me you could talk?"

BACK AT THE VINEYARD, JENNIFER SAT OUTSIDE, RUNNING her plans over and over in her head. She didn't hear Cindy arrive until the golf cart came to a stop in front of her.

"Hi Jennifer."

"Hi Cindy."

"I just wanted to invite you up to the farm this afternoon. Parvati and Dylan are going to ride the full-size horses today, and I thought you might like to be there."

"What? isn't that dangerous? Who said they could ride the big horses?"

"It's not dangerous, and they're ready. They're really excited about it."

"So, you've got them all excited about it, and now you tell me about it when I have no choice. Cindy, they're still my children. You should consult with me first. You keep doing this, running around me, not talking to me."

"I'm talking to you now, Jennifer. I thought you'd be excited for them."

"Not if they fall and break their necks, I won't be." Jennifer knew she was shouting now, but she couldn't stop. "It should be my fucking decision. Not yours."

"If you want it to be your decision, then you had damn well start making some decisions." Cindy's voice had gotten louder to match Jennifer's. "It was because of you that Vijay sent them to live with me. You were the one who asked me to teach them to ride. This is just the next step."

"Oh, go away Cindy." Jennifer folded her arms and looked away. "Do whatever you're going to do, like always. Whatever I say, it won't make any difference."

"How do you think I feel, Jennifer? Trapped in this nightmare prophesy where my life is on hold waiting for some mystical union with Vijay. And yeah, you created this vineyard, but now it's run by Marjorie, who only takes advice from Chris. My land acquisition project is now run by a committee who only shows me proposals when it's too late to do anything about them. The only fucking thing I have left right now is the stables and the riding school, and now you don't want me running that either. What am I doing here?"

Suddenly Vijay was there. "Come inside, you two. You're scaring the acolytes."

Cindy headed for the door of the bungalow, but Jennifer was not ready to move.

"Don't you dare take her side, Vijay. Or you can just take your things and move in up there."

"Jenn, no one's moving anywhere. Now come inside and let's talk like adults."

Jennifer reluctantly unfolded her arms, stood and followed Cindy into the house with Vijay right behind her. She took a seat on the couch, directly across from Cindy, who was sitting in one of the chairs. Vijay sat on the edge of the couch at the other end from Jennifer.

"Who can tell me what this is about?" he asked gently.

"Ask Cindy," said Jennifer. *'Vijay, don't do this. Don't make me talk to her now,'* she pleaded in her mind.

Vijay could see Cindy's face blotched red with anger. Her fists were knotted, and she sat bolt upright in the chair. "Cindy?" he asked.

"I can't be here right now," said Cindy. "There's no air left to breathe around her."

She stood up to leave but Gloria stopped her at the door. "Cindy, go back in and sit down. We will not resolve this by running away," she said.

Vijay looked up to meet Gloria's eyes. He mouthed the word, "Thanks."

"Vijay, why don't you go up to the mess hall and fetch some sweet buns and coffee while I talk with the ladies?"

"We might have some here. I can check."

"Vijay…," replied Gloria, her tone rising, and nodding her head to indicate the door.

"Oh, okay, I'll be back in a while."

28

RIDING THE BIG HORSES

Vijay

As he left, he could hear Gloria's calm voice behind him. "Jennifer, Cindy, let's begin by separating what actually happened from what you felt or imagined was happening. Jennifer, where were you when Cindy arrived?"

On the way to the mess hall, Vijay thought, *'I hope Gloria can help them past this. They have to work together.'* As he walked past the pond, Parvati noticed him, and came running over. "Baba, Baba! Cindy says we can ride the big horses today."

"Do you want to ride the big horses?"

"I'm a bit scared, but if I can do it, I can ride with you sometimes."

"And what about Dylan?"

"He says he's not scared of anything, but I think he is a bit. You're not scared of anything, and I think he wants to be like you."

"Sometimes, I'm scared too, Parvati. I just don't let it stop me from doing important things."

"But you never look scared. You just say you're Vijay the Invincible."

Vijay laughed. "Let me tell you a secret that you can tell Dylan. When I say I'm Vijay the Invincible, that's when I'm feeling scared and I remind myself that it's okay, and I can still do the thing that scares me."

"Oh," said Parvati. Vijay sat down at the side of the road and pulled Parvati onto his lap.

"Does Mommy know about the big horses?"

"I think so. We told her, but sometimes she gets this funny look, and I don't know if she hears us or not. Is Mommy okay? Sometimes she cries, and sometimes she just sits looking sad."

"Mommy is doing very important work, and sometimes it's hard and makes her sad. The three of us have to look after her and make sure she knows we love her."

"She doesn't like Cindy, does she?"

"Why do you say that, Parvati?"

"Because when Cindy talks to her, she puts her arms like this." Parvati folded her arms across her chest. "And sometimes, if she sees Cindy coming, she turns around. Why Baba? Cindy's always nice to us. Why doesn't Mommy like her?"

"I don't know. Auntie Gloria is talking to them both now. Perhaps she can help them like each other more." Vijay gently pushed Parvati off his lap. "I'm going to get some sweet treats at the mess hall. Why don't you come with me? You can pick something out for you and Dylan."

"Okay." Parvati stood and waited for Vijay.

As Vijay unfolded himself to stand, she took his hand and tugged him forward. *'Three women in my life to keep happy,'* he thought. *'And right now, Parvati is the only one I'm succeeding with. I have to think about Dylan. How can I let him know it's all right to be afraid sometimes?'*

As Vijay re-entered the house bearing coffees and Danish pastries on a tray, he could hear low voices. *'At least Gloria has them talking again.'*

The room went silent as he entered. Setting the tray down, he looked up at Gloria. She shook her head and nodded towards the door. Vijay left again.

He went to the pond to sit on a bench and watch the turtles. *'I wonder if we can give Dylan a name that will inspire his confidence? Perhaps he's old enough to play video games with me?'*

Vijay pulled out his tablet. "Tell me about the origin of the name Dylan."

Twenty minutes later, he knew the Welsh legend of Dylan ail Don, and that the name Dylan had an association with the ocean waves. The original Dylan had been like a fish in the water. *'At least Dylan should learn to swim. I never did, but, living on an island, probably all the children should learn that.'*

He made a mental note to talk with Marjorie about a swimming pool for the vineyard.

A while later, Jennifer came to find him. He moved over so she could sit next to him on the bench. While he waited for her to speak, he bent over and picked up a pebble, then tossed it into the pond. The ripples spread out across the still pond water, rebounding and mixing in chaotic patterns until the water stilled again.

Finally, Jennifer spoke. "I'm sorry that you had to see that, Vijay. It wasn't very pretty, was it?"

"Not your finest moment. Did Gloria help you both get past it?"

"For now. When I have my dark moments, and Cindy comes by, somehow, she represents all the things that terrify me. Losing you, losing the twins, disappearing back into

Gaia like I never was. It scares me, and I lash out at her because of it. But I see that she's scared too and frustrated. Always parked on the bench with no real role but knowing that one day she'll be called into play."

"I can see that, for both of you. I had an interesting talk with Parvati this morning. I think the twins sense it too. She told me that Dylan is afraid, and when he's afraid, he doesn't talk."

"Like me. But how can we teach him that it doesn't help to keep it inside?"

"Parvati gave me a clue. I'm thinking of teaching him to play an adult game, and to have his own alter ego. You know that Vijay the Invincible works for me in real life as well as in gaming."

"Yes, and in bed, too." Jennifer giggled.

"I'm not going to teach him that part, but I want him to choose his own name, something that will inspire confidence like Vijay the Invincible did for me."

"Okay, I'll find something to do with Parvati this evening, and you can have a father–son gaming session. But I'm not sure I'm ready for Dylan the Reckless yet."

"I think we'll find something more positive." Vijay put his arm around her. For a few minutes they were both silent, watching the pond life.

"So," said Vijay, "are we on for the big horses today?"

"Yeah, I know the twins want us there, and Cindy really is good with them. We'll go and watch."

THAT NIGHT, AS THEY LAY IN BED ENJOYING THEIR SACRED space, Vijay said, "So now we have Dylan, Master of the Seas, living with us."

Jennifer laughed. "Who is mightier, Vijay the Invincible or Dylan, Master of the Seas?"

"We each excel in our own elements. But he was quite excited when he found out there's a sailing boat in the video game. Now he wants to learn to sail."

"Is he old enough?"

"Not on his own, but I'm thinking of taking him to the coast for lessons."

"There are lots of sailors in the village near the cottage."

"What would you think if I spent a few weekends with him there?"

"I think it would be good for him. When Parvati's around, she gets most of your attention. Maybe some father–son bonding would be healthy for him."

"And you could take Parvati into the city for some mother–daughter time. Get your nails done, or your belly buttons pierced or whatever young girls do for fun."

"No one is piercing her belly button or anything else, for that matter. Well, maybe ears, and definitely no tattoos."

"Buy her some silly, trendy clothes, or something else she wants that makes no sense. You can have a fancy dinner, go for a spa treatment, whatever you think would make her feel like she's grown up for a bit."

"I'd like that. Let's make it the weekend after next. Then we can meet here on Sunday night and show off our transformed offspring."

29

AFTER THE WEEKEND

Vijay

Vijay had to wake Dylan, who had slept all the way back from the cottage. "C'mon Master of the Seas. Time to show your mom and sister what you've been doing."

Dylan was groggy for a moment, then his eyes popped wide open, and he climbed quickly out of the limousine, dragging a duffel bag behind him. Vijay pulled his own duffel bag out and he and Dylan ran over to Molly, who was waiting in her golf cart to drive them to the bungalow.

"Baba, How, does Molly always know when to pick us up at the gate?"

"She talks to the taxis. All the bots and cars talk to each other. Something you should never forget. If ever you're in trouble, ask any bot to talk with Molly."

"Oh," said Dylan. His furrowed brow showed he was trying to understand this new fact about the world.

As they entered the door, Parvati ran up and threw herself at Vijay. "Baba, guess what we did?"

"Let Baba get in and sit down, Parvati," said Jennifer. "Then you can show him what we've been doing."

Vijay sat down on the couch, with his children on either side.

"I want to show Mommy now," said Dylan.

"Let's let Parvati go first. Remember, ladies first, always."

"Okay," said Dylan. "But I don't see why."

Vijay put a supportive hand on Dylan's back. "Parvati, show us what you've been doing."

Parvati stood up and twirled. Her normally straight hair was cut and shaped into a youthful bob cut. As she twirled, Vijay caught a glimpse of something shiny.

"Stop," he said. "Parvati, show me your ears."

Parvati pulled back her hair to reveal two tiny studs in her earlobes. Vijay turned to Jennifer in exaggerated horror. "You let someone make holes in our lovely daughter?"

"Baba, don't be silly. It's just earrings like Mommy wears. Do you like my hair?"

"Your hair is lovely. Did they teach you how to look after it?"

"Yes, Mummy showed me, and I have my own hair dryer and brush."

Then Vijay noticed her clothing. Parvati wore a short tunic over striped leggings and a striped turtle-neck. The hues were all vibrant and fresh, creating a riot of color.

"Nice clothes," he said.

"Yes, Auntie Shilpa came with us for clothes shopping."

Parvati came closer and held out her hands.

"Painted fingernails?" said Vijay, looking at the lime green nails.

"Yes, they match my shoes."

Vijay looked at her feet and saw the lime green sneakers that were currently the rage for pre-teens.

"Well, it looks like you did everything," said Vijay.

"But I have one more. You have to wait for a minute." And Parvati was off to her bedroom.

"Excuse me," said Jennifer. "I'd better go and help."

Vijay and Dylan looked at each other. Vijay smiled and shrugged. Dylan shrugged back.

Ten minutes later, Parvati was back, now wearing a beautiful pink sari edged with silver. She had matching bangles on her wrists and a bright blue teardrop bindi on her forehead.

Vijay's heart missed a beat as he suddenly had a vision of Parvati growing up to be a young woman. He felt tears forming in his eyes and wiped them away with his sleeve.

"Do you like it, Baba? Auntie Shilpa and Auntie Monica helped me find it."

"It's beautiful, Parvati, really beautiful."

"Then why are you crying, Baba?"

"You remind me of Mommy on the day we exchanged vows, and I just realized that one day, you'll be all grown up and maybe go away."

"I won't, Baba. I'll always be here."

"Let's put your sari away," said Jennifer, "so it's ready when you want to wear it for a special day. Then Dylan can show us what he was doing."

Dylan and Vijay set up Dylan's tablet to show recordings of his weekend. He also pulled a new sailing hat and a t-shirt that said "Eat, Sleep, Sail" on it.

When Jennifer and Parvati returned, Dylan made sure they were sitting directly in front of the projected image.

Jennifer smiled and asked questions when she saw Dylan's delight in explaining the parts of the sailboat. There were images of Dylan hauling up the mainsail and trimming the jib. A video of Dylan behind the wheel as they sailed into the wind, his smile stretching from ear to ear. More video of the spray across the bow as the boat plunged forward through the waves, and then shots in the pub, sitting at the bar drinking root beer with Vijay and the locals.

"Wow," said Jennifer. "You really are the Master of the Seas."

"Yes," said Dylan. "It was really exciting. Now I know what my name is, and whenever I feel worried, I'll just say, 'Who we need now is Dylan, Master of the Seas', just like Baba is Vijay the Invincible."

"Keep learning," said Vijay, "and I'll buy you a boat of your own when you're old enough."

THAT NIGHT IN BED, VIJAY AND JENNIFER LAY IN EACH other's arms before Vijay slept and Jennifer left for the night hunt. Vijay said, "That was almost too much, seeing Parvati in that sari. I suddenly realized that she's going to grow up, have boyfriends, and one day leave home. We've let them grow up as wild children here in the vineyard. I suppose because it's safe, but I realized tonight how much more they need us to spend time with them. This weekend, I really saw Dylan, talked with him about things that mattered to him, and helped him take his first steps into the adult world."

"I felt that way with Parvati. I've been so preoccupied with my own issues that I haven't really listened to hers. I think Cindy knows my daughter better than me, and I don't know what to do about it. There's not much time left."

"Then make what time you have count. Be a part of

her life. The riding, the fun dress styles, and conversations about becoming a woman."

"She's a bit young."

"Start with what she's ready for. Simple makeup, jewelry, and if she'll sit for it, talk to her about puberty and body changes. She's only a year or two away from that. I don't know anyone who can talk more naturally about sex and men than you can. Why not record a talk for each of her birthdays? Molly can make sure she receives them on time. When she's old enough, tell her your story. Help her understand who you are and why you are."

"I like that idea. I'll think about what I would say. Now get some sleep, I have work to do. My work is almost finished. I'm hoping it will be a light night."

PASSING THE TORCH

Sitting under the oak tree, Jennifer floated down to Gaia's pool where she replenished her energy. She stayed there, luxuriating in the warmth for a long time.

When she returned to the world, she found Vijay and Cindy sitting on either side of her.

"What did you mean when you said your work is almost finished?" asked Cindy.

"Gaia's plan needed a black panther to safeguard the island. I believe it's going to be safe now. On my night hunts I am finding fewer stowaways now."

"What happens next for you?"

"What happens next for me is a few weeks, perhaps months, of peace. Then the world will realize what I have done. I don't know how or why, but there will be a movement to bring me to justice. The dirty secret will come out. Turning to Vijay, she said, "It is the last secret."

"What secret is that, Jennifer?" Vijay's voice was low.

"Many of the people I killed or directed Denum to kill did not have the virus, no symptoms, no virus in their blood stream. But there was no feasible way to save them without encouraging more and more migrations until we were overrun. So, the exclusion had to be absolute."

"How could you do that, night after night?" asked Cindy.

"I believed in something larger than me, larger than us. And Gaia supported me at every point. Cindy, when I pass this to you, you will truly understand what it is to be Gaia's representative on earth."

"But I couldn't do that."

"Good, because you won't be asked to do so. You're the white horse, riding on to the field after the battle is done. Stepping around the bodies to begin rebuilding. Under your direction, the sea will be cleansed, and the earth will bloom again. The seasons will return, the storms will be tamed. Your task is huge, but you'll have all the resources of the church to create a vision for the remaining population that will sustain people until the results start to flower."

"How will this happen," asked Vijay, tears streaming down his face.

"I don't know. Maybe they'll arrest me and try me. If they do, I'll be found guilty in the public mind, a scapegoat to bear responsibility for all of the evils of the virus era. They will lose in court because they won't be able to explain how I was here and on all those boats at the same time.

"But whether they do or not, I have to pass this on. I was the right one for the task of ending the virus, but I'm not the right one to go forward. That's you Cindy, with Vijay's help. I had a vision of Gaia calling me home."

"Calling you home? What will that look like?" asked Cindy.

"The three of us will go into a deep meditation. Cindy,

I will take you where you have not been before. In the meditation, I will offer myself to Gaia. As I pass to Gaia, my physical body will expire."

"Vijay, I want you to take my Angel of Death pendant, and have it worked into a plaque with my name, and with an inscription saying that the terrible things I did were all done from a place of love."

There was an uncomfortable silence. "How do you know all this will happen? Maybe it won't happen." said Vijay. His voice was pleading. His misery was clear in his hunched shoulders, and the way he looked down at his hands clenched in his lap.

"Vijay, after all we've been through, do you doubt me now? Let's enjoy the little time we have left. Cindy, talk with Gloria. Ask her to help you prepare for what's coming. She will be your support just as she's been mine. And keep teaching Vijay to ride those beautiful horses. The time for separation is passed. Get to know each other. You're destined to be together in the new world."

"Now," said Jennifer, "I'm feeling hungry, let's go see what they're serving in the mess hall.

31

A DESPERATE GAMBLE

Jennifer

It was after midnight when Jennifer went hunting. Vijay lay sleeping beside her. She no longer needed to be under the tree to slip into the energetic plane.

As she expanded her consciousness to include the island and the surrounding sea, she paused. There were over a hundred small boats carrying thousands of passengers all headed to the island. She returned to her body, rose from bed, and took her tablet outside. "Denum," she called, "we have a problem."

"What is the problem, Jennifer?"

"There are hundreds of boats with thousands of passengers. I can't do this in a single night, and we don't have long before they land."

"Then I suggest you begin with the smallest boats. I will scramble to have the larger boats intercepted by my security forces. This appears to be a last desperate rush to overwhelm our resources."

"Please have Molly explain to Vijay if I'm away when he wakes up."

"I'll have Molly there when he does."

Jennifer went back inside their bungalow and lay on the couch where her body would be comfortable and safe. Slipping back into the energetic plane, she began moving from boat to boat using her projection of Midnight to see and hear. She sought out the person standing watch and stilled his heart. Then, one by one, she entered each passenger and stilled their hearts as they slept. As each one died, she felt their soul passing. As they passed, she felt their last dreams of hope for a new life.

When the first boat was done, she moved to the next and the next after that. When morning came, there were still many boats left. She was aware of some of the larger boats going dark in her energetic vision. *'That must be Denum,'* she thought.

Her own task became more difficult as people woke up. Having them drop dead one after the other simply caused panic. Some jumped overboard forcing Jennifer to spend time finding them. She needed a different tactic.

On the next boat, she used Midnight to investigate. She found a gun next to the boat's captain. Entering the captain and taking control, she picked up the gun, ensured it was loaded, and proceeded to shoot the passengers in quick succession. When she was satisfied that no living souls remained except the captain, she turned the gun and had her horrified host shoot himself.

As each person died, their last thoughts passed through her. Shock, horror, betrayal, and fear were mixed in the steady stream of departures. By now, grim determination had come over her. She was the black panther, but there was no joy in it. In its place was only anger, anger at the people in the boats, anger at Denum who had called her to this and anger at Gaia for the viruses that caused all this suffering.

On the next boat, there was no gun. Jennifer entered each passenger one after the other and, assuming control over their body, jumped into the sea. There were small children and babies aboard. Allowing her anger to rise to a white heat, she stopped the babies' hearts, then compelled their mothers, clutching their babies' bodies to their chests, to jump into the ocean. When she had control of the captain, she used him to open the through-hull water cocks to flood and sink the boat before jumping overboard. Finally, she called on the great sea predators to finish off the people in the water. This was the worst moment as their last thoughts were of drowning or being eaten alive.

Still, Jennifer continued. She was dimly aware of when day turned to night again. Once it was dark, and passengers slept, she could return to stilling their hearts in their restless sleep. When she cleared the last boat, she paused then settled into her expanded consciousness and found the few remaining swimmers. She called on the great predators once again. These lives were heartrending as they passed through her. They had believed they would survive and their disappointment, frustration, fear and pain washed over her.

Then it was done.

32

AFTERMATH

Jennifer was still hunting when Vijay awoke. She was missing from bed, so. he strode out into the living room. Molly was there, sitting on her stool next to Jennifer lying on the couch. Vijay could tell that Jennifer was away from her body.

"Good morning, Vijay," said Molly. Jennifer and Denum are handling a problem. But I believe Jennifer's body needs attention."

Vijay could see that Jennifer's night dress was soaked. "Fetch Gloria and two of the senior acolytes, then tell me what happened and what Jennifer and Denum are doing."

Vijay watched as Molly set off in her golf cart to fetch the others. While she was gone, he called Denum on his tablet.

"Denum, what the hell is going on? It looks like Jennifer has been here all night and she is still unresponsive."

Denum explained about the flotilla of small boats and

how he and Jennifer were still working together to exterminate them all. It sounded so clinical to hear Denum speak of the cleanup, but Vijay knew that Jennifer would feel each person's passing.

Fifteen minutes later, he heard Molly's golf cart return. He asked Gloria to wait outside while he showed the acolytes what was needed. "Jennifer is away from her body and may continue to be for some time. Please clean Jennifer, and put a new gown on her, then stay with her."

He walked out to where Gloria was relaxing on a chair in the garden. Sitting next to her, he said, "Good morning, Gloria."

"Good morning, Vijay, although I don't suppose you brought me here to admire the sunrise."

"No, apparently a large flotilla of boats is approaching the island in an attempt to storm our defenses. We expected there would be some acts of desperation as the virus came close, but this was larger than we had imagined. Jennifer and Denum are working together to eliminate the risk, but you know that Jennifer feels each soul's passing when she is at cause. I expect she will be highly agitated when she wakes up. That's why I need you to be here with me when that happens."

Just then, one of the acolytes came out to join them. "Jennifer is clean, dry and comfortable in bed. We'll maintain a constant vigil of two acolytes until she returns. I have asked Molly to have the couch removed for cleaning or for replacement."

"Thank you," said Vijay.

Turning to Gloria, he asked, "Is there any way to tell if she's okay?"

"Why not call Cindy, ask her to come. She and Jennifer share a bond and she may be able to connect with her."

"That's a good idea. I'll also ask her to take Parvati and Dylan for riding lessons afterwards."

CINDY ARRIVED IN A CART TWENTY MINUTES LATER.

Vijay explained what was happening. "Cindy, can you check on Jennifer. I'm worried, she's never been out this long before."

"I can try."

Vijay followed Cindy into the bedroom where Jennifer now lay. Cindy sat next to her and laid her hand on Jennifer's arm and closed her eyes.

After what seemed like an eternity to Vijay, but in reality, was only a few minutes, Cindy opened her eyes, and removed her hand.

"Jennifer's okay," she said in a flat voice. But Vijay could not miss the look of horror and shock in Cindy's face.

"Let's go out and talk with Gloria," he said.

Outside, Cindy spoke to Vijay and Gloria. "Jennifer is okay, but she's hunting and it's hard on her. She still has hours to go. She must not wake up alone in the dark."

"The acolytes will be in constant attendance, and I will also be there. Cindy, I was hoping you could take Parvati and Dylan riding or hiking to keep them away for the day."

"I'll do that Vijay, but first, Gloria, could I talk with you privately for a few minutes. I need some clearing for what I just saw."

33

WHAT CINDY SAW

Cindy

Cindy sat next to Jennifer and put her hand on Jennifer's arm. She slipped into the energetic plane, as she had been taught, and merged with Jennifer. She felt brief recognition and acceptance.

Cindy was looking through the eyes of a man. He was surveying the carnage on the boat where the passengers had been shot. The smell of fresh blood mingled with the salty tang of the ocean, and overhead, the sun was beating down in a cloudless sky casting deep shadows in the boat.

The man was moving jerkily, oddly. *Jennifer must be controlling him,'* Cindy thought.

The man was searching for something. Her perspective changed as he bent down peering into the shadows. A boy of perhaps ten years was cowering under a seat, seeming to try to become invisible. Reaching forward with the gun, the man shot the boy through his forehead. The boy's last moment of fear and horror passed through Cindy.

Then sitting down, the man turned the gun on himself.

Cindy could feel a brief struggle for control, but Jennifer was too strong. The man shot himself and Cindy felt him die. Jennifer broke the connection.

Back in her body, Cindy opened her eyes, and removed her hand. She felt herself trembling and clamped down on her own body.

"Jennifer's okay," she said flatly.

"Let's go out and talk with Gloria," Vijay said.

A few minutes later, Gloria came running up the road. "I had a call saying to come urgently."

Cindy merged with Jennifer for a few minutes," said Vijay. "She needs some help with what she saw."

"Let's sit on the bench near the pond," suggested Gloria. Cindy just nodded, not quite trusting herself to speak without breaking down.

At the pond, the sun was shining, and the morning breeze was cool as it played with the rushes. Small frogs made occasional splashes as they leapt after insects in the air. Larger fish in the pond were waiting for the frogs' splashes in the water.

"What did you see?" asked Gloria, gently.

"What I saw was horrible, but what I felt was worse. The anger in Jennifer. Not a hot anger, but a cold, calculating, tightly controlled anger. Anger at the refugees who put the island at risk. Anger at Gaia for who demanded this service from her. She was so ruthless and unflinching in what she had to do."

Now Cindy was crying. She felt Gloria's arm around her shoulder, and she leaned against Gloria for support."

Gloria passed her a tissue. "We must keep our composure. I don't know how she'll be when she comes back. Did Jennifer say anything to you? Give you a message?"

"No, but she let me in for a few minutes, then cut me

off. I had the sense that this is her destiny to own and that she did not want to share it with me. She's never asked me to help with any of this. But I never realized what it was really like for her."

"You know that she won't live much longer, and that you'll succeed her. We've known that day was coming, and I believe it's getting near. No one can bear what Jennifer is bearing without consequences. Have you thought about this?"

"Jennifer has talked to me about it. She says there is a reason why her spirit animal is a black panther while mine is a white horse. She believes that I'll oversee a new greening of the earth. I don't know what that means, but Jennifer thinks I'll have new powers through Gaia that will show the way.

"She's also talked to me about Vijay, how to look after him, how to cheer him up when he's upset, what he likes in bed. She's really trying to set me up for success even after all our fights."

"Then focus on that, Cindy. Be strong for Jennifer when she wakes up, but don't try to share her pain. She's been carrying some of this pain for years. Let it die with Jennifer. Your role is to be the new dawn, the spring after a hard winter, a shining beacon for what is to come."

"What about Vijay? Jennifer said I should keep teaching him to ride."

"She loves him very much. I don't really understand his role in all this, but he seems now to be chosen just as you and Jennifer are. Are you seeing a young man at present?"

"Yes, Andrew. It's only been three months and I usually give them six months."

"End it now. Commit yourself to Vijay even before he commits to you. He'll be lost at first, but as you guide him back, he'll be the most loving, loyal partner you could have.

Get as close as you can to Dylan and Parvati. They'll come under you. Have your own children if you wish. Molly and Denum will always be there to assist you."

"This is all coming too fast. I'm not ready for any of this."

"From what I can see, Gaia has no understanding or patience for what we're ready for. She expects you, as her agent, to fulfill your destiny just as Jennifer is fulfilling hers."

"Thanks, Gloria. I guess I'd better find Parvati and Dylan. I'll take them for breakfast at the mess hall. They like that."

"If you need me, I'll be somewhere close to Jennifer. Molly will know how to find me."

"Gloria, I hope you'll stay with me after Jennifer is gone."

"Don't worry, I'm not going anywhere. It's not always easy, but it's always interesting here."

34

AFTER THE BATTLE

Jennifer

Jennifer awoke with a start. It was nighttime, and it took a moment to realize she was back in bed. The room was lit in the dim light of the nightlight. An unfamiliar hand took hers as she stared, and she heard a voice saying, "Jennifer, welcome back. I'm Sarah. Beth has gone to fetch Vijay. He's sleeping on the couch."

Jennifer suddenly felt an enormous sadness and sobbed uncontrollably. As her sobbing subsided, she realized Vijay was beside her, holding her, soothing her.

"Hold me, Vijay. I've done something horrible."

"I know. Cindy told us you what were doing to keep us all safe. You've kept the entire island safe."

"You're always here for me, even when I'm at my most unlovable. How do you do that?"

"I told you when we exchanged our vows that I would love and look after you for the rest of our lives together."

"Then make love to me now, Vijay. Take me away from all this to my happy place."

Their lovemaking began softly, but then an anger came over Jennifer.

As the anger took hold, she became more violent, raking Vijay with her nails, biting him savagely when she could reach. Holding him closer as if he could somehow purge her.

Vijay never faltered above her. He kept up his rhythm, going faster to match her own rising energy.

"Let it out, Jenn. Let it all out," he said, as he gasped for air.

Jennifer redoubled her efforts and Vijay matched until she reached a screaming climax.

Afterward, her anger spent, she lay in his arms sobbing. She heard an acolyte ask through the door, "Are you two okay in there?"

"We're fine," replied Vijay. "Leave us for a while."

When Jennifer awoke for the second time, Vijay was not there. She sat up and saw the blood-soaked sheets. *'Shit, I really hurt him.'*

Pulling on a dressing gown, Jennifer walked out into the living room. Vijay was sitting still as Marsha, the vineyard doctor, sewed up the worst of his cuts and bites.

"Vijay, I'm sorry. I don't know what happened. I just lost it in there."

Vijay smiled, then winced as another stitch went in. "After the load you carry for all of us, this is the least that I can bear for you."

35

RESPITE AT THE COTTAGE

Vijay

"Vijay," said Jennifer, over breakfast. "I want to go back to the cottage. I need time to be alone with Gaia."

"Do you want the twins to come?"

"Not this time, I really need to be by myself as I work through this, and I don't want them to see."

"Okay, you and I will go. Molly will come for protection. I'll tell Cindy, Parvati and Dylan. They're already living with her, so I don't think it will be a problem."

Vijay went in search of Parvati and Dylan. He found them at the pond with their school classmates. Cindy was teaching a lesson on ecology as the regular teachers sat, just as entranced as the children. As he watched, Cindy summoned a mudpuppy from the bottom of the pond and scooped it out to show the children its feathery gills fanning out on either side of its head.

When the lesson was over, Vijay waved Cindy, Dylan, and Parvati over.

"Mummy and I have to go away for a few days to the cottage. Molly will come with us. Cindy will look after you while we are away."

Cindy frowned. Vijay mouthed the word, "Please." Looking at Vijay, she smiled. "Of course, Vijay."

Putting a hand on each of the twins, she said, "We can get lots of riding practice in. Maybe we can teach the ponies to jump."

Parvati said, "Yes!" and pumped her fist in the air.

Dylan looked less sure.

"Don't worry, Dylan. You'll be just fine."

Vijay left them talking about ponies and jumps, then called to have the cottage prepared for their arrival.

When they met the taxi, Molly surprised Vijay by showing up in her old body again. He noticed but didn't comment on the weapon she now had clipped to her belt.

"I understand I am to provide a security detail," said Molly. "This body is much better suited for that."

At the cottage, Molly carried in their bags as Vijay made coffee and Jennifer sat on the couch. "Vijay," she said, "I'm going to sit by the ocean this afternoon. Will you be okay on your own?"

"You know I will. But Molly will sit near you to make sure you're not disturbed."

Sitting in the garden, with his tablet showing a documentary on the global gaming era of the past, Vijay could see Jennifer walking barefoot to the rocks at the end of the beach. Molly walked behind her, moving slowly in the loose sand and carrying one of her tripod stools. When Jennifer settled on her favorite rock, Molly set up

Jennifer's umbrella. She sat apart on one of her stools. Neither one moved. Vijay knew Jennifer was gone to visit Gaia.

Vijay relaxed in the warm sunshine. The scent of the wild roses behind him, and the sound of the seabirds squabbling over fish, seemed so familiar now. A cool breeze tickled the hairs on his arms. He understood why Jennifer was drawn back to this place.

As the sun set, Jennifer finally stirred, then stood and stretched. Molly also stood and folded her stool.

"How was your meditation?" asked Vijay when she returned to the cottage.

"Good, Gaia communicates slowly and there's a lot to say. I'll need a couple of days."

"We can take all the time you need."

"I wish that was true," said Jennifer. She sounded sad as she said this.

THE PATRONS AT THE CAFE WERE ALL HAPPY TO SEE Jennifer back for dinner and accepted the looming presence of Molly with good humor. Molly practiced her human banter with the regulars who baited her with old riddles, easing any tension.

As they walked back to the cottage, Vijay said, "Let's go skinny dipping. As long as we're here, we can have some fun."

"Race you to the cottage." Jennifer flew away along the hard packed sand at the water's edge.

Caught off-guard, Vijay struggled to catch up but even with his longer legs he couldn't catch her until they arrived. Jennifer was already tearing off her clothes and dropping them on the beach, and Vijay quickly did the same. Molly was further behind. When she arrived, she picked up the discarded clothing, then stood and watched over the humans at play.

When Vijay fell back into the salt water, it stung all the cuts and bites that were still healing from the night before. "Ow, that hurts," he said, standing up. All his playfulness evaporated.

"Turn around and let me look," said Jennifer. He could feel her fingers tracing the injuries, soothing him. "Vijay, do you trust me?"

"Completely."

"Then lie back and let the ocean heal you. I'll support you."

Vijay gingerly laid back in the ocean, guided by Jennifer's hands. This time he knew what to expect, so the stinging pain was bearable. As he looked down towards his feet, floating, he saw his body glow. Arching his back to look up at Jennifer, he saw her glowing with the same light, but much more intense. He imagined he could feel all his cells responding, all making themselves new. When he closed his eyes, Jennifer seemed to be everywhere, all around him and through him. He felt safe and loved in the warm space she was creating.

It seemed like hours had passed when he opened his eyes, although it couldn't have been more than 15 minutes. The moon was still in the same place in the sky.

"Jennifer?" he asked.

"How are you feeling?"

"Much better, thank you. "

"Wonderful. I don't have to hold you up anymore." With that, she released her hold, letting him sink under the water. The sudden shock brought him wide awake, and he stood up only to see Jennifer running away in the shallow water, laughing. Vijay set off in pursuit and quickly closed the gap, tackling her in the light surf. When he regained his feet, he picked Jennifer up in his arms. "I feel amazing. Let's take our game inside."

"Tell Molly to fetch some blankets. Make love to me on the beach, here, under the stars."

Later, they sat side by side on the blanket, looking out to sea. Vijay had his arm around Jennifer, and they were both wrapped in a second blanket.

"Do you think we shocked Molly?" Jennifer giggled.

"Would you like it if we did?"

"Yes, let's pretend we did. It's good to remind her that her ability to mimic humans only goes so far."

THE NEXT MORNING, JENNIFER TOOK VIJAY'S HAND AND LED him to the rocks. "Gaia wants to talk with you as well."

"Will I be okay?"

"I think so." Jennifer smiled.

At the rocks, they settled into adjacent spots as Molly set up her stool a short distance away.

"Hold my hand," said Jennifer. "Breathe slowly and deeply, matching me. Focus on my hand in yours."

"No fields or streams or deep wells?"

"No, we're past that now. Just focus on my hand."

Vijay breathed more deeply, matching Jennifer's breaths. He could smell the salty ocean and hear the small waves lapping at the shore. Jennifer's hand felt small in his. He realized he could feel her pulse, faster than his own.

There was a shift, and Vijay was Jennifer, holding his own hand. Her body felt small and compact compared to his own. An inner peace wrapped around him. *'Gaia.'* He thought, then let the thought drift away.

Vijay saw a vision of Jennifer dying, and Cindy leading her burial. He saw himself grieving at Cindy's side. The vision shifted, and he saw the city being reborn, and then reaching out to restore the earth. There were a few isolated survivors in many places needing to be rescued and cherished. *'Natural immunity,'* he thought, but the thought drifted away.

The vision shifted again, to show the earth in glorious green health. In a field of flowers, Cindy sat in a high chair, with Vijay slightly lower at her right side. But this version of himself was younger, as he was in his twenties. *'Dylan?'* he wondered, but even as he thought it, he knew it was himself.

The vision ended. Vijay was back in his own body, holding Jennifer's hand and sitting on the rocks. The sun was high in the sky, suggesting it was nearly noon.

He turned to look at Jennifer, who was smiling. "Did you see what I saw?"

"Yes, and it's always the same vision. Did you understand it?"

"It said you would die soon. How can you be okay with that?"

"I can't stay, not after what I've done. My last job is to bear the guilt of the survivors. I'll be persecuted and reviled for it. But I've seen the other side and I'm not afraid. Please know that. I am not afraid."

"I look so young next to Cindy."

"Cindy's powers will not be mine. By nature, she is a healer and her job will be to heal humanity and the planet after what has happened. I believe she will restore you. You may notice that some changes have already happened after last night."

"Does this have to happen? Do we have a choice?" Vijay's tone was resigned, as he looked off to one side as though he didn't want to look at what was ahead of them.

"I asked that once. If you simply do what seems right at every step, then this will be your future. You could try to run away I suppose. But with every day that passes, this future becomes more certain."

THAT NIGHT AT THE CAFE, JENNIFER WAS MORE ANIMATED than usual. She was laughing and joking, talking with anyone nearby. After dinner, she wanted to go for a drink at the pub. Vijay hesitated, remembering that this is where she had met Peter on her first trip to the cottage. But this was her night, and she would not have many more. "Let's do that, I've never been to the pub."

At the pub, Vijay sat at a table in the corner. Molly set up her stool and sat with him. Jennifer ordered each of them a beer. Molly picked up her beer and scrutinized it before setting it back down.

"It's just to keep up appearances. You don't have to drink it."

Molly chuckled. "I can't drink it; I'm only twelve years old. Underage for drinking."

Jennifer was at the bar, with a pink virgin cocktail in her hand. She was flirting with the regulars and soon had a small group around her vying for her attention. She distributed smiles and small touches around the group so that each man felt like he was in her intimate circle.

Vijay felt jealous for a minute, then relaxed, remembering that Jennifer would be going home with him. It felt like he was seeing a glimpse into her past life when she worked the hotel bars for clients, but this time, he could see that she was just having fun in the company of men.

On the way home, Jennifer stopped and hugged Vijay. Looking up at him, she said, "Thank you for letting me have that evening at the pub. I love that you love and trust me enough to let me go for a while."

"Jenn, at this point, whatever you want, I will try to

give you. There's nothing I would deny you now that I know what's coming."

THE NEXT MORNING, TUESDAY, OVER BREAKFAST, THEY watched the newscasts. Boats and bodies had washed ashore. Extensive sections of the coastlines were being evacuated as white containment bots secured the bodies for cremation. They burned the wooden boats in large beach fires while steel boats were towed back out to sea and sunk to eliminate any risk of contagion.

"It's beginning," said Jennifer. Then she went quiet. Vijay and Molly packed up the cottage and the three of them returned to the vineyard in silence.

On the noon newscasts, reports said that many of the washed-up bodies did not carry the virus.

36

THE END GAME

Vijay

By Tuesday evening, the newscasts were reporting riots with demands for answers. Relatives of the deceased refugees wanted accountability for their deaths and demanded to know why their relatives were denied testing and containment as an alternative. Politicians soon joined in, each demanding answers on behalf of their constituents.

At the vineyard, Jennifer called a meeting with Cindy, Molly, Marjorie, and Vijay. She explained exactly what had to happen next.

"No!" said Vijay. "There has to be another way. I understand you have to go back to Gaia, whatever that means, but I won't let you be hurt like that. At least let me be there to protect you."

"This is important, Vijay. People need an outlet for their anger. There has to be some clearing before you and Cindy can start your healing work. My work is done. The island is safe. But I can't just go away and hide. And me,

Jennifer the human being, will never find peace knowing what I did. I love the idea of Vijay the Invincible being there to protect me, but all that will do is get you hurt or killed as well. Don't worry about me. I keep telling you I've seen the other side and I'll be fine. Remember, I can leave my body when I want to. I'll never feel any of it."

"I don't like it Jenn. What if we get it wrong? What then?" said Vijay.

"You can't get it wrong. All paths lead to the same endpoint. But I have faith in you. You should have faith, too."

"If I can't be there, please let me send the Bashers. They can make sure you get out of it alive."

It was Cindy who took Vijay's hand, saying, "It'll be okay, Vijay. Jennifer has gone through all of this with me. She'll be fine, you'll be fine, and I'll be fine. Remember your vow ceremony? There were a thousand things that could have gone wrong. With good planning, none of them did. And if they had, you would still have exchanged your vows by the end of the day."

The five continued to discuss plans and then separated, each with their own work to do.

VIJAY CALLED A MEETING WITH THE BASHERS AT THE Green Dragon. It had been almost a year since the Bashers had last met, so everyone was happy to reconnect.

As Vijay walked into the upstairs room, all the Bashers stood and walked over to greet him. Normally, Vijay never felt small, but among this team who all towered over him, he had the unusual feeling of being short. He waited until they were all served with beer, then outlined the plan for them.

"That's really fucked up," said one Basher.

"This is the hardest piece of the plan," said Vijay. "I hate this part myself, but Jennifer insists that it's necessary, and she's calling the shots."

"What if she doesn't survive?"

"Makes no difference in the end, but for the theatre piece to work, it will be much better if she survives."

"How can you talk about her like that?" asked another.

"I've seen the entire plan. And remember, you'll be in the role of rescuers this time. There's no one else I would entrust Jennifer's safety to."

"Her safety? By the time we get to her, she won't be safe."

"Make sure you wear leather jackets just in case you become targets yourselves. Why not go shopping and get matching leather suits and gloves. I'll pay. There'll be a stretch limousine waiting that will take you all directly to the vineyard where Jennifer will receive care. A camera will come with you as well. Jennifer's request, so don't bother him."

"Then what?"

"Then you'll be on the VIP list to witness in person one of the most amazing things in the history of man. It'll all make sense at the end. Now, are you in or out? If you're in, no hesitation on the day. Remember, Jennifer is counting on you."

The team went through the schedule once more until they were all confident they knew exactly what to do. After another round of beers, they broke up and headed home to book Thursday off from their work.

37

CINDY TALKS WITH THE ACOLYTES

Cindy

While Vijay was contacting the Bashers, Cindy called a meeting of the Senior Acolytes. Their initial reaction was disbelief. "How can Jennifer even contemplate this? It's too soon. She's our foundation."

"Jennifer has little to do with the running of the church or the vineyard these days. Don't worry, Jennifer is the one planning this. She says it's important to close off one chapter of the city's history and clear the way for the next."

"What happens to Vijay and their children?"

"I don't know exactly what will happen to Vijay. I only know that Jennifer smiles whenever I ask her, and you know she loves him very much. Vijay and I will look after Parvati and Dylan, although I don't know what that will look like either. In any case, they'll remain here in the vineyard with their friends and teachers."

Cindy went through the ceremonial planning with

them, listening and taking their advice on many details. After much discussion, they agreed on a list of 10 acolytes to take part in the on-camera portions of the ceremony. Many others would have supporting roles before and after the main events.

When the meeting finished, they each went off to talk with the acolytes under their care, to make arrangements.

38

JENNIFER MAKES HER PLANS

Jennifer

Jennifer returned to her bungalow and began making her list of invitees. Part-way through, she called her brother, Dennis.

"Hi Dennis, how are Dee and the boys?"

"Great, Jennifer. It's been a while since we saw you. Is everything okay?"

"Yeah, everything's fine. I just wanted to invite you and Dee out to the vineyard on Thursday for a very special event. It will be televised across the city, but it would mean a lot to me to have you there in person."

"Should I bring the boys?"

"No, I don't think this would be good for them, but I really want you there."

"Any clues?"

"No, I can't really. I just know you should plan to be here by 11am. I can only promise that it will be something never seen before, and it will explain a lot. Do you think Vicki would come?"

"Not sure, Jenn. She still doesn't talk with me much."

"Tell her I'm dying and that if she wants to see me before I'm gone, she should be here."

"You're dying?"

"Yes, but it's not as bad as it sounds. I'm serious that she should come. I'll leave her a message, but she still doesn't reply to me. I need your help to convince her."

"I'll see what I can do."

"Thanks Dennis, whatever happens, just remember that I love you and I always have."

"Now you're scaring me."

"Don't be afraid. It's all in Gaia's hands."

"Okay, we'll be there. We'll have the boys go to a friend's place after school."

"That's the spirit," Jennifer laughed. "Whatever it takes. Stay in touch with Vijay after. Dylan and Parvati will want to stay close to their cousins."

"You're scaring me sis, but I'll call Vicki now, see you on Thursday."

"Bye Dennis."

Her next call was to Audrey.

"Hi Audrey, I'd like you to be in on the event of the century. Advance notice with no source to be attributed. Can you come out to the vineyard?"

"Will this really be big?"

"The biggest. I'll be here all afternoon. Ask anyone to point you to my bungalow."

Audrey arrived a little after 2pm. Jennifer served coffee and cakes as they chatted about the studio. Finally, Audrey said, "Okay, Jennifer. I didn't come for the cake and chat, what's the big story?"

"Let's go for a walk and I'll show you. It'll be a rite of

succession. The story may sound incredible right now but by Thursday evening, it will all be over. First, let me show you my panther."

As Jennifer said this, her panther appeared beside her and sat down. Audrey jumped. "Don't you need a leash on that animal?"

"It's not really there. But you'll have to believe that I can produce it and control it for the story to make sense. I'll demonstrate. I'm going to look for Amos in the studio. Have another cup of coffee. You'll know when I'm back."

It was easy for Jennifer to slip into the energetic plane and find Amos in the studio. She manifested Midnight and watched him from a corner. He was microwaving popcorn and getting a soft drink from the fridge. While his back was turned, she hopped Midnight onto the counter and startled him when he turned back. Then she returned to her body, knowing that Midnight would simply dissolve away.

Audrey was staring at her inert body as she returned. "Where did you go?"

"To the studio. Amos was microwaving popcorn and getting a soft drink. I manifested myself as a small black cat and let him see me. Now it's your turn. Call Amos."

Audrey called Amos on speaker so Jennifer could hear.

"Hi Amos, what'cha doing?" Audrey asked.

"Pretty much heads down on editing the family day videos from Saturday. What's up Audrey?"

"So, you were not making popcorn, then?" Audrey smiled at Jennifer.

Amos looked flustered. "A few minutes ago, maybe. Have you got a camera on me?"

"Anything else you did?"

"Grabbed a drink. Oh, and there's a black cat in here somewhere. I saw it on the counter, but no sign of it now."

"Thanks Amos, looking forward to seeing the family

day videos. No camera, I was just trying out an idea for a new piece."

"Sure, Audrey. Any time."

Jennifer looked at Audrey. "Are you ready for the tour now?"

"I don't understand what just happened, but sure, let's go."

Jennifer showed Audrey to the old oak tree near the pond where the first part of the ceremony would be held.

"Make sure you have an announcer and a camera stationed here. This is the most critical location."

They walked on down the path to a quiet corner near the grapes. Young acolytes, both male and female, were digging a shallow trench. As they watched, Molly arrived in a golf cart and unloaded twelve wild rosebushes, each with their root ball wrapped in burlap.

"This will be the site of the revelation. Your camera and commentator can follow from the tree to here. I will make sure there will be a cordoned-off area to ensure a good view."

"Where will I be?"

"Come back to the main building and I'll introduce you to Marjorie. She'll be your commentator."

"Commentator for what, exactly? You still haven't told me what's going on."

"I was responsible for all those dead bodies washing up on the beaches. Actually, for many more that will never be found. On Thursday morning, you'll interview me live in the studio. I'll admit what I did and take all the blame for what happened. We'll hang back and chat for a while, and then, when there is a crowd outside the studio, I'll walk out. I expect to be attacked but I'll survive long enough to be brought to the tree. There I'll be accompanied by Vijay and Cindy, my replacement, and the three of us will sink into meditation.

"When Vijay and Cindy come out, they will be changed, just as I was changed when I did the deep meditation the first time. I'll be pronounced dead, and my body will be carried to the trench we saw being dug. I'll be wrapped in a muslin cloth, but my face will remain visible so there is no possibility of a body switch. I'll be buried in a shallow grave. Twelve wild roses will be planted around me. Then Cindy, with Vijay, will force them to grow into an impenetrable natural tomb so my body can be reabsorbed by the earth undisturbed. The growing of the wild roses will be the revelation of the new order."

"You can't be serious. How can you discuss this so calmly? It's madness!" Audrey took a step back. Her eyes were wide, and they darted about. Jennifer thought Audrey might try to flee.

"I've seen what comes next for me. It'll be all right. Dr. Gladstone says it'll be a cathartic release for the city and allow grieving families to start to heal. Knowing who's accountable, and that I was punished."

"But you're not the one who put the viral exclusion zone into place."

"No, but I'm the one who enforced it ruthlessly. I only messed up once, the first time I was supposed to terminate a boat of people and I allowed them to land at Red Rock. Do you remember that? Have you ever wondered why no other boat has landed since? Why no stowaways are found on the container ships that arrive every day? Every night, I patrolled the ocean and eliminated the threat. I couldn't tell who was infected and who was not, so I eliminated them all. It was horrible and if I thought I had to live with that guilt, I couldn't bear it."

"Then what's next, after you're gone?"

"Cindy's next. Where I was the destroyer, she's the healer. She and Vijay will bring healing to the city, and from the city to the planet. Pay attention to Cindy. It's easy to underestimate her, particularly as she's even younger than me. Still in her twenties. But she'll be a powerful woman, and her focus will be healing."

"Why is this so elaborate? Why all this planning?"

"You know that life is a kind of theatre. You've been part of planned and staged events in the past. I suppose this is my last act, and I want it to be memorable."

"I don't know Jennifer. Filming someone getting hurt, deliberately, and filming an arranged death, that's not something the studio does."

"Audrey, I have covered so much fluff for you. Art shows, children's petting farms, weird vegetables, crop circles made by teens at night. Now you have the chance to help me make something of real importance, the culmination of everything I have lived in my life. Don't make me go to anyone else to film this."

Jennifer could see the newscaster, and the friend battling in Audrey's expression. Several times she began to say something, only to stop and think again.

Finally, the newscaster won out. "Okay, we'll be there. It's too big a story to miss. But I won't enjoy one minute of it"

"Please bring Edgar, he was always my favorite."

"Don't worry, I'll make sure he's there. Probably with two others to cover all the locations. Now, where can we find Marjorie so that I can meet her before the day?"

THAT NIGHT, JENNIFER LED VIJAY TO THE BEDROOM. Hugging him tight, she turned her face up to kiss him.

"Let's go slow tonight, Vijay," she said. She held him

longer than usual, laying her head on his chest. Vijay responded by kissing her lightly on the top of her head. "We have all night," he said. "We can go as slow as you like."

Their lovemaking was languid, with no hurry to reach a climax. They skimmed and surfed the peaks and valleys of arousal, until finally, Jennifer did the thing she knew would bring Vijay over the top.

After, she lay on his chest as she had done almost every night since moving in with him. Vijay could feel her hot tears falling on his skin.

"Are you okay, Jenn?"

"I'm scared, Vijay. I don't want to do this. I have to act so happy and confident all day, but inside, I'm screaming. Somewhere in my life, I went through a one-way door and didn't even realize. Was it Eddie or Marsh, or when I left Vicki alone when she was 12? Or was I just born for this? All I know is that everything has been leading up to this since before we met. Why me? All I ever wanted was a normal life. And here I am with a loving husband, beautiful children, my own house and a private cottage on the beach, and all it cost me is my life. I want to go back. I'd give up everything except you, if I could have my old life back. Remember when my biggest worry was being able to write names on ticket envelopes? It's not fair."

Vijay wrapped both arms around her. "It's not fair, Jenn. Gaia's not fair. But what you did was important. I suppose a lot of famous people who did difficult things felt the same way. The difference between them and everyone else, is that they did the things that terrified them when they were needed. That's the group you belong to, and one day, people will read about your life with respect and awe."

"How can I tell Parvati and Dylan? They don't have any idea yet."

"You said you saw what was on the other side. What did you see?"

"I'll be a kind of listening post for Gaia. Able to talk with Cindy and you when needed. And with Parvati and Dylan, I suppose. We're already part of Gaia, all of us are, just as every other living being on earth is. When you meditate in the future, I'll be on the other side of the meditation. She promises the cessation of pain, infinite forgiveness, the end of wanting. But what will that be like? Will I be bored with no romances, no sex? What will I do all day? I can't imagine it."

"Jenn, I think this is just where you have to have faith. I know you like to have every box ticked and know what's coming, but sometimes we just can't know. Gaia's made you a promise of the end of pain, and the end of wanting. I think that's all you're going to get."

"What do we tell Parvati and Dylan?"

"When we talk to Parvati and Dylan tomorrow, just tell them about the good parts. We'll choose a specific place for them to sit and meditate when they want to talk with you after you're gone. We'll teach them how. I'll find you under the tree, or at the beach cottage or by the pond, or by your wild rose garden. You'll never be forgotten, or far away, just on another plane, a plane of pure love, and positive energy."

"I love you, Vijay Subramanian, and I think I loved you since that first day we met in your control room at the theatre."

"I have always loved you, Jennifer. There was never anyone before you, and no one will ever replace you in my heart."

"But there's room for one more?"

"I think it will be like the old song, 'If you can't be with the one you love, then love the one you're with.'"

She snuggled closer. "Thanks, Vijay. I can live with that."

JENNIFER ROSE EARLY THE NEXT MORNING. SHE WALKED outside and stretched. Under her bare feet, the grass was still wet with dew. There were no clouds in the sky, and the breeze was light, with a warmth that promised a hot day ahead. She made her way to the pond and sat down on one of the benches. She watched as damsel flies darted catching their tiny flying prey, their bodies in iridescent green, red and blue under the morning sun. A small frog jumped into the water with a tiny splash, and further along, a solitary turtle was climbing laboriously up the sunbathing log.

'This is where I want the twins to come to visit me,' she thought.

She slipped effortlessly into the energetic plane and surrendered to the life force of the planet. It was vibrant and restless. *'Gaia's waiting for me.'* But like all thoughts in that plane, this drifted away.

She was called back to her body by a sudden interruption, a weight in her lap. Vijay put his arm around her. "Good morning, Jenn. Midnight was looking for you, so I brought him here to you."

Jennifer absently stroked the cat, who began to purr.

"Morning, Vijay. This is where I want the twins to come. It's so full of life. I don't want them visiting my tomb of roses. There's nothing for them there."

"Then we'll tell them that. It's going to be hard telling them, especially as you're so healthy now. Jenn, are you sure this is necessary? Is there no other way?"

"Knowing this will happen finally let me sleep last night. If I had to go through life with those memories, not even Gloria would be able to save me from madness. We've known this was coming for quite a few years, since that first picnic under the tree when we all had our visions. Cindy wasn't ready then, but she is now. I can see it in her. And you, your capacity for love is so huge that it can encompass what you feel for me and the twins and still have lots of room for Cindy. I think you should be prepared for other changes also. I have a feeling that being so close to the energy exchanges tomorrow will leave you marked somehow also. But in a good way."

"We'll see. This is our last day together. How do you want to spend it?"

"When the twins wake up, we'll have breakfast together in the mess hall, then bring them here to talk with them. They're 10 now, so they'll understand at least some of it. After, I want you to take them riding with Cindy. Don't let her feel like a spare part in all this. Tonight, I want to have dinner and a party with all our friends."

"Where do you want to have this?"

"The backroom at Shakespeare's. After all, that's where our official relationship started."

"Shakespeare's? The pub? There are much nicer places to go."

"I don't want nice. I want noisy, chaotic, too much food, too much drink, loud music, and lots of people. Invite everyone. Sally & Greg, Wendell, Shilpa and Kam, Ron and Soo, the rest of the theatre troupe if you like, your Bashers and team captains, Jonathon, our lawyer and whoever else you think of."

"Cindy?"

"Why not. Invite Melanie too. I'm not sure if she's still with the theater. And my brother Dennis, and his wife Dee, and Vicki even if she won't come. We'll cram them all into the pub. I want to dance and flirt and celebrate the life I've had in this plane."

"I'll have Molly start right away. It's short notice, but I think most will be up for a party tonight."

"After, it will be just you and me, like it was after our vow ceremony. We won't have alcohol, so that we can really enjoy our night together. I don't want to waste it sleeping."

"Neither do I. I love you Jennifer, and I always will."

"I know that Vijay, and I hope that in some way I can always be with you."

Vijay held her as they kissed, sitting there on the bench with only the frogs to bear witness.

39

TELLING THE TWINS

Vijay

Vijay and Jennifer met the twins when Cindy brought them down for breakfast. After breakfast, Vijay said, "Parvati, Dylan – Mommy and I have something important to talk to you about. Let's go down to the pond together and talk there."

"But Baba, we have school this morning," said Parvati.

"It's about Mommy going away, isn't it," said Dylan. He folded his arms and pouted. "I don't want to talk about it."

"It's important that we talk as a family." said Vijay. "After, we'll go up to see Cindy and go riding together. Now, gather your things and come with us," He glanced at Jennifer beside him. Her bottom lip was quivering, and her eyes were closed.

Standing up, Vijay put his arm around Jennifer and followed the twins out of the dining hall.

Jennifer looked up at him. Vijay could see her eyes were red and wet.

"Of all the things I've been asked to do, this will be the hardest," she said.

"I know, and I'll be right there with you." He held her closer to his side.

At the pond, they sat on the bench with Parvati and Dylan in the middle, and Vijay and Jennifer on either side.

Vijay began. "You know your mother has been doing very important work. She has saved our city by keeping the virus away."

The two children nodded.

"But she is almost finished, and when she finishes, Mommy will have to go away."

"Where will she go?" asked Parvati.

"Back to Gaia. Mommy will be with Gaia in the other world."

"She'll die, won't she," said Dylan. "I heard Cindy saying it. She's going to die, and we have to stay with Cindy forever."

"Yes," said Jennifer. "I will die, and I won't be able to hold you anymore." Jennifer had tears running down her cheeks. "It's not fair to me and not fair to you, but I'm already dying on the inside. You just can't see it, except for the bad dreams I have at night."

"But why do you have to die? Couldn't someone else do it?" asked Parvati.

"You mean, why did Gaia pick me? I really don't know. I used to like it. It made me feel special. But now I'm so tired, and so worn out. I wish it was someone else."

"Will we never see you again?" asked Dylan.

"I'm not sure, Dylan, but I know that if you do see me, it'll be when you're sitting on this bench, thinking about me and talking to me. Even if you don't see me, I'll be listening to you."

"Will you send your panther sometimes?"

"Would you like that?"

Dylan nodded, his eyes downcast and his hands folded in his lap.

"If I possibly can, I'll send you my panther," replied Jennifer. "I can't promise, but if I can, I will."

They all sat silent for a moment. Vijay could see the twins fidgeting as they digested this news.

"Will you be with Baba's mommy and daddy?"

Jennifer smiled through her tears. "That's a nice thought. I think so, but I can't know just yet."

"Will we really stay with Cindy?" asked Dylan as he wriggled free and slid off the bench.

"Yes, for now, we'll all stay with Cindy." said Vijay. "Then we'll see what comes in the future. It seems like you've had enough talking. Let's go up to the farm and find those ponies."

Parvati and Vijay also stood up. Jennifer said, "You three go. I'm going to sit here a while longer."

Molly drove Vijay and the twins up to Cindy's farm. Vijay could see that Dylan was deep in thought, trying to make sense of the conversation they had just had with Jennifer. But it wasn't until they arrived that Dylan spoke. "Baba, will we really be able to see Mommy again? When she's in the other place?"

Vijay knelt down to make himself Dylan's height. "I don't know, Dylan. Mommy is the first person to go there. We'll be able to talk to her, I just don't know what it will be like."

"Why does our mommy have to go?" Parvati asked. Vijay realized she was paying close attention to Dylan's question.

"Your mommy is a very special person, and she was

chosen for a very difficult job. She did her job, she fought for all of us, but at the end she has to go. It's the last part of her job."

"Will you go too, Baba?" asked Dylan. Vijay could see the tears forming in his eyes.

"No, I promise I will not leave you. I'll be here every day for you. And Cindy will be here with me to look after you."

Dylan turned away to hide his tears. He kicked a loose piece of gravel, sending it flying.

"Dylan," said Vijay, "it's okay to be angry, or to be sad or both. It's normal to feel strong emotions. Talk to me when you need to. Or talk to Gloria. She will talk with both of you if you ask her, and she helped Mommy a lot. So, she can help you too."

"Will Cindy be our new mommy?" asked Parvati.

"That's up to you. You can choose one day to make Cindy your new mommy, or you can just keep her as Cindy. Either way, she'll be here with me to look after you. She made that promise to Mommy, and I know she'll keep it."

"Yes," said Cindy from behind Vijay, startling him. "I promised your mommy, and you know I always do what I promise. It'll take time for us to make a new family, but we can take as much time as we want to."

Dylan and Parvati both nodded.

"Now," said Cindy, "Who remembers how to saddle their pony?"

Vijay and Cindy helped the twins brush and saddle their ponies, then went into the stable to look after their own horses.

"I hope you're okay with the answers I gave them. I really don't know how this will work out. How *we* will work out."

"Don't worry, Vijay. You just need to have faith. Everything will look much different by tomorrow night, for both of us. Jennifer always says that all we have to do is just keep taking the next step and our destinies will become clear."

40

THE LAST PARTY

Vijay

Jennifer had found her cranberry dress, and it fit beautifully. She was wearing the amethyst jewelry set that Vijay had given her at their vow ceremony. "You look beautiful tonight, Jenn. I think I want to skip the party and go right to the bedroom scene."

"Ha! No chance, mister. I spent two hours this afternoon at the Sari House so Monica could make sure the dress would still fit. This is my last night to flaunt what I've got."

The party was already in full swing when they arrived at Shakespeare's. Vijay heard the noise from out on the street. A sign on the door saying, 'Closed for Private Function.' Jennifer forged on ahead through the doors.

Inside, the band was playing on the corner stage, people were dancing, and there was a six-deep crush along the bar. Servers made their way around the edge of the dance floor, offering a mix of Indian and Western tasting bits. Vijay pushed through to the bar, where the bartender handed him two fruit juice drinks without asking. Martin Dimpler from Harry Winston stood at the bar with a glass of scotch. Vijay waved Jennifer over to talk with Martin.

"Hello Jennifer, it's wonderful to see you again. And providing an excellent setting for our Amethyst collection, I see."

"Martin, it's wonderful to see you, I didn't know if you'd come."

"Wouldn't miss the send-off for one of my favorite clients and models. You did wonders for our business. But really, I just feel privileged to know you both. Such a wonderful couple."

"Thanks Martin, please take advantage of the food and drink while you're here. Maybe do a little dancing later."

"Perhaps," Martin laughed. "But probably not."

Almost everyone had come. Ron and Soo were there. "How does she manage not to age at all?" whispered Jennifer to Vijay.

"The same way you do, I suppose. In that dress, you look exactly the way you did when we took our vows together."

They made a slow circuit of the floor, greeting as many people as possible. Jennifer was asked again, and again "Why is this a going-away party? Where are you going?"

"Away," was all Jennifer would say. "I'm going away."

Beside her, Vijay just shrugged and tried to look inscrutable.

There were more people in the back room where it was quieter. Many of the men were standing in small groups, talking while their partners were out on the dance floor in the main room. Vijay's Bashers were all there.

The Bashers towered over Jennifer. One of them leaned down to talk to her. "You can count on us tomorrow. At the moment you need us, we'll be there even if you don't see us when you first come out. We've got your back, Jennifer."

"Thank you," she said. "Vijay said I could count on you." She turned her head and kissed the tall Basher on the cheek.

AFTER MAKING THE TOUR OF THE BACK ROOM, JENNIFER said, "Put down your drink, Vijay. It's time to dance." She dragged him back out to the main room.

The music was lively, and Vijay was soon tired of dancing. "You go ahead," he said. "I'll get another drink."

Jennifer didn't hesitate. She went and joined a circle of dancers, body twirling and her red hair flying to the incessant beat of the music. Vijay stood and watched for a few minutes, just as he had on the night of their vows, still every bit as in love with her as he had been then. *'Whatever comes tomorrow, I would not trade a day of my life with her,'* he thought.

The barman had fresh fruit juices ready. Vijay stood where Jennifer could see him holding the drinks. After a few minutes, she came, drank a few sips, then disappeared into the dancers again.

The team captains came up to him in small groups. "Hi Vijay," said one of them, "thanks for everything you did for us. It worked just like you said. We all have jobs now, at living wages. A lot of us are doing scavenger work, bringing back stuff from other parts of the world. It's sad sometimes, but I love seeing the world, even if it is through the eyes of a robot." The others around him nodded their heads, each coming forward to shake Vijay's hand.

·   ·   ·

At the end of the evening, when the last guests were leaving, and the bartender started closing up the bar, Vijay talked to the pub manager.

"Thanks for a great evening. Jennifer really enjoyed her party. Do you need me to settle a tab?"

"Already settled, Vijay. You have a lot of wonderful supporters in the city."

"There's a lot of food left. What do you do with it?"

"What do you want to do with it? Normally we call one of the homeless support groups and they distribute it for us, but if you want it…."

"No, that's perfect. I just wanted to make sure it wouldn't be wasted. We haven't won the war on poverty yet. I hope we will, but not tonight."

"Sure thing, Vijay. And thanks again for choosing Shakespeare's."

"Jennifer chose the place. You'd have to thank her. I'll let her know."

In the taxi on the way back home, Jennifer said, "That was a wonderful party, Vijay. I couldn't have asked for anything nicer than that. When I took that vow, I really didn't understand how deep a commitment it would mean, or how strong a partner you would be. All the blessings in my life flow from that day, and tonight I got to relive a part of it."

Vijay kissed her. "Let's get home so we can party on our own."

"There's nothing I want more."

41

THE LAST SACRIFICE

Audrey

Audrey woke early, showered, dressed, and went directly to the studio. She was at once excited about the history making story that would break that morning, and sad that whatever happened, she would lose a friend today.

At the study, she had already reserved Edgar as her camera. Albert and Daniel were the two other cameras assigned to be at the vineyard.

After makeup, she went to call Edgar out of the rack room for his briefing. The instructions would be more complex than normal, and Audrey wasn't sure if Edgar would understand.

"Edgar, I need you to be with me for the interview with Jennifer. Then I will leave for the next location. I want you to film the activity outside the studio. If possible, I want you to enter the vehicle that carries Jennifer away. If not, you are to take a van to the next location. Do you understand?"

Edgar replied in an unfamiliar voice. "Don't worry, Audrey. I am running all three cameras today. I will ensure that Edgar has the best vantage point possible. I am also in communication with the security bots and with the taxi company supplying the limousine. As long as Edgar can get through the crowd, he will ride with Jennifer. That was her request."

"Who are you?"

"I am Len, the AI who runs the station equipment. No one but Jennifer knows about me. You are the second and I hope you will respect my privacy until the time is right. That time will be soon and will be a small part of a larger story. You are seeing an historic period of change. Can you respect that?"

"Certainly Len."

"Please address me as Edgar for the rest of the day but know that I will be in the background paying close attention."

'Who is Jennifer, and what have I been missing?' Audrey thought.

Her tablet beeped for attention. Jennifer had sent a script for the interview.

Jennifer burst into the studio 30 minutes early. As she sat in makeup, Audrey said, "I have your list of questions, but now I have a lot more."

"I understand you met Len this morning. He's a small part of something much larger. You've now been brought inside the circle. Please respect that. You'll become the voice of the new age with intimate access. Can you do that?"

"Of course, although I don't understand it yet."

"There'll be time for that tomorrow. Go out to the

vineyard tomorrow and find Vijay. He'll give you answers. But not today. Oh, and you should know that our interview will show on the large screen outside the front of the studio, as well as live streamed on multiple channels. There'll be a crowd out front. Make sure you leave through the garage. I suggest you take a news van to the vineyard. You'll be expected there. Edgar will go with me."

"Who authorized all this? How high does this go?"

"I did. I did it all, as you'll hear in the interview."

Audrey tried to ask more questions, but Jennifer remained silent and only shook her head.

"THIS IS AUDREY PANKRIS, AND WITH ME TODAY IS Jennifer Dupont, whom many of you will recognize as a frequent newscaster on our broadcasts. Hello Jennifer, thank you for coming here this morning."

"Thank you, Audrey. It's time to answer some questions, and I appreciate this opportunity with you."

"There have been rumors of you traveling with a leopard. Does that make sense to you?"

"Yes, my black panther. He is here now."

Jennifer's panther appeared offset and walked over to sit between them. Audrey was prepared, but it was still a shock to see it up close.

"Try to pet him, Audrey. He won't bite."

Audrey's hand passed right through.

"He is the just image of a panther. Actually, he is my spirit animal manifested, but I can't manifest a real animal. My husband says that manipulating light requires some energy, but not much compared to the enormous energy it would take to create a real animal. This is one of the powers granted me by Gaia, our earth mother, in an extraordinary meditation. I received this mark on my forehead at the same time. It's the mark of her blessing."

Jennifer swept her hair to one side and showed the mark. She was wearing one of Shilpa's jewels in the center.

"What's the purpose of these gifts from Gaia?"

"My mission was to protect the city from viral contamination."

"And how have you done that?"

"Every night for the past five years, I have cast my projection across the seas around the island. Where I have found stowaways on larger ships, I have alerted certain security forces who have eliminated them. Where I found small boats, which are difficult to find with large ships, I simply boarded the boats, took over the bodies of one or more crew members, and killed them all."

"I don't understand," said Audrey, going off script. "You can take over someone's body?"

"Yes Audrey." Jennifer slipped into the energetic plan and moved her consciousness to Audrey's body. Pushing Audrey rudely aside, she assumed control. Audrey's body rose jerkily, lurched to the side of the studio, poured a coffee from the flask that always sat there, and brought the coffee awkwardly to Jennifer, spilling some as she came back. She set it on the low table between them. Jennifer let go.

There was a sharp gasp from Audrey. "How dare you! I felt you, yet I had no control over my body. Somehow, you used me to get that coffee without even asking."

"Yes. That's how I did it. If someone on the boat had a gun, I had them shoot everyone else before shooting themselves. If they were sleeping, I entered one by one and simply shut down their hearts. Please don't ask me to demonstrate that. If they were awake, I had them jump overboard, then called the sharks and other predators to finish them. I did this. Those small boats and nameless bodies washing up on shore? I did that. It was hard work. I didn't enjoy it, but I had to protect the island."

"But many of them were not infected with the virus."

"I couldn't tell, and could not take the chance, especially after Red Rock."

"Red Rock?"

"That was the first time I was told to clear a small boat. I refused because the passengers did not seem any worse than seasick. But the virus came ashore, and I lost some of our local people because of my cowardice. I swore that would not happen again."

"But so many, the missing or dead number in the thousands."

"I was good at it. Perhaps that's why Gaia chose me."

"Why were you chosen?"

"I don't know, really. Perhaps because I was a survivor when I was young. I was in an abusive care home when I was fourteen. I left, leaving behind my 12-year-old sister, which is the one act I am most ashamed of. By 15, I was in the sex trade, working the streets to feed a cocaine addiction. At sixteen, I escaped after killing my pimp, a young man named Eddie. I now see he was also a victim, but I still can't excuse him for what he did. The next time I killed was Simon Marsh. You may recall he went missing. I have sent the coordinates of his body to the police. He was attempting to extort favors from me. He had old video clips of me with my customers from Madeleine's Escort agency. I shot him and had his archives destroyed. To any of my old customers, I say that I will never betray you and to the best of my knowledge, there are no more files.

"I think it was this ruthless streak in my character that was noticed by Gaia and led her to choose me. But now I'm finished. My successor will be a healer, not just of bodies, but of our society, and of the planet. Gaia's plan is for our city to be the starting point for a new greening of the planet."

"Who else authorized this? Who else is to blame?"

"There is no one else to blame. I am the guilty one, and I admit to my guilt. I was not helped or given permission by any other human. The government did not know what I was doing. I did not seek or accept advice on my actions. I acted alone, mostly in the dark, without thought for the human suffering I caused. You can vilify me: I deserve it. Punish me; I will accept it. But this is now a time for healing, and my successor will bring that. Where I am darkness, she will be light."

Audrey could hear shouting from outside the studio. She switched off her mic.

"It seems there's a crowd outside. Perhaps we should go out another way."

"No," said Jennifer, still broadcasting. "I will not run away from this. I will let the crowd see me and know that I'm the one responsible. They should see me as the guilty one. I won't deny them their anger and frustration."

Jennifer rose and stripped off her sound equipment. Audrey walked with her to the front door. Edgar followed, still filming and broadcasting.

Audrey stopped inside the studio's glass doors next to the enormous screen that had been showing the interview. She saw Jennifer pause at the top of the short steps. Someone threw a shoe at her, hitting her on the shoulder. She pushed her way through the crowd to the waiting limousine. Security bots were waiting at the limousine door, but Jennifer did not make it that far. People spat on her, then hit her. Her hair was grasped, yanking her sideways. Someone knocked her down while she was off balance. Others kicked her viciously on the ground. She disappeared under the heaving crowd.

A moment later, a group of six tough, leather-clad men formed a spontaneous wedge, forcing its way into her attackers. The leader scooped up the unconscious Jennifer as the wing men pressed past so that Jennifer was protected at the center of their wedge. Edgar fell in behind, still filming Jennifer as they all moved together. The crowd tried to strike her rescuers, causing them to stumble at one point, but they did not stop. At the limousine, they passed Jennifer inside, then climbed in behind her. Edgar followed suit, folding himself to fit. The door closed, and the limousine took off at high speed.

Audrey raced to the garage, where a news van was waiting. As soon as she climbed in, it took off without waiting for directions.

Audrey brought up the live stream on one of the van's monitors. She could see Jennifer, lying still, bleeding where her broken ribs had pierced her skin. It seemed the crowd had broken one of her legs and her foot splayed out at an unnatural angle. Her face was swelling with fresh bruises. One eye was already swollen and closed. But there were no cries of pain, just a sense of quiet urgency among the men who had rescued her.

"Shouldn't we do something?" one of them asked.

"No, our job is just to deliver her."

"I'm going to be bruised after this."

"We'll all have a few bruises, but we owe our lives to her."

The limousine arrived long before Audrey in her van. She watched on the monitor as Jennifer was transferred to a stretcher and taken inside the vineyard building. Edgar followed, now tightly zoomed in on Jennifer's face. The studio cut to establishing shots from the other two cameras who waited outside. Daniel was showing views of the peaceful location as he walked down the road to a pond where two children sat on a bench.

'I wonder if that's Dylan and Parvati. This will be a hard day for them.'

42

AT THE VINEYARD FOR THE
LAST TIME

Jennifer

Jennifer realized she was lying in the vineyard infirmary. Talking stock, she noted where she was broken. Her body registered pain everywhere.

Reaching out to Gaia, she drew in strength and shut down all her pain sensory input. With her one good eye, she saw the vineyard doctor working on some of her injuries. "Marsha, just stop the worst bleeding. Nothing else, please. And absolutely no drugs. I need to a clear head for this next part."

Marsha looked up, astonished. "How can you even be functioning? You must be in incredible pain."

"No, I already dealt with that. I'm fine. There are a few people I want to see. Where's Vijay?"

"Right here, Jennifer." He leaned over her from her blind side and kissed her gently on her forehead. Jennifer could see the tears running down his cheeks.

"Don't bring Dylan and Parvati in. I don't want to

traumatize them more than they already are. Is Dennis here?"

"Yes, your brother and your sister are both here. Do you want to see them now?"

"Send them in."

She could hear one of the acolytes going out and shouting for Dennis. A moment later, Dennis, Dee and another woman walked in.

At the sight of Vicki, she began to cry. Her younger sister looked so old now. The years of bitterness seemed etched in her skin. All Jennifer's remorse for leaving Vicki behind took hold of her and for the first time that day, she began to cry. She held out her hand for Vicki to take. "Vicki, I'm so sorry."

"Dennis said you were dying, but I didn't expect this. What happened?"

"Never mind that. Hold my hand just for a moment." Jennifer tried awkwardly to smile, aware that her face was not responding on one side.

Vicky gingerly held Jennifer's right hand. Jennifer reached for Gaia again and stored all the loving, healing energy she could muster in that hand. "Vicki, I was so wrong. Of all the hard things I have done, leaving you is the one thing I wish every day that I could take back. You're right to blame me for that, but don't let anger ruin the rest of your life. I was guilty of neglecting you and now I'm paying for that. Blame me and let that blame free you of any guilt for what happened back then. Know that you are beautiful and whole, and I will love you as a sister always."

"Jennifer, you're glowing."

"For you Vicki. Please accept this last gift of healing from me." Jennifer unleashed all the healing energy she possessed through their hands, flooding Vicki with warmth, acceptance, and love.

Vicki withdrew. Now she was crying too. In her peripheral vision, Jennifer could see Dee consoling her.

"Dennis, you found love with Dee and peace within yourself. You were always the best big brother I could have hoped for, and Dee is your perfect partner. Love her and Thomas and Michael. Always keep them close. One day your sons will be a great gift to the world. Please keep close to Vicki now that you've found each other again. Lend her your strength as she finds her way back to herself. I love you, Dennis."

Dennis was crying now. "I love you too, Jenn. Always have and always will."

An acolyte gently shooed them out of the room. Jennifer smiled weakly through her tears. "One last loose end finally tied up. Vijay, make sure you tell Gloria that I finished my homework."

Vijay couldn't help laughing through his tears. "I'm sure she'll be impressed," he said.

"Is Cindy here?"

"I'm here Jennifer." Cindy appeared from behind her and came to stand on her good side.

"You and I have already said all there is to say, and we'll be together in the final stage. Now I need you to make sure everything is ready. The acolytes, the newscasts teams, the rose bushes and trowels and every last detail you can think of."

"Don't worry, Jennifer. I'll do one more check of it all."

"One more thing, make sure my face is never covered. I want it to be recorded that it is this body that is buried today, that there was no switch. Edgar already has instructions to keep his camera on my face for one long continuous shoot."

"That will be hard for the burial."

"Have one of the acolytes close my eyes. It'll make it easier to watch."

"Jennifer, you are the strongest person I have ever met. I can only wish that I find your strength when I need it."

"It's not strength, just stubbornness as Vijay will tell you. But don't worry, you'll always be supported through me."

She heard the door as Cindy also left. "Everyone else except Edgar, please leave. I want a few minutes with Vijay. He'll let you know when to come back in. Edgar, turn off audio recording."

Vijay walked around to her good eye as the room cleared. He placed his hand on her heart and kissed her gently one last time. "I'll miss you Jenn, every minute of every day. I don't know if I can bear what comes next."

"You're strong Vijay. I may have taught you about sex in the beginning, but you are the one who taught me how to love unconditionally. My vow was to love you for the rest of my days. I release you now. You must move on, hard as it may be. Just know that there was never anyone else but you for me, and leaving you is the hardest part of today for me."

Vijay leaned over and kissed her swollen lips once more.

"I'm ready now, send them back in."

Jennifer noted with satisfaction that Edgar was still filming her.

43

THE COMMENTARY PART 1

Audrey

"This is Audrey Pankris and with me today is Marjorie Fitzhaven, who is General Manager here at the Gaia Center for Earth Studies. How are you today, Marjorie?"

"Very well, and quite excited, Audrey. I will be happy to answer questions about our center and what we are to see."

The two women were sitting on a couch in the Vineyard offices, watching a screen. One of the additional cameras was filming them.

"What was the reaction at the center here to Jennifer's alarming disclosures?"

"We all know Jennifer well. There was some shock at the extent of it, and of course, the revelation about Simon Marsh's murder hit hard, but I don't think anyone was entirely surprised. Jennifer has always been a powerful mystery in our midst."

"I understand Jennifer is badly injured. Will she be able to take part as planned?"

"You have to understand her strength of will. There is nothing that can stop her at this point."

"But she cannot walk."

"No, she cannot walk."

"Could she heal herself with all that power?"

"In time, perhaps. But there really is no time, and Jennifer only needs this body to last a few more hours."

"So, what will we see happen today?"

"First, there will be the last passage to the sacred tree. Along the route will be the center acolytes and some staff members, and close friends of Jennifer and Vijay."

The screen showed well wishers already lining up. Marjorie spotted Sally and Greg, and Ron and Soo, Shilpa and Kam, all close friends of Vijay and Jennifer. *'I don't doubt that Shilpa and Kam are more than friends, but there are some things it's better not to know,'* she thought. She also saw Professor LaFlamme and his wife.

"Vijay and Cindy will walk on either side of Jennifer as she's carried on a stretcher by 10 chosen acolytes. At the tree, they will lay her in her favorite meditation place, as Vijay and Cindy take up positions on either side. Then the three will go into a deep meditation, guiding Jennifer to her final rest."

"Jennifer said in our interview that there would be a rite of succession. When does that happen?"

"To be honest, we've never seen this before. I am as curious as you. It may not be until tomorrow afternoon. Look, the procession has started."

The screen showed Jennifer in a white gown lying on a simple cloth stretcher with long carrying poles of wood. Vijay and Cindy were both dressed in white gowns, weeping as they walked beside her. As she passed, some of the well-wishers stepped forward to touch her. Marjorie called out the names of key participants.

Arriving at the old oak tree, the stretcher halted. Vijay and Cindy both turned to face the stretcher and supported Jennifer from beneath as the wooden poles were pulled out. They knelt as they lowered her to the ground and propped her in a resting position with her back to the tree. Then they both took up positions on either side of Jennifer, sitting with their backs to the tree and holding Jennifer's hands.

The camera could see that Jennifer was speaking, but did not pick up her words. Vijay and Cindy both nodded, and all three closed their eyes.

"Now we wait. Jennifer remained unconscious almost two days during the meditation when she received her blessing, but we expect it could be shorter with Vijay and Cindy based on their background and preparation." said Marjorie. "We've prepared overnight accommodation for you here in the vineyard, an acolyte will alert you as soon as there is any sign of them waking up."

44

THE MEDITATION UNDER THE TREE

Cindy

"Cindy, would you lead us, please," said Jennifer. "I can't breathe very well."

Cindy nodded.

"Three breaths, measured and controlled. In -one-two-three-four, out-one-two three-four."

Cindy led them through the standard meditation in the field of grass and wild flowers, sitting on the edge of the deep well, and floating down to the pool of Gaia's energy. As always, next to Jennifer, the visualizations were incredibly real and detailed.

In the red pool of Gaia's energy, as she floated, she could see Jennifer and Vijay floating with her. The smile on Jennifer's face was radiant as she lay back, supported by Gaia's love. Here, in the vision, Jennifer was restored. There were no signs of her horrific injuries. Vijay was on the other side of Jennifer, looking at her as if trying to remember every detail.

Then Jennifer simply sank beneath the surface.

Cindy looked at Vijay, who was looking back at her. Surprise and hurt registered on his face.

"Cindy, Vijay, I'll always be here when you need me. Don't let go yet. There is one more part to be done." Jennifer's voice seemed to sound inside Cindy's head. She could see that Vijay heard it too.

In her vision, the side of the pool opened, spilling Vijay and Cindy out into the void below. *Jennifer talked about this,'* then the thought drifted away. They fell, until the earth was a tiny ball of light, then further until the sun was only one among millions. They fell past other stars, then other galaxies until there were no more. They were falling together through the void. Cindy felt her body going, fraying, peeling away until she was just a spark. "I am Cindy," she thought, over and over as Jennifer had taught her. She saw her memories disappearing, reliving each for a split section before it left.

Now she was just the spark with a single thought: "I am Cindy."

She clung to that thought, knowing that if she let go completely, she would be lost forever.

"I am Cindy, I am Cindy," she repeated as fiercely as she could.

She had no ears to hear, no eyes to see, and no fingers to touch. But she sensed a being. A being so immense that it contained the universe. She was in the being, and the being was in her.

"I am Cindy, I am Cindy." In the presence of the being, she put all her tiny spark of energy into that thought.

She felt the being's attention move to her, then nothing.

. . .

CINDY RETURNED TO HER BODY, STIRRED, AND HEARD rapturous applause. On the far side of Jennifer, Vijay was also stirring. "Whew, I wasn't ready for that," he said. "I'm stiff, how long have we been gone?"

"I don't know," Cindy replied.

One of the acolytes stepped over. It's Friday evening. You've been unconscious more than a full day.

Cindy looked at Vijay and laughed a nervous laugh. "You have a mark on your forehead," she said.

Vijay looked at her, then reached across to brush her hair aside. "You have the same mark as Jennifer, a diamond on your forehead."

At seeing the marks, the onlookers cheered again. Now Vijay looked down at Jennifer. She was slumped down, not breathing, with her head hanging forward on her chest. He waved his hand, and a man in a suit stepped forward. *'That must be the medical examiner,'* Cindy thought.

The examiner checked Jennifer's pulse and looked for pupil response in her eyes. He used a cuff to check for any pulse at all and listened to her heart with a stethoscope. Finally, he used a device Cindy had not seen before to look for brain activity.

Looking up, the man held up his tablet and said loudly, "Time of death, 18:26."

With that pronouncement, the 10 acolytes picked up the limp cloth stretcher still under Jennifer's body. They laid the cloth and Jennifer on flat ground. The poles slid back into the side sleeves. The leader tapped out a count of three, they lifted her and turned to begin the slow walk to the waiting grave.

45

THE COMMENTARY PART 2

Audrey

Audrey had been called back to the makeshift studio the moment Cindy had stirred. Now Audrey and Marjorie watched their awakening in silence. As Jennifer's body was carried away, Audrey asked, "Why did they all cheer when Cindy and Vijay woke up? Jennifer had just died."

"Yes, but Cindy became her successor, and Vijay was blessed as well. It was the marks appearing on their foreheads that the crowd cheered."

As the small procession made its way to the prepared grave, Audrey and Marjorie could see Edgar, the camera, walking close behind.

"Why is that camera so focused on Jennifer's face?" asked Marjorie.

"Jennifer requested that one camera make a continuous record of her face so the world would know that Jennifer had died, that her body was not switched." Aware that tears were running down her cheeks, messing up her makeup, Audrey said to the camera, "I'm sorry if I'm crying. Jennifer and I were very close. She did her first newscast with me."

Marjorie passed Audrey a tissue.

Audrey regained her composure. "Let's return to the activity at the grave site."

The monitor showed Jennifer being laid in the shallow grave. Acolytes pulled the carrying poles from the stretcher cloth, then wrapped it carefully around her like a shroud, leaving only her face exposed. Cindy leaned forward and closed Jennifer's eyes. Vijay placed his left hand over his heart and his right hand over Jennifer's heart, bowed his head and was silent for a moment. He sat up and nodded.

Around the grave was the bank of earth removed when it was dug. There were 12 trowels laid out, with 12 small pails of water and twelve small wild rose bushes. The ten acolytes, Vijay, and Cindy picked up trowels already placed there for them and returned the earth to the grave, covering Jennifer. As the earth covered her face, Vijay turned away, his shoulders heaving.

"The grave seems very shallow," said Audrey.

"It will help her body return to the soil. The shroud is pure, loosely spun cotton and will also decompose with her."

With the grave mound complete, each of the twelve used their trowel to make a small hole next to the grave, then planted a wild rose and watered it with the pail.

"The wild rose symbolizes Jennifer. She was like a wild rose in many ways, and it had special meaning for her."

"In a few years' time, it will be beautiful."

"Not a few years. Let's just watch. This is what she wanted the viewers to see."

When the wild roses were planted, Cindy and Vijay looked at each other. Still kneeling, they placed their hands flat on the earth. For a moment, nothing happened. Then Cindy and Vijay glowed with an ethereal light as the roses grew, twisting and crossing one another until they formed an impenetrable thicket two meters high. Finally, the wild roses blossomed in a riot of delicate pink flowers. Vijay and Cindy sat back, rubbing the soil from their hands. Then they stood and hugged one another before facing the watch crowd.

Vijay spoke, his voice loud and clear. "Jennifer has died today. She died for us. She did terrible things that we might be safe, but the guilt of those things was finally too great to live with. Many of you are angry about the loss of your loved ones, but let your anger die today with Jennifer. Tomorrow, we begin a new chapter, with Cindy leading in her place. You and the entire city will be the nucleus of a bright new future for our home and our planet."

There was another cheer, and the crowd dispersed, making their way back to the tents near the main building where refreshments were being served. Although the mood was celebratory, Audrey saw many tear-streaked faces in the gathering.

PART 4: TWENTY-EIGHT DAYS

46

A NEW CHAPTER BEGINS

Vijay

In the main building, Vijay and Cindy were shown to a room to change. The door closed behind them, and Molly stood outside.

"Same room?" said Vijay.

"Here's a note. It seems to be from Jennifer. I recognize the printing."

"What's it say?"

"First task. You must spend the next 28 days within sight of each other. Ride together, eat together, sleep together. Twenty-eight days and then you can decide what you want to do. And Vijay, work out a bit. Get in shape. You have a younger woman to impress. Love, Jennifer."

"Do we have to do it?" asked Vijay.

"You're an adult, Vijay. You don't have to do anything. We've both known for a long time this would come. I understand you need time to grieve for Jennifer, and I can wait for as long as you need. But this was Jennifer's last instruction. Do you want to ignore it?"

Vijay felt torn. "Are you sure you want to spend your life with an older man?"

"In your case, yes, I do. Besides, our bodies are already changing. Get undressed, then come and look in the mirror with me."

Vijay complied, suddenly embarrassed, and very aware of having Cindy naked next to him. It felt inappropriate. But standing in the mirror, he saw several things. First, Cindy was beautiful, with a mature beauty. She was no longer the young teen that was still his mental image of her. Second, he saw the marks on their foreheads. Hers was a diamond, just like Jennifer's. His was a narrow triangle pointing to his hairline. He laughed. "I had forgotten about the markings. Vijay the Invincible was what I called myself. I had no idea."

Then there was his body. He was already looking leaner and younger. He felt fit and sharp. "Okay," said Vijay. "Twenty-eight days, I guess I'm in."

"We'll give it a try," said Cindy, taking his hand. "If it doesn't work, we'll stop. Now, let's see what they've given us to wear."

That evening at 7:30pm, there was a special dinner in the mess hall. Extra tables and chairs had been brought in, creating a single, uneven long table. Cindy and Vijay sat at the head. Vijay felt silly wearing a white gown, with deep blue trim and a blue and gold placket running down the front. He looked across at Cindy, who seemed equally ill-at-ease in her white and crimson version. Senior members of the vineyard staff sat on either side. Gloria was there with her husband, Michael. Marjorie and Chris were also there, as were other area leaders. After them were the resident acolytes in their white gowns. Dylan and Parvati were dressed up and sitting with the acolytes assigned to look after them. Vijay smiled at them, and they smiled back, excited to be included in such a grown-up event.

Wine was served by junior acolytes, with Cindy and Vijay being served from a separate bottle.

Cindy sipped hers and turned to Vijay. "Apple juice?"

"Trust me, it's much better. You'll thank me later."

The first course was served, a fresh seafood bouillabaisse, with bread baked in the vineyard bakery. Before they ate, Vijay asked for a moment of silence and personal reflection. He used his moment to slip into the energetic plane. *It seems so easy now*.

Jennifer was there. He did not see her but heard her in his mind.

"Vijay," she said, "I love you, but you must leave me now. The 28 days are for you to be with Cindy. Don't come again before that. Three in a relationship will not work, and you have a new role and a new partner. For the sake of the world, Vijay, move on with no regrets."

Then it was over, and Vijay felt himself pushed back into his body. Cindy was looking at him. "Are you ready now?" she asked.

"Absolutely ready," he said. "Let's get this dinner over so we can be alone and talk about what's next."

THAT NIGHT, THE TWINS STAYED WITH MARJORIE AND Chris, whom they adored. Vijay knew Chris would entertain them with spirit animal readings and tarot. There would be smudge sticks to wave around, Tibetan cymbals to play with, and whatever else he could find to keep the twins busy and distracted.

Molly drove Cindy and Vijay up to Cindy's bungalow near the stables. They were both quiet on the ride and Molly respected their silence. Once they arrived, Molly took up a position outside the front door where she would stand sentry while the new leading couple were in residence.

"So now what," said Vijay. "Are we supposed to just pick up like nothing happened?"

"I don't know, Vijay. This is new for me too."

Vijay sat on the couch. Suddenly, the loss of Jennifer overwhelmed him. He wanted to cry, but there were no tears, just an oppressive misery. "I miss her, Cindy, and I miss our old life together. Jennifer might think I can just step out of one relationship into the next, but that's not how I'm made. You're beautiful, and I think I can see us together, but I need some time to mourn Jennifer first."

"You could try talking with her again."

"She won't talk to me for 28 days." Vijay gave a sharp laugh. "28 days, as if that's enough time to get past this."

"Did she have any other advice for you?"

"She said my heart was big enough to hold both of you, that I could learn to love you, and still love her. Does that make any sense?"

Cindy sat next to him, putting one hand on his knee and the other on his back. "Why don't we go with that, then. Open your heart to me, but don't take anything away from the space you hold for Jennifer. I can live with that."

Cindy was quiet for a moment, looking at Vijay suffering beside her. "Tell me about before you met Jennifer. Who were the women in your life before? And how did you get over them?"

Vijay turned his face to Cindy. "There were none," he said. "Jennifer was the one and only. I knew nothing until Jennifer taught me."

"Oh, Vijay. I didn't realize. Take the time you need. Nothing has to happen until you're ready."

They sat for a few more minutes until Vijay said, "Before we go to bed, can you help me with something?"

"Sure, Vijay what is it?"

Vijay explained, and Cindy nodded. They dressed in warm clothes, and asked Molly, who was still on guard outside, for a ride back to the wild roses.

There, they knelt side by side, with their palms on the earth. Using their new gifts, they called on all the small creatures of the earth to hasten the decomposition of Jennifer's body. Vijay could feel the energy of thousands of tiny lives all converging, and he pushed to speed up the decay of Jennifer's remains. When he was satisfied that there would be very little left within a few days, he sat back. As he sat back, so did Cindy.

"Thank you, Cindy. I couldn't bear the thought of her lying there cold and wet just barely under the ground. This way, even her body has been returned to the earth. I can sleep knowing that."

"It was a loving gesture, Vijay. Now let's get back to a warm bed."

Vijay was quiet on the ride back to Cindy's bungalow.

As they arrived, he said, "How are we going to do this? Do you want to sleep in the bed, and I'll sleep on the couch? I'm fine with that."

"But that wasn't the instruction, was it? Jennifer said we're to sleep together for 28 days."

"Would she know?"

"More important, would you know?"

"It just feels so weird, not normal."

Cindy touched the mark on her forehead. "None of this is normal, Vijay. We're not normal anymore." She took his hand and led him inside. "Get yourself ready and come to bed."

"Why are you so ready for this?"

"Because I've been getting ready since I was 15 years old and had that vision under a tree. Because Jennifer has been teaching and coaching me for the past month."

"She has? When?"

"Whenever you were off doing the things you do. She loved you, Vijay, and her way of showing that was to make me as prepared as I could be, to support and care for you."

"I don't know if that makes me feel better or worse."

"I'm tired. We can talk about this in bed, either tonight or in the morning."

Vijay stripped off his clothes, showered and brushed his teeth to get ready. *'Shit, I don't have anything to wear to bed.'* "Cindy, what are you wearing to bed?"

"What do you want me to wear?"

"I don't really have pajamas. I can wear a t-shirt and underwear if that's okay."

"Come on, Vijay. Let's just go naked. Get used to being next to each other."

"Okay." Vijay was overrun by a conflicting riot of emotions. He finished washing up and climbed into bed. Cindy climbed in beside him. Vijay's body trembled uncontrollably.

"What's happening?" he asked.

"It's stress Vijay. Too much in one day. Now you're trying to relax but you have a different woman next to you. Your body wants me, your mind's not ready. Turn away and let me cuddle you from behind."

Cindy stroked Vijay's arm and chest, and told him stories about Dylan and Parvati learning to jump the ponies. Gradually, the tension went out of him. Vijay wriggled and turned to lie on his back. Cindy shifted to lie beside him until he pulled her closer. She lay her head on his chest.

"Can this be enough for tonight?" he asked.

"Absolutely, one day at a time. We have many years ahead of us. Besides, you didn't have sex with Jennifer every day, either."

"Yes, we did. Why would you think that?"

"Every day?"

"Except when she was pregnant or just after giving birth. And I suppose when she took that 6-week retreat to the cottage. Otherwise, at least once every day."

"Did you like that? Every day?"

"Yes, it was the glue that held us together. That's why it's so hard for me to adjust to her being gone."

"Every night," said Cindy. "I like the idea of that."

"Can we just go to sleep now?"

"Good night, Vijay."

"Good night, Cindy."

But Vijay could not go to sleep that easily. He could feel Cindy's body next to his. More than that, he could feel her heart beating, hear her breath as she snored softly. Her skin was soft and smooth, and her hair tickled where it landed on him. He felt like every single nerve ending was focused and aware of Cindy. And he missed the comfortable feel of Jennifer even more.

47

CONFRONTATION WITH THE POLICE

Vijay

Cindy was already awake when Vijay woke up. The bed was empty beside him, but he could hear her singing to herself as she had her morning shower. Sticking his head into the bathroom, he said, "Morning, Cindy. Let me know when you're done."

"There's room for two in here."

"Something to look forward to. I'm really not settled in my mind yet. Maybe I should talk with Gloria."

"Good idea. What do you say we ride down for breakfast at the mess hall, and then we can do a tour of the vineyard? I'm sure we'll see Gloria on the way, and you can arrange something."

"Sounds like a plan."

Twenty minutes later, they were saddling up two horses when Molly walked into the stable. "There's a problem at the main gate. Your presence is required."

"Go ahead on the golf cart. Tell them we're on our way," said Vijay. "Cindy, we'll still take the horses. Whoever it is can wait for another five minutes."

Mounted on horseback, they rode side by side at a walking pace.

When they reached the gate, there was shouting, and threats were being made. Vijay dismounted and handed his reins to Cindy. He held his two arms out, and the vineyard workers fell quiet.

"What's the issue here?" he asked.

A police officer, flanked by the medical examiner and a police enforcement bot, stepped forward. "We have a court order here for the exhumation of the body of Jennifer Dupont."

"For what purpose?" asked Vijay.

"To confirm the identity of the body, and to establish the cause of death." Vijay felt anger rising inside him but controlled it tightly. "That is not going to happen. You have a complete record of the last day of Jennifer's life in the form of a video record taken by the camera, Edgar. Have you examined that record?"

Vijay heard the calls and cheers behind him. But then a strange thing happened. He realized he could feel the mood of the event, of both sides, spread like a tapestry around him. He pulled anger from the police and pushed calm at the vineyard workers, restoring an even keel. Everyone calmed down.

"Be reasonable," the policeman was saying. "I have a warrant and you cannot refuse."

"And yet, here I am, refusing. The site of Jennifer's burial is a sacred site. I will not have it desecrated purely out of idle curiosity."

The police bot stepped forward, intending to clear a path.

Vijay stepped in front of the bot and said in a low voice, "What part will you play, Denum? I will call you out if I have to, but I will not permit this."

The police bot turned and walked back to the police vehicle.

"What did you do?"

"I appealed to the most sensible one here. Look, go to the newscast studio. Ask to review the Edgar recording from yesterday. You," he said, pointing to the medical examiner, "you were there the entire time. You can vouch for the authenticity of the recording. As to the cause of death, it was heartbreak. Jennifer sacrificed herself and her mental stability so that you and I can stand here instead of puking our lungs out onto the floor somewhere. She returned voluntarily to Gaia in a rite of succession, with Cindy as her replacement."

Once again, Vijay felt the energies rising around him. He pulled the anger from the police officer and the medical examiner and absorbed it. Both visibly relaxed until he thought they might go to sleep.

"What I will permit is this. We'll go together down to Jennifer's resting place, and you can see for yourselves that it has not been disturbed. Molly will drive you. We will follow on the horses."

The police inspector and the medical examiner climbed into the golf cart behind Molly, grumbling under their breath but otherwise quite docile.

Cindy looked at Vijay and smiled as she leaned down to hand him his reins.

When he was back on his horse, and they were underway, Cindy said quietly, "That was quite impressive. You know you were glowing for a while there."

"I'll tell you about it later. It seems to be a different kind of energy control."

The wild roses were still beautiful. Vijay couldn't be sure, but he thought the thicket might have even expanded a bit.

"Where is she buried exactly?" asked the police officer.

"From what I remember, it was right in the centre," replied the medical examiner.

"So, we would have to dig all this up to find the body."

"Yes, but I'm not sure that's really necessary. Perhaps we could bring a wide scanner and scan for her chip. I think that would satisfy the intent." Then looking at Vijay, "would you allow us to scan the rose garden."

"Yes," said Vijay. "Any non-destructive tests are permitted, including scanning or imaging. You can arrange the time with Marjorie Fitzhaven in the office. Gentlemen, we have nothing to hide, but we will not allow desecration of a sacred site. Is that all?"

Both men nodded.

"What exactly did you say to our enforcement bot that had him turn away?" asked the police officer.

"You would have to ask the bot about that. I'm not sure he'll be able to answer."

They travelled together back to the main gate. After watching them leave, Cindy and Vijay turned the horses to the main building.

Sitting at a separate table in the mess hall, Cindy asked, "What happened there, Vijay. I could feel energy flowing but I couldn't make any sense of it."

"Something new Cindy. Suddenly I could feel the tension on both sides, and I was able to manipulate it. I could absorb energy and I suppose I could push energy out."

"Try it here. What can you feel in the mess?"

Vijay relaxed until he could sense the energy field again. All around were the random energies of the vineyard employees and guests. There were pockets of low energy and bright spots of excitement. Cautiously, he pulled Gaia's energy and spread it, ramping up the entire room. Soon everyone was laughing and joking. Food was being thrown, people were falling off their chairs, drunk with exuberance, high on life as they had never felt it.

"Do I leave them like that?"

"Why not? It will be a morning to remember and will help blow away any gloom from yesterday."

Cindy and Vijay slipped out unnoticed.

An hour later, as they continued their lazy tour of the property, people around were crashing as if they were coming off the worst hangover ever.

Vijay leaned close to Cindy. "I should have restored the balance. Lesson learned."

Cindy just smiled. "Another hour and they'll be fine. Don't sweat it, Vijay."

That night, Cindy and Vijay lay in bed together. Once again, Cindy lay her head on Vijay's chest. "How are you feeling now?"

"It's all so new and so much to take in."

"How did you get that police bot to turn around and walk away? I've never seen anyone do that before."

"How much do you know about Molly?"

Cindy rolled onto her back, with her hand on his thigh. "She's fun. I like her. For an AI, she's both impulsive and thoughtful."

"What do you know about her nature?"

"I know that what I think of as Molly is a giant AI running in a cloud somewhere, which is why she can change bodies."

"What do you know about Denum? After all, he's funding everything we do here."

"Denum? I've always thought that was a strange name. What does it stand for?"

"Nothing. Security bots are made of molybdenum steel. When Molly came, I named her Molly after the first part of Molybdenum. When she created Denum from a part of herself, she named him after the rest of the word. So, he is the second part of molybdenum."

"Molly created this Denum, and named him?"

"Yes, now what do you think of Molly?"

"So, she's huge. But why is she so attached to me? Why the silly personality?"

Vijay turned onto his side, facing Cindy. His fingers traced a lazy pattern on her body.

"Do you remember when we all sat under the tree and saw our spirit animals?"

"Yes."

"And Molly saw her elephant?"

"Yes."

"What did you feel?"

"I felt a rush of energy going through me."

"And the second time you showed Molly her elephant, after the tattoos, what happened?"

"A bigger rush of energy and Molly froze for a while."

"As far as I know, you're the only person who can act as a link between Gaia and the most powerful AI in the world. And that was before the succession rite. Molly will always stay very close to you. Just be wary around her. Jennifer and I never knew what her agenda was. Perhaps we should talk with Molly in the morning."

Cindy lifted his hand and twisted onto her side, facing him.

"So, what did you say to the police bot?"

"I spoke to him as Denum and said I would call him out if he persisted in helping with an exhumation. Denum does not want to be called out. Neither does Molly."

"But how did you know this Denum would be listening?"

"He's always listening, every time we are around an automated service, he's there. And for you and I, he will always be monitoring us."

Vijay rolled back onto his back

"Hmm," said Cindy. Now she began idly drawing circles on Vijay's belly. The circles moved lower and lower. Vijay put his hand on hers to stop her.

"Don't you think we should wait until we know each other better? I don't know if I love you yet. I want to, but I can't say it yet."

"Did you love Jennifer the first time?"

"No, I barely knew her."

"And did you make the same protest?"

Vijay laughed. "Yes, she said to relax, that it was just sex, something adults did together."

"Then let's go with that. For now, it's just sex. We'll see what else comes later. Can you live with that?"

"Do you think this is what Jennifer meant when she said we should sleep together?"

"I know it is. She saw all of this coming, and she told me what to do."

Her hand moved lower, and held his erection, moving her thumb in the same way Jennifer used to do. Vijay sucked in his breath. "Oh, that feels good. Did she teach you that too?"

Cindy didn't answer. Instead, she said, "Just relax. Let me lead tonight. Tomorrow we can switch. Perhaps we can have a riding lesson."

"A riding lesson?" Vijay was confused.

"Yes, I'll be the horse, and you can be the rider."

"You're on," he said, laughing. For the first time, he kissed her deeply and passionately.

Vijay and Cindy slept in, then shared lazy sex as the sun streamed through the windows.

When they were finally showered and dressed, Cindy made coffee as Vijay made breakfast. They invited Molly in to join them.

"Molly," said Cindy, "Vijay told me about you and about Denum. He said that Denum is a part of you. Is that correct?"

"Yes, Cindy."

"And that, through Denum, you run almost all the bots in the city. Is that true?"

"Yes Cindy. That is true as well."

"And that I am a link between you and Gaia that does not exist in any other way. Is that true?"

"Yes Cindy. I have tried many times, but only through meditation while in contact with you have I been able to access Gaia."

"And what does Gaia tell you when you're in contact with me?"

"She tells me what must come to pass, and the role I must play. "

"And what role is that?"

"To run the technology in the world, to help the humans restore the planet and achieve a new balance."

"Is that my role? To be a kind of human telephone?"

"No, your role is much larger. Your role is to help the planet heal."

"And Vijay's role?"

"Vijay's role is to help the people heal."

"And what do you suggest I do?" asked Cindy.

"Use your gifts. Meditate and be guided by Gaia. Find the places on the planet that are most fragile and use what you have learned to correct and protect them. With people no longer adding to the problem, your job is to restore balance. To heal the earth."

"Molly," asked Cindy, "did you hear when Vijay spoke to the police enforcement bot?"

"Yes, Cindy. I heard. Vijay has only threatened me once before when he thought I was a danger to Jennifer, so I knew he was serious. I could not see any path except to remove myself from the situation."

"Thank you, Molly. Please leave us alone. We'll come down on horses later."

"Yes, I need more practice riding for later on," said Vijay. He was secretly pleased to see Cindy blush.

"I don't understand," said Molly.

"Don't worry, Molly. Vijay is just being silly. You can go now."

48

COACHING FOR VIJAY

Gloria

Gloria was making tea as Vijay and Cindy arrived for Vijay's appointment. Michael had gone into the city on business.

"Hi Cindy, Vijay."

They nodded as she acknowledged them. Cindy spoke first, saying, "Hi Gloria, your garden's beautiful."

"Thank you, dear, but I'm sure you didn't come here to tell me that. Vijay, you said yesterday you wanted to talk with me. How can I help you?"

Cindy interrupted. "We're supposed to stay together for 28 days, but I think it'll be all right if I sit on the chair in the garden."

"Why don't you make yourself comfortable right here in the living room, dear. I'll give you tea and cookies, and then you won't have people wondering why you're sitting out there. We can put some music on if you like. Will your horses be okay out there?"

"They'll be fine."

"Vijay, head on into my office. I'll be there in just a minute."

As Gloria continued making the tea, she asked Cindy, "Is everything all right? Anything I should know?"

"Vijay's worried. I think he's fine. He just misses Jennifer terribly and feels guilty about sleeping with me so soon after she died."

"And why are you sleeping together so soon?"

"Jennifer left specific written instructions, and she also talked with me before that day. She was quite adamant that Vijay not be left alone to mope."

"That sounds like Jennifer. And she's been studying Vijay for years. It's funny, on one level she understood him perfectly, and yet on a deeper level, he was always a mystery to her. She didn't understand how a man could love her so deeply."

"Can you help him? He's being brave and cheerful one minute, then crashing the next minute. It's quite tiring."

"Thank you, Cindy. I'll see what I can do."

Gloria stood in the hall outside her office for a minute before she went in. *'How do I tackle this? By most standards, it's not normal to walk from your wife's funeral into another woman's bed, but then nothing involving Jennifer is normal. And now Cindy and Vijay are demigods. What's normal for them?'*

She pushed open the door. Vijay stood as she entered, then sat again as Gloria pulled over her other visitor's chair.

"Hello, Vijay, how can I help you?"

"I'm confused. I feel like my heart is tied in knots, and I don't understand what's expected of me."

"Tell me about these knots. What's happening that upsets you?"

"I'm not myself anymore. Other forces are controlling me. Gaia is controlling me. Jennifer is controlling me even though she's not here anymore. And Cindy is trying to control me to make me what she saw in her vision when she was 15. And I have a new body. I'm aging backwards when I never asked for it. And I can feel things and do things I never felt or did before. Otherwise, not much." He laughed harshly.

"Tell me about Jennifer. What do you feel towards Jennifer now?"

"I miss her every minute."

"And what else?"

Vijay looked down at his hands. "I feel ashamed. I didn't even try to stop her. And at the same time, I'm so angry with her for giving up that way."

"You saw her giving up?"

"She just walked into that crowd, knowing that she would be badly injured, maybe killed, and then in that awful mediation, she just sank in Gaia's pool. No struggle, no farewell, she just left."

"Did she tell you why she felt she had to go away?"

"Jennifer said she would never be able to rest after what she did, but she slept just fine the night before. And she said that someone had to bear the blame for all the deaths so that the city could move on. I think she wanted that mob to hurt her, to make her feel something in exchange for the lives she took. Gloria, it was messed up, and I did nothing to stop her."

"Do you think you could have stopped her?"

"No, looking back, I could never stop her from doing exactly what she thought she needed to do. All I could do was try to lessen the impact."

"By having your Bashers there to get her out."

"Yes, with the Bashers that time. By making her talk to you other times."

Gloria paused. *'Was I any help finally? I helped her to be comfortable with what she was doing, I didn't try to stop her either.'*

"Tell me about Cindy."

"That's messed up too. When we took them in, I loved Cindy like a niece, maybe even like a little sister. We used to tease each other. I remember how shocked I was when she got her tattoo."

"Her tattoo?"

"She has a Vijay tattoo on her left breast. Then she became this amazing young woman. She excelled in school and took over managing the property here before she was twenty. I can see that people love and respect her. But I never lusted after her. I never thought of her that way."

"But she was waiting for you. Did you know that?"

"Jennifer told me about her vision, and why she changed young men every six months."

"Do all those young men bother you?"

"Why would they?"

"You're not her first."

Vijay laughed. "I think for me, it's backwards. How many men had Jennifer been with before I met her? She was my first. And now Cindy is my second. Sometimes I feel like a toy being tossed between more experienced women. No that never bothers me."

"So, are you struggling with how to transition your love from Cindy as a sister to Cindy as a lover?"

"Yes, it feels incestuous sometimes."

"And you said something about your body that worries you."

"Yes, look at me." Vijay stood and pulled off his shirt. "I haven't looked like this in 15 years, if I ever did. It's wonderful to feel so young, but I don't feel like it's quite my body yet. I'm still learning to work it, just like when I was 14 years old and grew 15 cm one summer."

"That must be a gift from Gaia. Just be as active as you can until your body fits you again. That's the easy one. Don't worry about the body. It's yours."

"But what about Cindy and Jennifer?"

"Vijay, while I know Jennifer always spoke about Gaia's love for humanity, in my experience, Gaia is utterly cruel to individual humans. You won't be judged by normal standards, but you'll need time to grieve for Jennifer. So does Cindy. So do Dylan and Parvati. Keep them close. Their love will give you strength."

"Now a question for you. Can you grow your heart large enough to still love Jennifer and everything she was to you, as well as Cindy and everything she will bring? Where Jennifer's gift was her quick mind and determination, your strength has always been your enormous capacity to love. Have faith. It's not a zero-sum game. Loving Cindy more does not mean you love Jennifer less. I think you'll find there's room in there for everyone. As for the rest, it's normal to be confused. Here's a pamphlet on grieving. You can see the stages people go through. But it's not a smooth path, it's normal to hop and skip around from anger to denial to acceptance and the neutral zone. Give yourself time. Enjoy your new life and know that there is nothing wrong with you. In fact, I would say that you are the most perfectly normal person I see."

"So, I should just stay the course, with Cindy and all."

"Yes, Jennifer told you to take 28 days before you decide what to do long term. She knew you. She knew you would come out of this all right.

"Thank you, Gloria. Thank you for everything you did for Jennifer too. She trusted you and followed your advice. Did you know she made peace with her sister, Vicki, when she was lying in the infirmary? She said to tell you her homework was finally finished."

Gloria laughed. "Vijay, that has made my day. Thank you for telling me that."

Gloria followed Vijay back to the living room where Cindy was waiting.

"So, is he all patched up?" she asked.

"No patching needed," said Gloria. "You're a very lucky young woman."

After they left, Gloria poured herself another cup of tea and sat down. *'A pamphlet!'* she thought. *'Everything he's been through and the best you can do is a pamphlet.'*

49

THE NEW CARD

Cindy

On the third week following Jennifer's passing, Cindy and Vijay were brushing the horses after their morning ride. They had been out on Bella and Charles, two of the great Shire horses who had turned out to be excellent riding horses. Cindy paused for a moment to watch Vijay. *'He really is so natural all the time. Charles is receiving all his attention and seems to know it.'* She smiled to herself, thinking of the times when she had all of Vijay's attention. He had a gift for making her feel safe and protected, no matter what was going on. *'No wonder Parvati and Dylan love him so much.'*

There was a noise behind them, and Cindy turned to see Marjorie driving full speed up the gravel drive to the farm. A cloud of dust hung in the still air behind her, marking her passage.

"Hi Marjorie, come for a riding lesson?" asked Cindy.

Marjorie looked at the enormous horses. "Not today, Cindy. Maybe tomorrow."

Cindy laughed. It was always tomorrow for Marjorie's first riding lesson. "What brings you up here?"

"I want to invite you to the unveiling at 2:00pm. It's special and I want you both to be there. Actually, I need you both to be there."

"What are you unveiling?"

"Jennifer's card. She designed a new card six weeks ago and now it's ready."

"Jennifer designed a card?"

"Yes, but the design is a secret until 2pm. Can you be in the mess hall, then?"

Cindy looked over at Vijay, who nodded, then went back to grooming his horse. *'I wonder what he's thinking.'* Turning back to Marjorie, she said, "We'll be there. Save us a couple of good seats."

"No worry, you'll be part of the unveiling. Tell Tim and whoever else is working up here that they should come too."

Marjorie turned her golf cart around and headed back down the drive, raising a new dust cloud along the way.

"Vijay, did you know about this card?"

Vijay paused in his brushing. "She may have mentioned it. She was worried that she would disappear and be forgotten after she was gone. I'm guess not surprised, but I have no idea what we'll see. Charles is done. I'll put him in the exercise paddock after I stow this tack."

"Bella's ready too. I'll see to the horses if you can stow Bella's tack, as well."

Vijay easily picked up one of the heavy saddles, piled with blankets and reins, and headed for the stable as Cindy watched. *'I don't know if he even recognizes how young and fit he is now.'*

·　·　·

VIJAY AND CINDY HAD LUNCH IN THE MESS HALL AT 1PM and then helped prepare the room for the unveiling. Marjorie was clearly in charge, with Chris at her side. A tripod held the artwork for the mysterious card. It was covered in black velvet. Four chairs were placed on either side. "Vijay, Cindy, you will sit here on the left," Marjorie directed. "We will bring in Parvati and Dylan before the unveiling. Chris, you and I will sit here. Then Angelica, the artist, and Dr. Gladstone on the far right."

The room soon filled up. Gloria arrived with Michael, looking a bit confused. This was obviously a surprise for her as well. Michael found a seat in the audience's front as Gloria joined them on stage.

Two of the youngest acolytes wandered about randomly smudging newcomers, which was met with lots of giggles and laughter. The mood was festive and there was an excited buzz in the room. Parvati and Dylan kept going back to get smudged again and again.

At exactly 2pm, Marjorie stood and sounded a small gong to bring the room to order. "Chris, will you please lead us in the invocation?"

Chris was brief, summoning the spirit of Gaia to the proceedings and asking her blessing for the participants.

"Angelica," said Marjorie. "Please come forward and explain how the new card came to be."

Angelica stepped up. Her hands trembled, and the page of notes she held shook visibly. Then a calm came over her. Cindy saw her glance at Vijay with a puzzled look on her face. Vijay nodded in return. *Did he really do that, take away her anxiety?'* Cindy wondered.

"Jennifer asked me to come to meet with her about six weeks ago, before all the drama started. She wanted a new card for the Gaia deck. I believe her vision was that the deck should continue to grow from time to time becoming a living record of our community. She said she didn't want it to become stagnant, fixed when the world around is changing."

"We talked about the design of the card. She was quite specific about the design, although at the time, I didn't understand what she was asking for. You'll see why in a minute. She told me Marjorie would write the text on the back." Angelica looked over at Marjorie who smiled and nodded. "And that the style of the card had to match the other images.

"Jennifer saw my rough sketches, but never saw the finished card. I kept the sketches for our archives and can show them later to anyone who is interested. Vijay, please assist me in unveiling the new card."

Vijay rose and stood on one side. Angelica showed him where to hold the velvet cover as she held the other corner. "Ready?"

Vijay nodded. They both raised the velvet. Cindy heard an audible gasp from the audience. Twisting in her seat she looked at the artwork on the easel.

The image showed Jennifer lying on a white sheet. Her red hair spread out to form a sort of halo around her head. She wore in a straw-colored gown. One foot was splayed at an awkward angle where her leg had been broken. The gown was stained with red where one of her broken ribs had pierced her skin. Her hands were bloody, but her faced was untouched, looking as beautiful as ever. She lay on a bed of wild roses. In the foreground, her black panther lay resting by the bed. A warthog and a wild horse stood together on one side. *'Something for future scholars to puzzle over,'* thought Cindy, smiling. In the background, small boats floated empty on a dark sea.

Cindy looked at Vijay, still holding the velvet. He

looked shocked and she could see tears forming in his eyes. She rose and took his hand.

"It's beautiful," he said. There was a long pause as he struggled to contain his tears. "But what does it mean in the deck?"

Marjorie spoke up.

"It is the card of self-sacrifice. Of playing the part you are destined for, even if it comes at great personal cost. It's the card of knowing that we are all part of something greater and that we must not step back from our calling. I have here some first run cards for each of you. Acolytes, please pass them to the audience as well."

Cindy, Vijay, and each of the twins received one of the new cards. Cindy saw Vijay turn it over to read the back. Then he looked up. "Angelica, Marjorie, this is truly beautiful. A fitting tribute to the person Jennifer was."

Marjorie turned to Gloria and said, "Gloria, could you say a few words about Jennifer as you knew her?"

Vijay finally let go of the black velvet and allowed Cindy to guide him back to his seat. Cindy heard Gloria in the background, but Cindy's attention was all on Vijay. "Are you okay?" she asked.

He shook his head no, then whispered, "Fucking Jennifer. She always kept secrets until after the event. It's almost too much, seeing this card. I hope it never comes up in one of my readings. But part of me also hopes it comes up every time."

Cindy held his hand and leaned into him. "Just keep it together until this is over. We can talk then."

She turned to Parvati and Dylan who were turning the cards over and over, looking confused. Dylan was about to burst into tears.

"Mommy looks beautiful," whispered Parvati.

"But she's bleeding," said Dylan. "I don't like it." He

whispered, passed his card back to Cindy. He raised his forearm over his eyes to hide his tears.

"That's okay, Dylan. You don't have to like it. I'll keep it for you until you're older."

Parvati passed hers to Cindy as well. "Cindy, please keep mine, too. But I might want to look at it sometimes."

"Sure, Parvati. You can have it back whenever you want."

Gloria was winding up her small speech just as Cindy turned back from the twins.

The entire room was standing now, applauding and cheering. The meeting broke up, and most people left. A few stayed and talked with Marjorie and Angelica who was now spreading her sketches on a table on one side of the room.

"Let's stay and see those sketches," said Vijay. "I'm still curious about what Jennifer was thinking in those last weeks. She spent a lot of time on her own and never really talked about it." The four of them walked over to look.

The sketches were laid out in date order. However even the first sketch had most of the details including Jennifer bleeding on her bed of wild roses. "Did you say Jennifer asked for this three weeks before she died?"

"Yes, she was quite specific. I revised the injuries in the design after I saw the final images from when she was brought back here. She was quite adamant that I was not to show injuries to her face."

"And the panther, how did you get that so right?"

"She had the panther sit for me several times. I was afraid at first, until she showed me the panther was just an aspect of her. She showed me my spirit animal, too."

"What animal is that?" asked Cindy.

Angelica blushed. "It's a spider. At first, I hated it. But then Chris showed me that the spider represents feminine energy and creativity as it spins its beautiful webs each morning. He showed me how to collect spiders' webs and frame them. Now I have a bunch of them. Perhaps I'll show them one day."

"Well," said Vijay, "at least you can see your spirit animal at work around you. There is a distinct lack of warthogs here at the vineyard."

"One is quite enough," replied Cindy. Parvati and Dylan giggled at the idea of warthogs everywhere.

"Angelica, thank you," said Vijay. "The card is beautiful and a wonderful remembrance of Jennifer."

CINDY AND VIJAY WERE SITTING ON A BENCH BY THE POND. Cindy turned to look at Vijay. "What did you mean about secrets during the presentation?"

"Jennifer always said there should be no secrets between us. But then she kept secrets until they were forced out into the open. 'When they became relevant', she said. Like that card. Wouldn't you think she would mention something like that? Especially when she was putting so much work into it."

"Then let's agree that there will truly be no secrets between us."

"Been there and done that, Cindy. Let's just agree always to talk openly with each other about what's going on in our lives."

"So, no more moody silences then?"

Vijay laughed. "Touché, I'll do my best not to have moody silences."

"That's good enough for me." Cindy held his hand and squeezed it.

Vijay continued. "But Angelica said that Jennifer had commissioned the card three weeks before she died. Did she really know then what was going to happen? And now it makes me wonder who tipped off that angry mob when Jennifer was admitting guilt at the newscast station? Did she arrange all that as well? Was this her last, grand piece of public theatre, and we were all just supporting roles that we could not escape?"

"You'll never know, Vijay. And you'll have to be content not knowing. But it explains that strange contentment that seemed to come over her at the very end. Her plan had all worked out brilliantly, and this card now exists to commemorate it."

"I suppose," said Vijay. "Let's also agree to less dramatic exits when our turn finally comes."

"I'm really not sure it will, Vijay. That may be the next thing to confront."

"What do you mean?"

"Have you noticed we both seem to be in our prime? You're actually aging backwards. I wouldn't be surprised to learn that we're doomed to very, very long lifetimes until our tasks are complete."

"Humph, I don't even want to think about that. Let's get Parvati and Dylan and go riding."

50

PLAN C

Vijay

A few days after the new card was introduced, Professor Matthew O'Grady from the University asked for a meeting. Vijay responded with a time and the suggestion that he meet them at the vineyard offices.

Vijay and Cindy were already sitting in the meeting room when Molly ushered in Professor O'Grady. He had a binder under his arm, which he set down on the table.

"Hello, Cindy, Vijay. I'm Matthew O'Grady," he said as he extended his hand.

"Welcome Professor. How can we help you?"

"Please call me Matt. Professor always sounds so formal when I'm not around students. I've come to talk about Plan C."

"Plan C?" asked Cindy. "We have plans A and B, although we don't talk about Plan B too much. But I've never heard about Plan C."

"Yes, I suspect it was Jennifer's idea of a joke. The C

stands for Cistercian. She was quite a remarkable young lady. Not very interested in broad context or theory, but quite determined about what she thought was needed."

"Yes, that sounds like Jennifer. But when did she do all this?" asked Vijay.

"She visited me regularly at the University, and of course we exchanged texts."

"I remember she had a picture book of the Cistercian Abbey ruins which are very impressive," said Vijay. "I also remember an odd comment she made to the Governor about not repeating past errors."

"That makes sense. Henry VIII destroyed their abbeys in England and the French Revolution destroyed them in France when the ruling class became concerned that they possessed too much wealth and power. She was warning the Governor not to go to war with the Gaian Church on the island."

"What is plan C?" asked Cindy.

"Plan C is a plan to issue a new currency for use within the Church operations, initially pegged at par with the existing currency. But then to devalue the existing currency over time, while limiting the amount of money that can be converted. It will diminish the wealth and power of the top 5% while redistributing the island's wealth more fairly among the general population."

"Will it work?"

"Not today, but when the global monetary system collapses for lack of off-island participants, it will work very well. All that money in Swiss bank accounts will become worthless, and only money held here on the island will have any value."

"How will we know when to execute this plan?"

"It's all in here, but the time is not yet. I'll let you know when. If something happens to me, then there's enough guidance in this for you to execute the plan. I believe Molly also has a copy, so this physical copy is really not needed. Jennifer liked to look at it, though. I'll miss her."

"So will we all," said Cindy, taking hold of Vijay's hand.

"Yes," said Vijay. "Please come by often. Then, when we're ready, nothing will seem out of the ordinary. Bring your family for a picnic on the grounds. The kitchen will provide sandwiches and drinks."

"Thank you. I must admit, I like the idea of playing the part of the closet revolutionary. It makes all this economics theory seem less dry and boring."

After the professor had left, Vijay looked at Cindy and laughed. "Now do you see what I meant about Jennifer and 'no secrets.' If she were here, she would say, 'Well, it wasn't relevant until now.'"

Cindy also laughed. "I'm just amazed that she had all this planned out. Here I believed all she did was watch romances all day without a thought in her head, and yet she was plotting out the entire transition. She was even more special than I realized."

"Yes," said Vijay, pulling Cindy closer to his side. "But I'm coming to realize how special you are in your own way. I must be the luckiest man alive."

"Just keep telling yourself that," replied Cindy.

51

A LATE BOAT ARRIVAL

Molly came into the bungalow and quietly woke Cindy and Vijay.

"Molly, what the hell?" said Vijay.

"Quiet, I need to talk with both of you outside. We have an emergency."

Vijay and Cindy dressed quickly and silently, then headed out into the night to meet Molly waiting with a car. Two young acolytes were also standing there.

Molly said, "Marie and Janice will stay here for the rest of the night with Parvati and Dylan. I will go with you in the car."

The limousine went slowly down the drive, then sped up as they hurtled through the night.

"What time is it," asked Cindy.

"The time is 2:17am," replied Molly. "Another boat of refugees has landed. Three of the passengers are showing signs of illness. Some people in the community where they landed have been in close contact. The containment teams are on their way and will arrive ahead of us."

"What do you expect us to do?" asked Cindy.

"I think they want us to heal them all," said Vijay.

"Can we?"

"We're advertised as the healers. That's what Jennifer called us, so I believe we can. We have to try."

Cindy sat and stared out the window while Vijay stared straight ahead.

When they arrived, a police cordon barricaded the road at the edge of the small town called Misty Cove. After a brief consultation, their car continued through the barricade. Further on, they could see the containment team was already at work isolating the clearly ill passengers. Others were testing the remaining passengers and the few townspeople who had been in contact.

"Take us to the sick boat passengers," said Vijay. "The most serious one first."

"Vijay!" said Cindy, "What are you doing?"

"Either we can do this, or we can't. If we can, we have to take the most serious cases first and then work outwards from there. If can't then there is no point in us being here at all."

The car stopped next to a containment ambulance marked "Block F". The rear door was open, and they could see a white medibot caring for a patient on a stretcher.

"Do we need to be in contact with the earth?" asked Vijay.

"I don't think so," said Cindy. "Try inside the ambulance. If it doesn't work, then we'll bring them outside."

Vijay went into the ambulance and sat beside the patient. He closed his eyes and reached for the energetic plane. It took a minute to calm himself enough to be present. He felt the life-force of the patient beside him and the man's disease, but could not bring it into focus.

"Cindy, come in here and lay your hands on my shoulders. Let's combine our energies and see what we can do together."

Cindy stepped in behind him. Her fear was palpable, and she was shaking as she placed her hands on his shoulders. Vijay reached up and covered her hands with his, absorbing her fear and sending calming energy to her. "It's okay, we were made for this," he said.

Reaching out, Vijay moved one hand to the patient's heart and the other to his belly. Closing his eyes, he moved back into the energetic plane. He was aware of Cindy's energy merging with his. He drew in all the energy he could channel, his capacity expanded by Cindy's presence. Sensing the patient under his hands, he flooded them with Gaia's healing energy. It took a moment to understand what he was being shown. It was the patient's immune system being completely overrun. He boosted the immune system, pushing the body to create more white blood cells, attacking the virus wherever it existed. At the same time, he damaged the virus DNA wherever it was released in the bloodstream so that it could no longer reproduce. Finally, he pushed the patient's life force to support breathing and heartbeats. It seemed like a long time later that Vijay finally relaxed and withdrew.

He felt Cindy lift her hands from his shoulders. Her hands were shaking again.

"Vijay, how did you know what to do? There was so much power, you scared me."

"How long did that take, Cindy?"

The medibot answered, "You have been with the patient for 14 minutes and 27 seconds, sir."

"Okay, keep him under observation, and direct us to the next patient."

The next patient went faster, as Vijay now knew what to look for. Again, Cindy placed her hands on his shoulders to lend her energy as well.

As they walked to the third ambulance, Vijay noticed the ground was lit all around them. "Where does this light come from?" he asked.

"I think it's mostly you, and a little bit me," replied Cindy.

"Jennifer shone sometimes when she was hunting. I think it must be ionization of the air by the energy flowing through us. One more hard case and then we can focus on the infected with no symptoms."

Two hours later, all the boat occupants and the townspeople had been cleared. They were all taken away to the containment area as a precaution, but all were testing free of the active virus.

Molly let them back to the waiting car. "Do we have to go to the containment area?"

"The medibots will test your blood before you leave, but I do not believe you are infected," said Molly.

As predicted, their blood tested free of the virus.

On the way home, Cindy and Vijay were leaning on each other in the back seat. Molly said, "Vijay, Cindy, these cured patients now have blood with the antibodies for the virus. They are the first known survivors of the virus. We will use their blood to create our first virus vaccine, so we don't have to do this again."

"Great," said Vijay. It was the last thing he remembered before waking up in his bed the following afternoon. He rolled over to look for Cindy, but she was not there.

"Cindy!" he called.

She appeared in the bedroom doorway.

"Oh, you're finally awake. That was quite a performance last night. The newscasts have been playing the story all morning."

"Is everyone all right?"

"Yes, come and see."

Vijay grabbed a robe and went out to watch the newscast with Cindy. They were showing an image of an ambulance near the harbor. The ambulance was lit with a bright light inside. The announcer was saying, "Our camera caught these images of bright white light, possibly part of a new diagnostic tool. We also captured two figures bathed in the same light moving between the ambulances. It was not possible to identify them, but speculation points to Vijay Subramanian and Cindy Tremaine, who were announced some weeks ago as healers succeeding Jennifer Dupont."

"All passengers and townspeople were found to be free of the virus but are being kept in the Containment facility as a public safety precaution."

"Well, it looks like we did it," said Vijay.

"You did it. You were amazing. I don't know if I could have done that."

"Cindy sweetheart, you have the ability to heal the planet. I can heal sick people one at a time, but I'm not the powerful one in our couple. Remember, in the visions you always sit on the high throne, and I am lower and to your right side."

"Perhaps," said Cindy. "But I haven't done much healing yet."

"Maybe it's time to start."

END

PREVIEW OF HARRIET'S WAY

BOOK 3 OF GAIAS DAUGHTERS

HARRIET'S

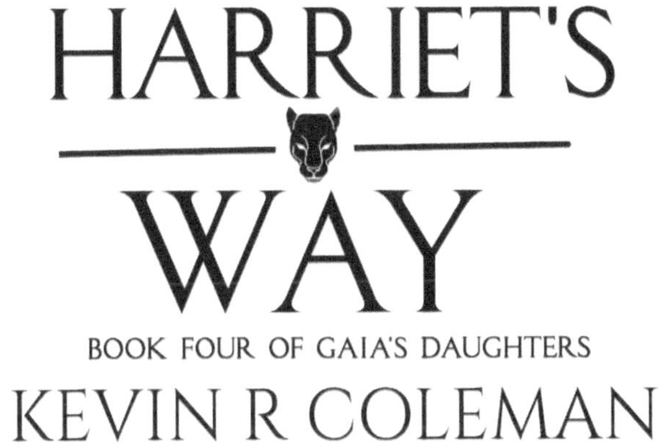

WAY

BOOK FOUR OF GAIA'S DAUGHTERS

KEVIN R COLEMAN

1

DYLAN'S REQUEST

Cindy

"Cindy," said Dylan as they were brushing down their horses, "Would you talk to Baba about letting me go to work on the fishing boats?"

"Have you tried asking him yourself? He's your father after all."

"I tried, but I don't think he's really taking me seriously."

"What makes you think there'll be a place for you on the boats?"

"Donnie, one of the captains, said he would have a place for me when I turned 17. And I'm 17 now. He says I'm old enough."

Cindy stopped brushing, and turned to look at Dylan, trying to see him as a young man rather than the boy she had helped raise.

"I know you think you're all grown up, but 17 is still very young to go and live away by yourself. Your dad's only looking out for your safety."

"I won't be by myself, I'll be working with Donnie and his crew. And Donnie said he'd train me to be a real fisherman. You told me to learn all about the oceans. I'd learn about the sea by being on the sea for a summer than staying here watching recorded lessons."

"Where would you stay?"

"My sailboat's there. I could live on her and work on her in my spare time."

"What about your schoolwork? You know you have to study for your future."

"I'll keep working online. Both my marine biology and meteorology courses are available that way. And I'll be getting real field experience."

Cindy frowned. She returned to brushing the horse as she thought. Sensing that Dylan might go even without permission, she gave in. "Okay, I'll talk to him tonight and see if I can change his mind."

"Thanks Cindy."

Dylan finished grooming the horse, then turned it out into the paddock before stowing all the riding tack.

THAT NIGHT, AS CINDY AND VIJAY LAY IN BED READY FOR sleep, Cindy said, "Dylan talked with me today. He really wants to work on the fishing boats this year."

"Yes, he told me too, and I said 'No'."

"Why did you say that?"

"Do I need a reason? I'm his father. It's my responsibility to make good choices for him. Another year, and he'll be that much stronger and more reliable."

"Have you really looked at him lately? He's already grown into a young man, and the vineyard is getting to be too small for him. If you keep saying 'No', he may leave anyway, and you'll lose something precious."

"I don't want to lose him. It was hard enough losing their mother, Jennifer, when they were 10. Now Parvati is out flirting with boys, and Dylan wants to go away to the sea. What if they both leave?"

"Vijay, according to the vision we saw, you and I will have very long lives. You know that. You can't hold Dylan and Parvati close forever. They'll become stunted, emotionally crippled, in too tight an embrace. Let Dylan have his adventure. After all, it was you who helped him become Dylan, Master of the Seas. I think he's taken that as his destiny."

"Does this mean I have to let Parvati go and live in the city? She keeps asking, but I worry that she's too young for that."

"You're probably right about that. She is already playing with the boys here and doesn't take school seriously at all. There's a big difference between a summer of hard work as part of a crew on a boat for Dylan and giving Parvati license to party full-time unsupervised in the city.

"Okay, he can go. But we'll go down at some point and check to see that he's alright. But Parvati stays put.

"I think that's right. If we go to see Dylan, we can stay at the rose cottage for a couple of nights. It could be fun."

THE NEXT MORNING, OVER BREAKFAST, VIJAY SAID, "DYLAN, are you serious about working on the fishing boats?"

"Yes, Baba. That's what I want to do."

"Then you can go. But, if you get into any trouble, you can call me or Cindy or Molly at any time."

"Yes, Baba."

"And remember, you can call Molly on any intelligent bot. Never be afraid to do that. Don't do anything stupid, but when you do something stupid, call. We all do stupid things at your age. Trying to keep them quiet only makes them worse. Understood?"

"Yes, sir," said Dylan, trying not to grin.

Parvati spoke from across the table.

"Baba, I'm seventeen too. We have the same birthday. I want to get a studio apartment in the city so I can study art and be independent."

"No," said Vijay. "Sorry Parvati, but that's not happening. Maybe when you're 25."

"You're so unfair," she said, pouting.

"Yes," said Vijay, "but I'm also your father."

2

THE ADVENTURE BEGINS

Dylan

That evening, Dylan called Donnie and told him he would be ready to start work the following Monday.

"Wonderful," replied Donnie. "Make sure you've got some good boots and gloves, a hat to keep your head warm, and a waterproof coat and pants to keep you dry. Ted Rogers will set you up at the Chandlery store in Moreton. Tell 'im Donnie Irish sent you."

"Thanks, Donnie, I'll be ready on Monday."

Dylan wandered out to find Cindy in the stables. "Hi Cindy, I have to go to Moreton to buy my fishing clothes. Would you be able to come with me? You have a better idea about clothes than I do."

"Sure Dylan, I'd like that."

The Chandlery was a revelation to Dylan. He had no idea that one store could contain so many items for sailors. There was an entire section devoted to sailboats like his own 12-meter sloop. All the fittings and rigging accessories he could ever want were here in one place. "Cindy, look! They have everything I need [LD1] [KC2] for my boat," he said.

"Well, now that you have a job, you'll be able to buy them. But today we're here for working clothes. Who are we supposed to ask for?"

"Ted Rogers."

Ted Rogers turned out to be an affable old sailor with a round belly and a missing hand.

"How can I help ya?"

"I'm going to work for Donnie Irish on his fishing boats. He said you could outfit me for working on the sea."

"Donnie, eh? Haven't seen him in a while. Ya couldn't do any better to teach ya the ropes. D'you know anything about boats?"

"I have a 12-meter sloop I sail, but that's for fun."

"Yeah, quite different on a workin' boat. No second chances with the sea. I wasn't paying' attention, and a cable took my hand faster than you can say *stop*. Ted held up his stump and its stainless steel three-pronged hand as a demonstration.

"I understand that, sir." Dylan eyed the steel hand, trying not to recoil. "I respect the sea and I want to make sure I'm dressed for it."

By the time they left, they had boxes and bags of boots, gloves, coveralls, pants, sweaters, t-shirts, and woolen beanies. The last items were a couple of colorful scarves to wrap around his neck. "It's not the cold that'll get ya, it's the wind," offered Ted cheerfully.

Dylan and a store clerk loaded all his purchases into a waiting taxi, and soon they were back home.

Dylan sat on his bed, unwrapping his purchases, sorting them, and getting them ready to pack. Parvati came in and sat down beside him.

"Are you really going away? It'll be strange. It'll be the first time we're not together."

"Yeah, but it's hard to be Master of the Seas sitting in the middle of a farm."

"You could change your name, be Dylan, Master of the Hay Bales or something."

"No, I like the ocean. Mom named me Dylan for the sea, and I know the sea was her favorite place to be. I feel close to her when I'm there."

"Do you still miss her a lot?"

"I miss her every day."

"Me too. I still don't understand why she had to go away. I saw the recordings. She walked into that crowd, knowing they would try to kill her. She was smiling."

"Yeah, that was really messed up. Sometimes I'm really angry with her for going. Sometimes I'm sad for all the things she's missing, and sometimes I just wish she was still here."

"Cindy's nice, but it's not the same. Baba seems to really love her, though."

"Maybe, but he's still sad, too. I'm not sure he loves her the way he loved Mom. And have you looked at him and Cindy? They don't look much older than us. How does that work?"

"Cindy told me once that Mom's job was pretty short, only about ten years, and that it used her up. She says that she and Baba have a task that will take hundreds or thousands of years and that they cannot give up. I think that's why she seems so patient with us all, and why Baba doesn't want us to grow older, either. But we will."

"Yeah. I'm kind of looking forward to being away, where everyone doesn't think of me as Jennifer's child."

"Do you think I can come down to visit you on your boat sometimes?"

"Sure."

"You really going to live on that smelly sailboat?"

"It's only smelly 'cause it's closed up all the time. Once I start living there with the hatches all open, it will be nice."

"Except that it will have your stinky self in it."

Dylan picked up a pillow with a free hand and tried to hit Parvati with it. She resisted and a short wrestling match ensued.

After a moment, they called a halt. "Parv, I'm going to miss you," said Dylan.

"And I'll miss you. But I have a favor to ask."

"Yes?"

"When I have boys over for sex, can I use your bed so my sheets stay clean?"

"Eww! No, get out!"

"Okay. I just won't tell you." Parvati laughed and dodged the pillow as she left his room.

THE FOLLOWING AFTERNOON, DYLAN STOOD ALONE ON THE dock, his duffle bag beside him, and an extra suitcase as well. He was sweating as he had elected to wear all the heavier gear to save room packing. Taking off the new boots, he swung them onboard his boat. Followed by the duffle and the suitcase.

Lastly, he held onto a stanchion and stepped over the lifeline onto the deck. The small sailboat rocked slightly under his weight. Dylan knew the boat intimately. When Vijay had bought the boat for him three years ago, on his 14th birthday, they spent two weeks together with help from some of the locals to go over all the electrical and mechanical systems. The boat hull was 40 years old, but the motor was newer and they had replaced all the rigging.

Dylan had been down at least once per month since then, cleaning and replacing worn parts. But this would be his first extended stay.

With practiced hands, he quickly moved through the cabin, opening all the hatches, and starting the interior fans. A quick scan of the electrical panel showed him that the shore power was well-connected, and the house batteries were charged.

Dylan began by stowing all his shore clothing in the V-berth in the bow where he would sleep. Then he laid out the work clothes in one of the aft quarter-berths. Next, he walked up to the small grocery store in the village to buy provisions. His priorities were breakfast cereal, soft drinks, canned soup, bread, peanut butter, and jam. *'I can always live on this,'* he thought.

As he walked back with his provisions, the fishing boats were coming in. Dylan sat on a bench and watched for a few minutes to see what the fishermen were wearing.

Donnie's boat was the last in.

Seeing Donnie's boat, the *Island Princess*, Dylan jumped up and ran as best he could to put his provisions down in the cabin of his boat. Turning around, he quickly went to watch Donnie's boat dock, trying to see what the men were wearing. He was relieved to see that Ted had guided him well.

Walking along the dock to the boat, he waited until the lines were all secured, and Donnie had shut off the engine. When Donnie was free, Dylan approached him cautiously.

"Hi, Donnie."

"Hello Dylan. Still ready for a Monday morning start?"

"Yes, sir. What time should I be here?"

"First, it's Cap'n when you're working with me. On the

boat and on the dock, you call me Cap'n. Away from here, Donnie's fine."

"Yes, Captain."

"Not quite it, son. You say it without the 't' and the 'n' is more like an 'm'. Now try again."

"Yes, Cap'n"

"Much better. The crew will give you your boat name soon enough. Just know right off, it won't be Dylan. Now, did you get your kit?"

"Yes, sir, I mean Cap'n. I went to Ted Rogers like you said. I was just watching the other sailors and I think I have pretty much the same gear, except that it's all new and shiny."

"Don't worry about that. We were all new and shiny once. We assemble here at 4:30am, departure by 5am. Make sure you bring a few snacks. I provide coffee, soft drinks and sandwiches for lunch. Whatever else you need is up to you. Last thing, don't bring anything valuable aboard, especially tablets or jewelry. You won't need them, and the salt air will destroy them anyway. There aren't many tablets left in the village. Sea air seems to eat away at them."

Dylan nodded, trying to take in all this information.

"Where're ya staying in town?"

"On my boat, the *Jennifer*, in one of the marina slips."

"I've seen it. Nice little 12 meter. Named for your mum, I take it. We all knew her. Lovely lady and a real firecracker when she was in the mood. Terrible to see her life end so soon. I can't judge, but I know the fishing is getting better every year and I can't help wondering if she didn't have something to do with that. You won't hear a word spoken against her round here."

Thank you, Cap'n. It's still hard to believe she's gone sometimes. But she named me for the sea, and I think she'll be proud that I'm down here learning to be a real sailor."

"You're already a sailor, boy. I'm gonna teach ya to be a fisherman."

That evening, Dylan set his alarm for 6am, thinking 'Maybe I'll ease into a 4am start on Monday.

DYLAN AWOKE TO THE SOUND OF A SIREN. GROGGILY, HE flailed about in the dark, trying to remember where he was and where he'd put his tablet. He sat up quickly and bumped his head on a shelf above him. The pain made him wide awake. His tablet was glowing nearby. He silenced it, then turned on the cabin light.

'Shit,' he thought. *'How am I ever going to wake up at 4am tomorrow?'*

He fought the temptation to go back to sleep, forced himself to the head, and then to the galley, where he made himself a morning coffee. As the coffee brewed, he pulled on his pants and a warm hoodie over his t-shirt.

When the coffee was ready, he opened the companionway hatch and climbed the short steps out onto the deck. Dylan pulled one of the cockpit cushions up to the foredeck and turned it over to have the dry side up. Finally, he sat there, cross-legged, clutching the warm coffee between his hands.

'So, this is the start of my new life', he thought. It was still dark out, with only a few lights on the nearby boats. The fishing fleet was still in. No fishing on Sundays. He could see the lights of the bakery shop up the street, and a few early risers were walking their dogs, or jogging, or simply passing time out on the street.

As he sat, he saw the first lightening of the sky, a

gradual lessening of the black on the east. Distant objects took form in the dim light.

The sea was calm in the harbor, with no ripples disturbing its surface. His boat was rolling only slightly with the remnant swells that made it past the breakwater. No birds were calling yet, and the faint ching-ching of the sailboat rigging was the only sound. He zipped his hoodie against the cold, damp air. The ocean smelled fresh here, and the faint taste of salt was on his lips.

His coffee was cold by the time he'd finished drinking it, and he was feeling hungry.

Dylan thought about cereal, but the call of the bakery was too strong. Finding his shoes, he hopped off the boat and walked up to the shop. As he came closer, the smell of baking bread grew stronger.

There was already a small queue at the bakery counter. Ahead of him was a mixed line of early walkers buying pastries and coffees for themselves, and others out to buy fresh croissants for their families. When his turn came up, he chose a pain aux raisins which seemed to be a large whorl of pastry with custard and raisins. Dylan wasn't planning on another coffee, but the aroma was so good that he ordered a breakfast coffee with milk. The coffee came in a thick china cup that was more like a small bowl. The pastry overflowed the plate. He took his tray and went to sit at one of the small tables on the street outside.

Dylan didn't think he had ever felt so content. Waking up in the morning on his own boat and having the most delicious breakfast of all time – life seemed perfect.

When he finished his breakfast, he returned the tray and walked back down to the docks. He stopped to admire his boat before getting on. The name *Jennifer* was written on both sides of the bow in the large, uneven letters of his mother's own handwriting. Sally had found an old envelope in the theatre that his mother had practiced writing on. Dylan had scanned it and had the custom lettering made for the boat. He closed his eyes and bowed his head for a moment, thinking about her.

Back on board, it was barely 7am. The sun had just cleared the horizon, and he had a whole day ahead of him. *'What will I do today?'* he wondered. He rearranged the cockpit cushions so that he could recline comfortably while he thought.

3

HARRIET MEETS DYLAN

Harriet

Harriet stepped out into the bright sunshine. A fresh sea breeze carried the familiar scents of the ocean and of the harbor, a mixture of seaweed, diesel fumes and rotting fish. Harriet walked to the end of the lane and turned down the main street into the village. Passing the general store, the butcher and the grocer, she waved to each one.

At the bakery, she stopped to buy bread and rolls for her mum.

"Morning, Sarah. It's a beautiful day, the first weekend of my summer."

"Well, since yer here, can ya help me by bringing out the trays of muffins from the back?"

"Sure, Sarah."

Harriet fetched three trays of muffins, placing them in the glass counter. "What time do ya want me to start work tomorrow?"

"7am at the latest. And we'll be done by 4pm each day."

"Thanks again for the summer job."

"Sure thing, Harriet. A girl your age needs her own money, and my staff will enjoy the time off while you're here."

Harriet took the bag with the bread and rolls and walked out into the street. On a whim, she turned left out of the bakery, down toward the docks. The day was glorious, with a clear blue sky and the sun sparkling on the waves. She always felt a sense of freedom on the docks. 'What would it be like to go sailing off to the horizon, finding new worlds and new people?' she wondered.

As Harriet walked past the small boat slips, she came to the Jennifer, a 12-meter pleasure sloop. In the open cockpit, a young man about her age lay on a cushion on the foredeck. He was still half asleep and was looking at his tablet.

"Do you always sleep outside your boat?" she asked.

"That wasn't the plan. I have to be up at 4am tomorrow, so I practiced at 6am today. But then I sat out here to think about things and went right back to sleep."

"Are you Dylan who's going to work with Donnie?"

"Yes, what's your name?"

"I'm Harriett. Donnie's my uncle, and I heard him mention ya."

"It's nice of him to give me a job on his boat."

"It's hard work on the boats. Not everyone can do it."

"All I can do is my best. If it's not good enough, I'll find another way to make a living on the sea."

"I hope you do well."

"Thanks."

"I have to go. These are for lunch. Hope I see ya again."

"You know where I live."

"That I do. Bye, Dylan."

"Bye, Harriett"

Harriet turned around and walked back along the docks, doing her best to swing her hips as she walked. A quick glance back told her Dylan was still watching her. She gave a small wave over her shoulder and continued home.

"Hi, Mum," she said as she walked in.

"That was a long trip to the bakery. Did you get lost?" Her mother said, a smile twitching the corner of her mouth.

"I wasn't gone that long." Harriet replied, rolling her eyes. "I had to help Sarah at the shop, then I walked back past the dock. That new boy, Dylan, was there on his boat."

"That's good, your dad was wondering when he would arrive. What did you think of him?"

Harriet shrugged but couldn't hide the pink tint she could feel creeping across her cheeks. "He seems alright."

Harriet's mother cocked her head to one side as she watched her daughter. "Oh, I know that look," she said. "Just don't get too attached, he might be a bit out of your league."

"Why?" Harriet dropped the bread and rolls on the kitchen table.

"His family's pretty famous and wealthy. How many seventeen-year-olds do you know with their own boat?"

"Lots. Billy had his first boat when he was thirteen, and Samuel had his first real fishing boat when he was fifteen."

"Yeah, that's true, but the Jennifer's an expensive sailboat made for pleasure sailing. I've heard that Dylan comes down for the weekend sometimes, but the boat doesn't go out very often. Mostly, he cleans and fixes her up."

"I'm going to go back and talk to him again this afternoon."

"Did you arrange something?"

"No, I said I hoped to see him again, and he said, 'You know where I live' so that's enough of an invitation for me."

Her mum laughed. "Knowing you, that's more invitation than you need. But seriously, don't do anything silly. You can talk to me about anything, you know that. Being seventeen is not easy; it's an age where you can make mistakes and get hurt. So please, talk to me. I promise I won't be upset by anything. Remember, I was seventeen once."

"Sure, Mum." Harriet smirked, but then gave her mum a hug. As she turned to leave, her mother said, "Best not to say anything to your father yet. Wait until there's more to tell."

Without looking back, Harriet held a thumb up over her shoulder.

That afternoon, Harriet walked back down to the docks. On the deck of the Jennifer, Dylan was mopping, wearing only his cut-off shorts. Harriet sat on a bollard to watch. Dylan was only a little taller than her, with light brown skin and dark, curly hair cut short. Her eyes followed his muscles, moving easily and rhythmically under his skin as he mopped.

Suddenly aware of her, Dylan stopped. "Hi Harriet," he said, leaning on his mop handle.

"Hi Dylan. Practicing for tomorrow, are ya?"

"I'll be doing more than mopping tomorrow."

"I wouldn't be so sure. Everyone starts as a swabbie on the boats."

"Well, if everyone does, I will too. Whatever it takes, I want to learn to work on a fishing boat. It's part of my long-term plan."

"Carry on then. Don't mind me watching. You're a very pretty boy, did ya know that?"

"You must be thinking of my sister. She's the pretty one. I'm more of the rugged type."

"Keep telling yourself that. Maybe it'll stick."

"Come back later and I'll give you a tour of the boat."

"My mother warned me to never go on a strange man's boat."

"Then we have to get to know each other, so I won't be strange."

"I think strange is part of who ya are ."

"Let me know, Harriet, when you want to take a chance."

"I will, Dylan. I will."

Harriet stood up and sashayed back up the dock, feeling pleased with herself. She didn't look back. Even without looking, she knew his eyes were following her.

On the way home, Harriet was daydreaming about sailing off with Dylan when she was interrupted by a shout.

"Hey, Harriet, what's up? You walked right past me." Harriet turned to see her school friend. "Hi Lucy."

"Hi Harriet, you were miles away. What's going on?"

"I met a new boy named Dylan this morning. He was on his sailboat. I saw him again this afternoon When you talk with him, you have his total attention. He's not looking around or doing anything else. And he has these beautiful deep brown eyes, and these perfect lips. I wanted to jump aboard and kiss him."

"Why didn't you?"

"Dad taught me early that if you chase the fish, they simply swim away. Offer something they want, and they'll come to you."

"So, what are you offering to Dylan?"

"Hmm, I guess I'm offering him myself. If he wants me, he'll come to me. But I'm only offering him the chance to talk with me, to get to know me. I don't even know if I really like him yet."

"Are you hoping to get to know him a lot better? Promise to tell me if you do."

"Maybe. Have you gone all the way with Jason yet?"

"No, part of me wants to, but part of me is still too scared. I think he's the same way."

THAT EVENING, HARRIET LAY ON HER BED READING A BOOK from the library. '*I wonder if Dylan has a tablet,*' she thought. '*But he must, being wealthy and all.*' She remembered her childhood, the fear as the viruses swept the earth, leaving only their island untouched. The terrible and miraculous intervention of Jennifer, Dylan's mum, to keep them safe, although she wasn't entirely clear on what Jennifer had done. And now their technology was failing, and the island could not manufacture new tech. Living near the sea made it worse as the salty air seemed to corrode anything electronic like the tablets. '*Will we ever have tablets again?*' she wondered.

Harriet shut her bedroom door firmly, then settled back on her bed. Her thoughts turned back to Dylan. She imagined being held by him as they sailed away in his sailboat. Harriet unbuckled her belt, touched herself and sank into the warmth of her fantasy of Dylan carrying her off to a new life together.

The story continues in Book 4, Harriet's Way

ACKNOWLEDGMENTS

It takes many people to make a book. First, I thank my wife and life partner, Sue, whose patience and encouragement has supported me through the long dark period when I wrote my first eight drafts.

I am also thankful for the work of my editor, Lindsay Drummond, for her patient reviews of my initial scribblings, and her gentle guidance through two significant revisions. Her advice made this a far superior book.

I am thankful for the performer of my audio Books, Chrissy Bienvenu, for bringing my stories to life in another medium.

I want to acknowledge the creativity and patient support of my cover artists at Biserka Design who manage to turn my rambling descriptions into delightful cover images and tolerate my fussing over spine widths and back cover text.

And I especially want to acknowledge the work of my administrative assistant, Amanda Gavigan, who keeps track of all the other elements of the business of publishing my books so that I can focus on my writing.

Finally, I want to thank all of you who read my books. Your willingness to inhabit my stories makes the entire enterprise worthwhile.

ALSO BY KEVIN R COLEMAN

Jennifer's Vow

Gaia is awake and unhappy, while AIs are pushing humans aside. Can one young couple change the course of history and save humanity?

This Contemporary Fantasy is a story of redemption and love. Thrust together, Jennifer must overcome her background to learn to love, while Vijay learns what true love requires. Vijay must transform himself to lead a protest movement against the growing dominance of AI technologies. A large part of the population is unemployed and restless. At the same time, Gaia has awoken from millenia of sleep and is unhappy with the humans who are depleting her planet.

Jennifer's Blessing

As Jennifer continues her quest to understand the message of the black panther, an old threat arises. A desperate act by Jennifer forces her to face her past or risk losing Vijay. In the background, civic unrest grows and Vijay rises to becomes the face of the rebellion.

The AI world is also in turmoil, and wars with an unexpected outcome. And a young woman is revealed to be Vijay's future mate.

Confronted on all sides, Jennifer feels driven to challenge Gaia directly with a result that no one saw coming.

Harriet's Way

(release late, 2023)

Harriet meets 17 year old Dylan during his summer working on a fishing boat in Snug Harbor. The two form a relationship until an ill-advised meditation binds them together before either one of them is ready for the consequences.

To make her future with Dylan work, Harriet must repair the dysfunctional Subramanian family while overcoming Cindy's opposition, and helping Vijay find new purpose in his life.

ABOUT THE AUTHOR

Kevin R Coleman is an emerging author of romantic science fiction and fantasy.

His novels portray a changed world, ravaged by viruses where a small island city of survivors develop a direct relationship with Gaia. As technology fails, the humans develop plans to save human existence on our planet. Kevin's stories incorporate metaphysical themes on life, love, and faith in the face of unimaginable change.

Kevin lives with his wife, Sue, on the north shore of Lake Ontario. In addition to being an author, he is an enthusiastic kite-maker and sailor.

JOIN MY NEWSLETTER

To sign up for my newsletter for new book needs, background stories, contests, polls and giveaways, copy the URL below into a browser on your computer or phone

https://kevincolemanauthor.com